Gabriel Hawke Novels

Murder of Ravens

Mouse Trail Ends

Rattlesnake Brother

Chattering Blue Jay

Fox Goes Hunting

Turkey's Fiery Demise

Stolen Butterfly

Churlish Badger

Owl's Silent Strike

Bear Stalker

Damning Firefly

A Gabriel Hawke Novel
Book 11

Paty Jager

Windtree Press
Hillsboro, OR

This is a work of fiction, Names, characters, places, and incidents either are the product of the author's imagination or are used fictitiously, and any resemblance to actual persons living or dead, business establishments, events, or locales, is entirely coincidental.

DAMNING FIREFLY

Contact Information: info@windtreepress.com

Windtree Press
Hillsboro, Oregon
http://windtreepress.com

Cover Art by Covers by Karen

PUBLISHING HISTORY
Published in the United States of America

ISBN 978-1-957638-82-9

Author Comments

While this book is set in Wallowa County, Oregon, I have changed the town names to old forgotten towns that were in the county at one time. I also took the liberty of changing the towns up and populating the county with my own characters, none of which are in any way a representation of anyone who is or has ever lived in Wallowa County. Other than the towns, I have tried to use the real names of all the geographical locations.

Special Thanks to Tim and Nickie Norman for joining me on my trip out Starvation Ridge and Tim for changing my tire that popped from the rocky roads. Also my critique partner, Karen McBride, my beta readers, Danita Cahill and Louis Brewer, my editor, Maggie Holcomb, and my final proofreader, Dalice Peterson. Without all of their input and guidance, this book wouldn't be here.

Prologue

She studied the young woman sitting across from her. There was a definite resemblance to her mother. And of course, the father.

"Mrs. Towman—"

"Please, everyone calls me Rosa. What can I do for you?" She smiled and softened her gaze on the young woman clutching her purse as if it held her courage.

"My mother, Eloise Laude, lived here as a child. She left when she became pregnant with me."

"I remember your mother. You have her light brown hair and heart-shaped lips." Rosa smiled. As the midwife for Wallowa County and surrounding areas, she met all the young girls who became pregnant and didn't want to go to a local physician for fear the whole county would know their status in an hour.

"Do you remember what caused her pregnancy?" The young woman had found her courage through anger. Her eyes had narrowed, her cheeks reddened, and her voice held grit.

"Yes. She had been raped." Rosa hated that word. Hated the men who preyed on innocent girls and women.

"And you know by whom?" The young woman's deep blue gaze was identical to the man who'd conceived her.

Rosa knew and wished someone would do something about the man. He'd raped too many young women and no one in the community would listen. He told the girls no one would believe their word against a man of the cloth. And that seemed so. When she had tried to talk to Reverend Betz, he'd given her the same line. When she'd talked to the sheriff years ago, he'd also said she was crazy. If she was crazy, it was because she didn't like terminating so many pregnancies with herbs. But she'd be damned if she'd let that fornicating man of the cloth populate the earth with his seed. Then there were the young girls, like Eloise whose family was so religious that they wouldn't let her do anything other than bring the child into the world and give it up for adoption. Rosa studied the determined young woman in front of her. It seemed Eloise had outsmarted her parents.

She halted that direction of the conversation while she decided how much to say. "What is your name, Dear?"

"Jayne. Jayne Laude."

"Your mother didn't marry?" Rosa asked.

Jayne's face scrunched up with ugly wrinkles around her nose and eyes. Hatred darkened her pale irises. Rosa knew the woman was thinking about how she was conceived and how her mother had been treated.

"How could she?" Anguish flashed in Jayne's

azure eyes. "She'd have to tell the man how I was conceived. Out of fear and shame. She felt no man would want to be my father nor her husband."

Rosa wanted to give Jayne a hug, but she could sense the woman wouldn't be receptive to any kindness at the moment.

"Do you know who hurt my mother?" Jayne questioned. Her gaze heated with anger as she peered into Rosa's eyes.

Rosa gently redirected the question to the young woman. "Have you found out who is responsible?"

"All my mother would tell me is he was the preacher of the church, her family attended." Jayne's voice didn't waver as she said firmly and without inflection. "I will find him and I will make him pay for my mother's suffering."

"Don't do anything rash. When you discover who he is, come to me. Then we will find a way to make others see him for what he is. Because your mother wasn't the only one."

Chapter One

Fish and Wildlife State Trooper Gabriel Hawke admired the snow-capped Wallowa Mountains in the distance as he drove toward Alder. Their majestic pine and granite-covered peaks had called to him sixteen years ago when he'd transferred here to work the fish and wildlife division and honor his ancestors. As much as he wanted to head into the wilderness, it wouldn't happen until more of the snow had melted. Today he was looking forward to a leisurely day of checking on turkey hunters out north. He enjoyed this job in the spring, except for the fact it was too easy to get stuck in the mud with run-off from the melting snow.

He topped the hill that gave visitors their first view of Alder and stared at a growing black plume of smoke on the southeast side of town.

Ash settled on his windshield as the radio crackled to life followed by dispatch requesting fire trucks, ambulance, and all available law enforcement to the Lighted Path Church.

Hawke switched on his sirens and lights,

navigating the hill into town and making his way through the back streets to avoid interfering with the ambulance or fire truck on the way. He stopped half a block away from the Lighted Path Church as a woman stumbled out of the fire-engulfed, single-story building.

The woman collapsed as two onlookers reached her.

As the first officer on the scene, Hawke hurried over.

"He's in there," the woman said and coughed into a handkerchief she held in her hand.

"Who is 'he', Mrs. Betz?" Hawke asked the wife of Pastor Betz the head of the Lighted Path Church.

"My husband. He was in his office." She coughed as another woman ran up and threw her arms around Mrs. Betz, ignoring the smoke and charred spots on the coughing woman's clothing.

Hawke stood and studied the orange flames leaping out windows and flicking through holes in the roof. He couldn't go charging into the building without knowing where he was going.

Oliver Taylor walked up. He was a deacon of the church.

"Mr. Taylor, where is the office in the church?" Hawke asked.

"It's clear in the back. Is Gordon still in there?" The man's rheumy eyes widened.

Hawke didn't reply. He headed to the side of the burning building as the shrill sirens wailed to a stop. If the firefighters didn't get the blaze out soon, it could catch the buildings on either side on fire.

Holding an arm in front of his face to ward off the

heat, he ran to the back of the building. The charred back wall was being devoured by flames, it would be suicide to try and enter the building.

A loud "woosh" was followed by the "thump" of the roof collapsing. Sparks and ash danced in the air. If the pastor had been in his office, they would only know after the fire was extinguished and the embers cooled.

Hawke made his way back to the front of the building. Firefighters doused the flames, and EMTs, Roxie and Bonnie, tended to Mrs. Betz.

Alder City Officer Craig Herold stood back watching the firefighters' efforts as Deputy Corcoran parked and joined him. Hawke circled over to stand beside the two officers.

"When I arrived, Mrs. Betz stumbled out of the church." He told the officers what the woman had said and how he'd gone around back to see if there was a way to get in and save the pastor. "Since this is more your jurisdiction and territory than mine, I'll get back to my job. I'm headed out north to check on turkey hunters."

Herold nodded and Hawke walked back to his vehicle. Before pulling away from the curb, he made a note of the people gathered around watching. He recognized most of them as locals. None of them had ever been pulled in for setting fires. The church wasn't as old as other churches in the county. But there was no accounting for how well it was built. He wondered if an electrical problem had caused the fire.

《》《》《》

Hawke chugged his vehicle along a road made from fist-sized and larger jagged rocks cradled in mud on Starvation Ridge. He was headed toward an area where he'd found a large flock of tom turkeys the week before the season opened. Scanning the trees and ridge around him, he was surprised as the road curved to the left and down the side of the ridge. A blue compact car was wedged between trees sixty feet from the road.

His first thought was what the hell was a car doing up here this time of year and his second thought jumped to the conclusion he'd find a drunk sleeping it off.

He stopped his truck on the road, not wanting to get stuck in mud, and shut off the engine before stepping out and listening.

Not a gobble, whistle, or chirp. Not even the rustle or whine of wind in the trees. This wasn't good. For all the birds to have gone quiet there was something amiss with the vehicle.

He pulled on his jacket and grabbed his small day pack before locking the doors. The sun was warm on his back. Spring sun was always welcome. While it felt good after the cold start to the morning, it made his walk over the thawing earth slow. Every other step, his feet slid making his progress more difficult.

Watching his footing and nearly falling on his ass twice, he stopped at the back of the blue compact car with Washington license plates. He wrote down the number in his logbook and studied how the vehicle was wedged in between two trees. One tree had the passenger side door blocked and the other tree was against the driver's side front wheel.

Hawke walked up to the vehicle, studying everything he saw which included a woman in the driver's seat who wasn't moving.

He knocked on the window.

The woman rolled her head in his direction. Her dilated blue eyes peered at him as if she didn't see him.

Grasping the door handle he gave it a tug. It was locked.

"Ma'am, can you unlock the door?" he asked loudly and gestured to the lock button.

She continued to stare at him.

Hawke unzipped his day pack and grabbed the safety hammer. He walked around to the passenger side of the car. The tree was against the back half of the door. He slammed the pointed head of the tool into the window. It cracked and he soon had a hole large enough to slip his arm in and unlock the doors. He pulled his arm out of the window and caught a whiff of smoke. Not from a cigarette or marijuana. It had a hint of campfire scent to it and something else that could have been the same as what he'd smelled on Mrs. Betz.

Returning to the driver's side, he opened the door. A heavy scent of smoke lingered in the air, and the woman's shirt and pant leg were stained with black scorch marks.

"Can you stand?" he asked, holding onto her arm.

She swung her legs out of the car and stood, but wobbled. Hawke settled her back onto the car seat. That's when he noticed the blood in her light brown hair.

"How did you get here?" Hawke asked, grasping his mic to call for an ambulance to meet him out on the highway.

"I-I don't know. The last thing I remember was standing inside a church and then waking up here." The woman moved her head as if looking around for the first time.

"What's your name?" Hawke pulled out his logbook and started writing down what he'd encountered and the time.

"It's…" She peered up at him, her eyes scrunched and her brow furrowed. "I don't know."

He studied her. Was she making this up because she started the fire at the church or had the blow on her head and possible fear for her life caused her to forget? A quick glance into the car didn't reveal a purse or anything that looked like it would have her identity.

"Do you have any idea why you are in Wallowa County? Do you live here?" He doubted she did with Washington plates, but she could have borrowed the car. He'd know soon enough when he ran the plates.

"Wallowa County?" She scanned the trees around them. "Where is that?"

"Northeast Oregon."

Her brow furrowed, again. "I don't understand. What am I doing in Oregon? I'm sure I don't live here." She sighed. "Anyway, it doesn't sound like home."

"If you can walk, I'll take you to my truck and we'll meet an ambulance out on the highway." Hawke grasped her elbow again and helped her to her feet.

She swayed a fraction but remained standing. "I think I can make it."

"We'll go slow."

As they walked back to the truck, Hawke called in what he'd found and requested to meet the ambulance at Charolais Road and asked that a deputy or another trooper join him. Even though he didn't know who she was or why she had ended up where she did, Hawke was treating this as a possible connection to the fire.

He continued to ask the woman questions, which she couldn't or wouldn't answer, as they drove back toward Highway 3 and the ambulance. He didn't understand how she knew she didn't live in Oregon, but couldn't remember her name. That didn't make sense. He figured it had something to do with smelling like she'd started the church fire.

Chapter Two

Hawke delivered the woman to the waiting ambulance and led Deputy Novak back to Starvation Ridge. Hawke parked his vehicle on the road and motioned for Novak to do the same. Not only was this the scene of an accident, but he also wanted to make sure he reported all the details. They walked down to the car, watching the ground for traces of tire prints.

A faint shifting of debris and bent grass showed the direction the car had entered the trees. The car wedged between the trees had to have been driven into the area while the ground was still frozen leaving minimal tracks. If it had only been a couple of hours earlier, there would have been mud on the tires and obvious tracks.

He didn't understand how the vehicle had navigated through the trees so carefully before wedging as it had between two of the largest trees. The compact car hadn't taken a straight path to the resting spot. Both he and Novak took photos. Hawke with his phone, and Novak with a digital camera.

"How do you think she ended up here? Drinking or high?" Novak asked.

"She was out of it, but it appeared more like she was drugged than drunk or high. We'll know for sure when they run tests at the hospital." Hawke opened the three car doors that could be opened and took photos before digging under the seats and through the glove box and console. There wasn't a scrap of paper. Either the woman was an immaculate person or someone had cleaned the car out so they couldn't identify her.

The key was in the ignition. A small replica of the Seattle Space Needle dangled from the key. This could corroborate the fact they believed the woman was from Washington.

He took a picture of the key chain, then found the latch to pop the trunk. Walking to the back of the car, Hawke noted a small window sticker in the back window. STOP VIOLENCE AGAINST WOMEN

The owner of the car seemed to have the same feelings as his mom who steered the MMIW movement at the Umatilla Reservation where Hawke grew up. He was proud of the work his mom, and now his sister, Marion, did within their reservation and others where they joined forces to bring the matter of the murdered and missing Indigenous women, children, and men to authorities and the public.

While the front of the car had been cleaned out, the trunk had not. A small overnight bag appeared to have been flung to the front of the space from the impact of the car stopping between the trees. Unopened water bottles scattered about the floor of the trunk and a pretzel bag lay empty, its contents broken and crushed under and around the bottles of water.

Hawke snapped a picture with his phone and called Novak over to get a photo with the county camera before he leaned in and snagged the handle on the overnight bag. Maybe now he'd have answers. Unzipping the bag, he was surprised to see folders, papers, and a worn journal.

Opening the scuffed faux leather cover, he studied the penmanship of what appeared to be a teenage girl. He remembered the girls in high school passing notes back and forth that were covered with loops, swirly lines, and hearts for dotted i's. The date on the first page of the book was January 1, 1999.

The first entry was all about a boy named Wade and the writer's hopes of getting asked to the homecoming dance by him.

Hawke glanced at the inside of the cover. The name Eloise Laude was written in the looping cursive with a heart over the i. The woman he'd helped out of the car wasn't old enough to have written this. The name Laude was one he remembered. There was an older couple by that name who lived out Hurricane Creek. He'd been called there when he'd first transferred to Wallowa County as a Fish and Wildlife Officer. They were having trouble with poachers shooting the deer feeding on their garden. He'd learned little about them other than they wanted the poachers caught. After he finished here and checked on the woman, he would go see if they could enlighten him.

"What did you find?" Novak asked, taking photos

of the open bag.

"I'm not sure. But look at this trunk. I would say someone put this car and that woman here for a reason and cleaned out the front. But they didn't think about cleaning out the trunk." Hawke pulled a file out of the bag.

"Foul play? How do you come up with that other than the difference in the cleanliness of the car interior and the trunk?"

"The way the car was wedged in between the trees, the fact the woman had a cut on the top back of her head and not the front, and she smelled of smoke." Hawke read down a list of names on the sheet in the folder. "These all sound like names of people who live in the county." He handed the sheet to Novak.

"They are." Novak studied Hawke. "Why would someone have this list?"

"I'm going to find out right after I run the license on this car."

《》《》《》

As Hawke entered Alder and drove toward the hospital his radio crackled to life. "Hawke, the license is registered to a Jayne Laude." Dispatch rattled off an address in Yakima, Washington.

"Copy." Hawke parked in front of the single-story, twenty-five-bed hospital and entered through the emergency entrance.

"Hawke, what are you doing here?" Donna Lenski asked. She worked the emergency desk and took X-rays.

"Do you know if the Jane Doe, Roxie and Bonnie picked up, is still here or in a room?" He stopped in

20

front of the registration desk.

"She was given a room. Just a second." Donna picked up the phone and asked someone for the room number of the Jane Doe. Hanging up the phone, she smiled. "I'll escort you over to the room."

"Thanks." Hawke fell into step beside the woman in her forties and the mother of two teenage boys. "How did the boys do in basketball? I didn't make it to any of the games."

She chatted about her boys and the basketball season until they stopped at room number 17.

"Do you want me to find a nurse to tell you what they know about her?" Donna asked.

Hawke knew what he wanted to say to the woman and the questions he planned to ask, but it would be nice to know her condition before he probed. "That's probably a good idea."

Donna put a hand up as if telling him to stay and walked on down the hall to the nurse's station. Hawke waited, listening to the machines in the rooms on either side of Jane Doe beeping and making sucking sounds. This side of the hospital had the antiseptic smell that made the hairs in his nostrils twitch.

A young woman with braided blonde hair walked toward him. "Trooper Hawke. I'm Vicky Ford. What did you want to know about Jane Doe?"

"Will asking questions be okay for her condition?" Hawke asked.

"You can ask. I'm not sure she can answer them. The doctor believes she has suffered short-term amnesia from the hit on the back of her head and perhaps she saw something that she wants to forget."

"Did you bag up her clothes for forensics?" Hawke asked.

"They are in a bag. I didn't know the police would be interested in them."
She watched him with her head cocked to one side like his dog did when listening intently.

"She smelled of smoke and had scorched marks on her clothes. There was a fire at the Lighted Path Church this morning. I just want to see if she was there or is connected to the church." Hawke smiled, trying to assure the nurse he didn't believe Jane Doe to be a threat to anyone.

"I did hear about that. Mrs. Betz refused to come to the emergency. I hope she sees her regular doctor. She's a good woman. Always in here visiting the sick and bringing them magazines and books. It's going to be hard on her without her husband. I was told her neighbor, Mrs. Larsen, is taking care of her." Vicky waved a hand to the hospital room. "Is there anything else you want to know?"

"That's good for now. I might have more questions after I talk to her." Hawke walked to the door, knocked, and entered.

The woman's eyes were closed. She had a bandage around her head and was in a hospital gown. She didn't have an IV or machine hooked up to her.

He walked over to a chair, placed it next to the bed, and sat down. "Ma'am, I have a couple questions if you feel up to answering them."

Her dark lashes fluttered up and sapphire eyes peered at him. Her lips quivered and a shy smile appeared. "You are the officer who found me."

Hawke smiled. "Yes, I am. I have some questions for you. Do you feel well enough to try to remember?"

"I'd love to remember who I am and why I'm here." She grabbed the control for the bed and raised up into a sitting position.

"Does Eloise Laude mean anything to you?" Hawke asked.

Her tranquil composure transformed. Multiple expressions darted across her pale skin and flashed in her blue eyes. "The name makes me feel happy and angry at the same time." Her full dark brows drew together above the bridge of her nose. "Why do I feel two such different feelings?"

"I don't know. I believe you live in Yakima, Washington." He studied her eyes and face.

A light came on in the blue depths of her eyes and her lips tipped into a genuine smile. "Yes! I have an antique store. It was my mom's…" her voice trailed off. "Eloise. That is my mom's name. Eloise Laude. I'm Jayne. Jayne Laude." Her face lit up at the memory, then drooped. "But why am I here? You said I'm in Oregon?"

"Wallowa County. The towns of Alder, Prairie Creek, Winslow, and Eagle." He watched as she processed what he'd said.

"I have been here once before. Mom brought me. We went to a house where there was an older couple. She left me in the yard playing with a black and white dog. There was shouting and then mom stomped out of the house, picked me up, and said we'd never come back here again. The devil had his claws in everyone." Her eyes widened. "Who is the devil and why did I come here?"

"From what I've discovered, you have grandparents living out Hurricane Creek by the names of Jerome and Anita Laude. Can you remember if you visited them on this trip?" Hawke had pulled his logbook out of his pocket and was scribbling down everything Jayne said.

The woman barely shook her head back and forth. "The names don't sound familiar. Grandparents?" She rested her head on the pillow and stared at the ceiling. "I don't have any recollection of any grandparents, siblings, aunts, uncles, or cousins. It had always been just me and Mom."

A pang of sadness squeezed his chest at the thought of the woman not remembering she had a family. He might only see his mom half a dozen times a year but he tried to talk to her every week. And now that Marion was back in their lives, he spoke to her once a week as well. And then there were all the cousins, aunts, and uncles that he didn't visit often but he knew they were there.

"I'm going to go talk to your grandparents after I finish talking with you. What about The Lighted Path Church? Have you ever heard of it?" Hawke watched the woman's soft expression of thought harden and when she peered at him there was a glint of anger in her eyes.

"We didn't go to church or pray or believe in God."

Her hatred of all things religious could have been sparked and she lit the first church she came to on fire. But he didn't take her for a crazy or a zealot. There was a reason for her fury.

"Was there a particular reason?" Hawke asked.

"I just know we had nothing to do with any religion and Mom never opened the door to anyone who spoke of God." She reached out with a shaky hand and picked up a glass of water, sitting on the table beside her bed. Sipping from the straw, she drained the cup to half before saying, "I just feel rage at the thought of church and anyone connected to it."

He figured it was a response her mother had instilled in her. But why? "When I found you, you said the last thing you remember was standing in a church…" He let that sink in.

Jayne's eyes widened. "A church?" Her blue eyes moved back and forth in her sockets as she thought. "I do remember a church. There was an old man standing in front of Jesus on the cross. He studied me with…" She shuddered. "His eyes were blue and his eyebrows thick and white. The smile…I remember feeling dirty as he looked at me."

"What did you say to him?" Hawke asked.

"I-I don't remember words. Just the feelings and then…I woke up and you were tapping on my window." She closed her eyes. "What was I doing?"

"I'll see if I can find out." Hawke crossed to the door and gripped the handle. "Get some rest to help your memory come back." Hawke left the room and pulled out his phone. He needed to let his superior know that he had come across the woman and a puzzle. One he would have to crack before he could get back to checking on turkey hunters.

Chapter Three

Hawke drove away from the hospital as he updated his superior on his morning activities.

Sergeant Spruel cleared his throat and said, "We only have fishermen and turkey hunters this time of year, that keeps everyone close in. Don't forget to watch for shed poachers at the Wenaha Elk Refuge while you search for clues as to why that woman was out at Starvation Ridge."

"My gut tells me she was at the church that caught fire." Hawke didn't want the young woman to be the one who started the fire. She'd not only have the arson conviction but manslaughter as well. He'd type up his notes and would hand them over to whomever he worked with on this case.

"The locals would be happy to pin this on an out-of-towner but keep an open mind. There could be a good reason she was at the church. Work with the city police, they are the lead on the fire." The sound of shuffling papers came through the phone from Spruel's side.

"Do you happen to know if Wes had a chance to look the church over?"

"He's at a Fire Marshal convention or something. He'll be back tomorrow."

Spruel sounded busy, but Hawke had another question. "Did they find a body in the office?"

"Yeah, they did. Talk to City about that." Spruel ended the call.

Hawke hoped Dr. Vance was called in to look at the body. But would anyone suspect the fire to be a crime scene until Wes made his findings known?

Hawke pulled over and parked across the street from the blackened church. He rolled his window down and regretted the action. The soggy charred remains filled the air with an acrid sweet heaviness. The Lighted Path Church no longer looked like a sanctuary, but a war zone.

He'd never been much of a churchgoer. Not when he'd prayed to God as a child to make his father come back to them and then to stop his stepfather from beating his mom and him. But he believed in the Creator. The bounties that he put on this earth to feed, clothe, and house people. However, people had to remember to care for those things or they would no longer be around. His ancestors had known they couldn't kill every buffalo or stop the fish from making their journey from smolt to full-grown salmon. Their bodies depended on these creatures for nourishment. He enjoyed the First Foods ceremonies held at the Rez.

Those ceremonies were his church.

Drawing his thoughts away from baked salmon and fry bread, he studied the half a dozen people standing on the sidewalk staring at the building. He wondered if they were parishioners or just curious.

Hawke called Dr. Vance.

"Dr. Gwendolyn Vance's office," a young male voice answered.

"This is State Trooper Hawke, I'd like to talk to Dr. Vance."

"She's at the hospital checking on a patient."

"Could you tell her to call Hawke, please?" He rattled off his number even though he was sure the county medical examiner had his number from previous homicides they'd worked together.

Scanning the crowd, he noticed a woman smiling as she stared at the burnt rubbish that had once been the church.

《》《》《》

Rosa stood on the sidewalk, her heart light. When she'd heard the church had burned down with Pastor Gordon Betz in it, she would have shouted Hallelujah if she hadn't been standing in the grocery store.

She knew it was wrong to feel such satisfaction but maybe the Lord had finally heard her prayers to rid this earth of the man who had preyed on innocent girls.

Someone tapped on her shoulder. She slowly turned and stared up into State Trooper Gabriel Hawke's brown watchful eyes. "Trooper Hawke, I heard you were the first on the scene."

He studied her. "Mrs. Towman, what are you doing here?"

She shrugged. "I heard about the fire and like the others," she waved her hands at the people standing around, mostly women who she knew had been raped by the pastor, "I wanted to see if it was true."

When his russet brow wrinkled, Rosa realized by his interest she needed to tone down her excitement or he would think she'd started the fire. "How awful for Mrs. Betz," she said. Even though in her heart she believed the woman would be happy to rid herself of the egomaniacal man she'd married.

Thinking of Diane, Rosa wondered if the woman had finally gotten up the courage to go against one of the commandments… "Do they know yet if it was accidental?" she asked.

Trooper Hawke took her by the arm and led her over to his vehicle. "Why would you ask that?"

She shrugged. "Things I've heard. His flock was getting smaller and smaller. Many didn't like the things he preached." Or his raping their daughters and sisters under the ruse of preparing them for marriage, she thought to herself.

The trooper continued to study her. He pulled off his baseball cap with the State Police emblem and scratched his short-cropped graying temple with long fingers on a wide hand. "What do you know about Pastor Betz?"

Would he be the first law enforcement officer to take her claims seriously? She peered back at him. She'd heard only good things about the State Trooper standing before her. How he stuck up for the underdog and didn't leave a murder alone until he'd found the killer. This was one time she hoped the killer wasn't found. Whomever it was had saved more young women and girls and freed those who had been 'chosen' from the pastor's clutches.

"Not much. I don't go to this church." She glanced around. "Can I go now? I have groceries in my car."

Hawke studied the woman. He knew as a midwife for the area she knew a lot of people, and he was sure she knew more about the pastor than she was telling. But why?

"Yeah, you can go. But if you hear anything about anything," he handed her his card, "give me a call."

"I will." She shoved the card into her purse and walked over to a small SUV.

Hawke's phone buzzed. He glanced at the screen. Dr. Vance.

"Thank you for returning my call," he answered.

"What did you want to ask me?" Dr. Vance's voice always held a hint of humor. She was fun to take by horseback into the wilderness for suspicious deaths.

"Did anyone ask you to take a look at the body that burned in the church today?"

"Is it suspicious circumstances?" she asked.

"We won't know until Wes can take a look when he gets back. Which will be tomorrow. But I have reason to believe it wasn't an accident." Hawke told her about finding Jayne and the circumstance around it.

"I'll take a peek tomorrow morning before I go to the office and hold the body until we get a clearance from Wes."

"Thanks. That's all I can ask for." Hawke slid into his vehicle and headed for Hurricane Creek. He had a number of questions for Mr. and Mrs. Laude.

《》《》《》

Hawke drove up a dirt and gravel lane that ran through the middle of overgrown dead timothy grass pastures and dilapidated wood fences. It was obvious the owners of the land and house, with peeling white paint, could no longer take care of it as they once had. There was still a pile of snow at the shady side of the leaning barn.

He parked in front of a two-story older farmhouse tucked into the pine and fir trees. There was a large willow off to the side of the house with a swing dangling by one rope.

The gravel path to the house crunched as he walked up to the porch. The odor of rotting wood and stale bacon grease met him as he knocked on the door. Behind the closed door, he heard a scrape of chair legs on a wood floor. Wheels rolling on wood followed by a clank of metal grew louder and the door opened. A woman with gray hair pulled into a ponytail at the back of her neck stood at the threshold gripping a walker. Her back was hunched, making her head nearly touch the aluminum walker. She tipped her head sideways to peer up at him.

"What do you want?" she asked in a rusty voice.

"Mrs. Anita Laude?" Hawke asked.

"Yes. We haven't driven anywhere in five years, what do you want with us?" She didn't offer to have him come in.

"I have some questions for you and your husband. May I come in?" He waved a hand toward the interior of the house.

She shook her head. "Jerome hasn't been doing too

well. You'll just upset him if he sees your uniform. What questions do you have of us?"

"Did you have a daughter named Eloise?"

Tears appeared in the woman's faded hazel eyes. "Yes. We could use her about now, but Jerome was set on her not bringing shame to the family. I doubt we see her before we die."

Hawke was sad for this older couple who'd shoved their daughter out of their life. But their being alone was on them if they pushed her away. He said, "I'm afraid that's true. It seems she passed away last year."

The woman opened and closed her mouth several times as if she wanted to say something but only retrieved a white handkerchief from a pocket of her pants and wiped her nose. "She would have only been forty-three. I had her when I was thirty. Kind of late. Messed my bones up."

Hawke wondered at the family dynamics. "Was she your only child?"

"Yes. I told Jerome when she came back with the child that we should just say she was married and her husband died, but he refused to do that because she insisted that she was raped."

Hawke peered at the woman. "By who?"

The woman became agitated. "We figured it was that Wade Archer who took her to the dance. They didn't get home until three in the morning. But she insisted it wasn't him. That it happened at the church." The woman shook her head. "No one would do something like that in a house of God."

That explained Eloise's hatred of all things God and the church. He had something to tell Jayne.

"Did she name who did it?" Hawke asked.

The woman's cheeks reddened. "She did." The woman's voice rose. "And I told her she was a liar."

Hawke pulled out his logbook. "Why was she lying?"

"Because there is no way our pastor would rape a teenage girl or any girl for that matter. Especially when he is married and everyone loves him." The woman's eyes no longer glittered with tears, they shone with conviction.

"Who is this man?" Hawke pressed.

"Pastor Betz." The woman proclaimed his name as if he were God.

Hawke wrote the name in his book and thought about Jayne Laude. Had she started the fire to avenge her dead mother?

"Why didn't you listen to your daughter? Surely you asked around?" Hawke questioned.

"She only had eyes for Wade, and why would we question the word of our pastor? He and Diane were happily married. We thought Eloise made it up to take the heat off her boyfriend and get back at us."

"Why was she unhappy with you?"

"Because when she told us that Rosa could help her make the baby go away, we told her she would bring it into the world and put it up for adoption. No daughter of ours would take a life." The woman nodded. "We sent her to my sister in Portland. Away from Wade and Rosa. After she had the baby, she ran away with the child and we didn't see her again until three years later when she showed up here asking us to be that child's grandparents."

"I'm guessing you turned your back on her again?" Hawke knew his question was accusatory, but the woman didn't seem to hear it.

"We told her she had disobeyed our wishes in keeping the child and we weren't going to have anything to do with it." A tear trickled out of her eye and slid across her nose into her other eye. "I tried to get Jerome to change his mind, but he was firm that no illegitimate child would be linked to our name."

Hawke debated and finally asked, "If she wants, would you be open to seeing that grandchild now?"

The woman's face lit up. "I would! We could do it outside, here, where Jerome won't see."

"I can't guarantee anything. She's bitter toward you. Eloise told her all about the times you turned her away."

Tears streamed down the woman's face. "If I could take it all back, I would. A mother needs their children around when they are growing old."

"I'll see what I can do." He turned and walked away, then retraced his steps. "Is there anyone looking after you?"

"The neighbor up the road stops in a couple times a week and brings us groceries. When we have a medical appointment, we call Community Connections for a ride." Mrs. Laude glanced over her shoulder into the house. "If I hadn't felt Eloise was lying and Jerome hadn't been adamant about an illegitimate grandchild, I would have let Eloise marry Wade. But she insisted it wasn't his child and there was no way she'd ruin his life."

Chapter Four

Driving back to Alder from visiting with Mrs. Laude, Hawke was sifting through the information he'd collected. The woman he'd found had come to Alder to confront the deceased pastor. Her mother had said the pastor raped her and now the grandmother had basically confirmed it, even though she still didn't believe it. He called Spruel and asked him to look up a Wade Archer and see if he still lived in Wallowa County. Hopefully, the man would remember his high school girlfriend and be able to shine a little more light on what happened.

Hawke arrived in Alder and drove straight to the city police station that was in the same building as City Hall.

At the reception desk at City Hall, he asked for Officer Herold, believing the man would be in the office typing up all the notes he'd made that day.

"He left for the night. Would you like to speak to

Chief Browning? He's the only one still around." The young woman picked up the phone on her desk.

"Yes. Tell him it's State Trooper Hawke, please." Hawke stood, holding his hat in his hands, waiting as the woman delivered his message. A faint reflection in the glass she'd moved aside to speak to him revealed his bright brown eyes. He'd witnessed this brightness in his eyes many times as he stared in a mirror thinking about a puzzle that needed to be solved.

His hair was cut short this time of year since he rarely made a trip into the mountains until May. Then he'd let his dark hair, with patches of silver, grow and he'd be in heaven riding his horse around the Wallowa Mountains checking on fishermen, hikers, and campers. By the time he spent most of his hours in the mountains checking on hunters, he'd be wearing civilian clothes and have long hair so no one would take a potshot at him as an authority figure. Spending time in the mountains was the reason he took this job. He wanted to give back to the land that had sustained his ancestors.

The woman hung up the phone with a clank, drawing his attention to her. "Chief Browning said for you to go on back to his office. It's down that hall, the third room on the right."

"Thank you." Hawke had been in this building a dozen times since transferring here with the Fish and Wildlife division. Every time he came, he found a new entity housed within the structure. This time he was surprised to see the Chamber of Commerce had moved in.

At Browning's door, Hawke knocked and waited for a reply.

"Come in," Browning called.

Hawke opened the door and entered a small room. Chief Browning was a tall, thin man with red curly hair and a pale freckled complexion. He sat behind his desk, a pile of papers in front of him.

"Have a seat. It's good to do something other than paperwork," Browning said, shoving the folders to the front of his desk. "You'd think with as small as we are there wouldn't be so much of it." He held up a mug. "Want a cup of coffee?"

"Only if it's no trouble," Hawke said, as the man stood and walked over to a one-cup coffee maker on the top of a bookcase.

"No trouble at all." Browning put a pod in the machine, pushed a button, and faced Hawke. "Are you here about the fire today?"

"Yes."

"Damn shame losing the newest church in town and the pastor all at the same time." The machine finished sputtering. Browning picked up the cup, handing it to Hawke. After putting another pod in the machine, the man stepped over to his desk and picked up a folder. He handed it to Hawke before retrieving his cup of coffee.

Hawke opened the file. Herold had been diligent. He'd questioned everyone present, including the wife before she refused medical help and was whisked away by the neighbor. Herold's interview with the woman was exactly what Hawke had witnessed.

"Herold did a thorough job," Hawke commented and glanced at Browning.

"He did. One of my best men." Browning laughed

and said, "I guess I can't really say that. Both of my men are the best."

The Alder City Police consisted of two officers and the chief. In a county of 3,100 square miles and 7,400 people, the city, county, and state police covered their areas and more when dispatch called. Whoever was closest to the altercation dealt with it first. The county had to cover the towns of Winslow, Eagle, and Prairie Creek as they didn't have city police.

"Have you had anyone bring up concerns about Pastor Betz?" Hawke asked.

"Betz? Like what?" Browning sipped his coffee, watching Hawke over the rim of the mug.

"He was too friendly with the young women," Hawke said with disgust.

Browning set his cup down and studied Hawke. "What do you mean, 'too friendly?'"

"A woman told her parents over twenty years ago that Pastor Betz raped her and they didn't believe her." Hawke sipped, watching the chief.

"Betz? I don't believe anyone has ever brought a complaint against him." Browning picked his mug back up. "But I take it you believe what you heard?"

Hawke told Browning about finding Jayne and what she'd told him. "It was this woman's grandmother I talked to who said her daughter was adamant Betz raped her but they believed it was Wade Archer."

"Wade? I'd believe it less of him than Betz."

This interested Hawke. "Why?"

"Wade has been the Alder High School girls basketball coach for nearly twelve years and there hasn't been a single whisper of anything inappropriate.

He has pep talks with them while his wife is in the locker room and then he leaves and the wife oversees that the girls change and get to the bus or wherever."

"And Betz?" Hawke asked, picking up his cup.

"He walked and talked like no one would refute anything he said. At least not his flock. If you asked them, he could have been God's other son." Browning shook his head. "I don't take to preachers who think they are God rather than the voice for God."

This was giving Hawke a good picture of the dead pastor. "I've asked Dr. Vance to hold the remains until Wes can look the site over. I just have a gut feeling this wasn't an accident."

"I'll let Craig know. Do you want to take the lead if it turns out to be a homicide? After all, you were first on the scene."

Hawke peered into Browning's eyes. "I don't have to take the lead, but I will be investigating. If I'd only shown up this morning and helped out, I'd be less likely to be involved. But finding the woman and hearing her comments, she could be the one who set the fire, but, again, my gut isn't following my head."

"We'll bring her in when the hospital releases her. You want in on the questioning?"

"Yeah, I do. And I think it will make her speak more freely." Hawke could tell the woman was appreciative he'd found her.

Browning picked up his coffee cup. "I've heard a lot about your gut instincts from Sheriff Lindsey. You can be the lead and Craig will help with the investigation."

"I'll be in touch with him tomorrow." Hawke

shook hands with Browning and headed out to his vehicle.

His stomach growled. Dani, the woman he lived with, was up at her lodge in the Eagle Cap Wilderness preparing it for the onslaught of guests she already had booked from Memorial Day through October. Dog, his mid-sized mutt, was most likely over at their neighbors, the Trembleys. Dog hadn't decided if he should hang out with the Trembleys who had been Hawke's landlords for over a decade or if he should stay home by himself all day. Most days, he hung out with the horses in the pasture, but come evening, he wandered to the Trembleys for human company and scraps. That meant Hawke didn't need to rush home. He'd stop by the Treetop Café for dinner and gossip.

Hawke called in he was off duty and walked across the street to the Treetop Café. It was a small restaurant on the corner across from City Hall and the Courthouse with the County Sheriff's Department. The food wasn't as good as the Rusty Nail in Winslow, but he'd have to drive past his house to go there for dinner.

Stepping inside the door, heads turned at the sound of the bell. Hawke smiled at the people he knew and made his way to the counter. He always sat at the counter when he was alone. It didn't make sense to take up a whole table when he was by himself. If he hunched over his meal, looking like he didn't want to be disturbed, people left him alone.

Even though he sat at the counter, he still wanted to hear any gossip about the fire.

Janelle, a waitress with bleached blonde hair pulled up in a ponytail, asked him in her raspy smoker's voice,

"You here for dinner or just coffee?"

"Dinner. I'll have the chicken-fried steak and mashed potatoes, please." He held up the coffee cup that had been upside down in the spot he chose.

Janelle filled the cup, smacked her gum, and went over to the window separating the dining area from the kitchen. "Mort, chicken fried and mashed," she called through the window, before wandering down the counter and refilling other coffee cups.

Hawke scanned a group of five women at a round table in the far corner. They all had their heads together as if whispering. Why would you come to a public place and then whisper?

Several of the group straightened and he stared into the face of Rosa Towman. Her eyes widened at the sight of him, then a smile slid across her lips and she bowed her gray curls to speak quietly to the group.

One by one the women rose from their chairs and left the restaurant.

Hawke picked up his coffee and walked over to the table where Rosa sat. "Mind if I join you?"

Rosa glanced up at the trooper and nodded. She had nothing to fear from the man and everything to gain if she could get him to believe her about Pastor Betz. "It's a free country, Trooper Hawke."

The man sat, sipped his coffee, and set the cup on the table in front of him alongside his cap. "Do you know a woman named Jayne Laude?" he asked.

"Jayne? What do you know about Jayne?" she asked, unsure if she should be worried for the young woman.

"She's in the hospital."

Rosa's heart leaped into her throat. Why would Jayne be in the hospital? What had happened to her? She shot to her feet and grabbed her purse. Finding her voice she said, "I must go to her."

Trooper Hawke put a hand on her arm. "She's not going to die. You can answer some questions for me first." He removed his hand and picked up his coffee.

Rosa settled back in her seat, watching the man. What wasn't he saying? She'd heard about how his instincts had helped solve more than a dozen murders over the years since he'd moved here. The rumor that went around about him said he was a descendant of the Nez Perce Tribe that lived in the valley most of the year before the treaty moved them to the reservation in Lapwai, Idaho.

"What's wrong with Jayne?" Rosa asked, holding her cup out to Janelle when she walked by with a coffee pot.

"She was hit on the head. I found her out at Starvation Ridge."

Rosa sat straighter and stared at the man. Her mind buzzed with why the woman had taken off in that direction. "Starvation Ridge? What was she doing out there?"

"She doesn't know. Didn't even know who she was until I discovered her mother's diary in the trunk of the car." His deep brown eyes studied her. "Then I talked to her grandmother—"

Rosa placed a hand over her mouth to muffle the harsh laugh. She couldn't hide her bitterness toward the parents who didn't listen to their daughters.

Trooper Hawke's eyebrows rose. "Do you have

something to say about the Laudes?"

She nodded her head. "I sure do. If they had listened to their daughter and taken action against Pastor Betz, there wouldn't be a dozen of his offspring living in this county." Rosa kept her voice low for only the trooper to hear. She didn't need one of Pastor Betz's followers to hear this and start calling her a liar.

"You knew what this man was doing?"

Chapter Five

Hawke leaned back in his seat and studied the midwife. He was appalled Rosa had kept the man's behavior from the authorities for decades.

"I tried to get Sheriff Oswell to listen to me after I'd found out from Eloise that she'd been raped by Pastor Betz. He told me I'd been inhaling too many of my herbs. Then several months later another teenage girl came to me with the same story." Rosa sipped her drink and peered at Hawke over her cup.

He could see she had a lot more she wanted to say on the matter of Pastor Betz.

Janelle arrived with his dinner. He placed the plate in front of him and waited for the gossipy waitress to leave. Lowering his voice, Hawke said, "If you can wait for me to finish eating, I'd like to take this conversation somewhere more private."

Rosa set her cup down and gathered her purse.

"You'll find me in the yellow house at the end of Elm Street. I'll have my records ready for you." She stood and walked out of the café.

Hawke's gaze followed her until she'd settled in her car and driven away.

A coffee pot appeared in his peripheral vision, and Janelle asked, "You seeing Rosa on the side when your lady is up on the mountain?"

Hawke glared at the nosey waitress. "I'm a one-woman man. Too bad there aren't more people around here like that." He cut into his steak. Even though he was thinking about Betz and a few others, he knew the woman would think he meant her.

She said something too quiet for him to hear, threw him a glare, and flounced back to the counter.

Janelle flirted and slept with any male that smiled at her. She'd tried several times to get him to ask her out, but she wasn't his type. He liked quiet, business-minded women, not ones that dressed twenty years younger than they were and flirted with anything that had whiskers.

Hawke ate his meal in peace, staring out the café window watching the world grow gray and fade into darkness briefly before the street lights came on illuminating patches up and down the street.

As soon as he finished, Hawke placed the plate on the end of the table and slid a twenty underneath. He picked up his hat and headed out the door, wondering how many women the pastor had raped.

Ten minutes after leaving the café, Hawke parked in front of the yellow house on the end of Elm Street. The cheery color seemed appropriate for the work Rosa did.

He placed one foot on the porch and the door opened.

"Come in," Rosa beckoned. "As soon as we finish, I'm going to visit Jayne."

"It will be past visiting hours," Hawke said, following the woman into the old Victorian house with many rooms off the side of the hallway.

"This was the first hospital in Wallowa County. It was built in the early nineteen hundreds. I couldn't believe my luck when it came up for sale ten years ago." Rosa led him into the kitchen. The room was decorated in muted yellow with chili peppers and cacti decorations.

There was a pile of folders on her kitchen table next to a plate of miniature cupcakes.

"Have a seat. Do you want coffee or milk to go with your cupcakes?" Rosa stood halfway in between the fridge and the stove.

"Milk, please." Hawke hung his hat on the back of the chair and sat down, pulling the folder on the top of the pile over to him. "These are all patients who said Betz," he couldn't go on adding pastor to the front of the man's name knowing what he did, "raped them?" There had to be close to twenty files. His hand clenched the one he held. Anger burned the back of his throat that this had gone on so long.

"Not all of them called it rape. He used his calling as a way to 'make young women receptive to their husbands.'" The woman said the last as if she were about to vomit.

Hawke stared at Rosa, believing he'd heard wrong.

"He had sex with young women about to be married?"

The anger on the midwife's face drove home the ugly realization.

"How could you have let this go on for so long?" He waved a hand over the folders, thinking about all the ruined lives.

"I tried. Every time there was a new sheriff or city chief, I would go to them and say, what about arresting this guy now? But they would go talk to the good pastor and he'd only tell them I was angry that he had saved the lives of children by talking their parents into putting illegitimate children up for adoption. He made me sound like I wanted to poison young women to make them abort their children." She picked up a folder halfway down the pile. "This was his youngest victim. I did give her a drink made of herbs that allowed her to abort the child. But that man raping her and his hold over her to keep it quiet, drove her to kill herself with drugs when she was eighteen. He'd first raped her when she was fourteen. As far as I know, she was the only one he'd forced himself on more than once. She was a beautiful girl. Silver-blonde hair, large blue eyes, and thick eyebrows."

Rosa studied the photo and for the first time realized just how deranged the pastor had been. How had she been so blind to not see the resemblance? Anger thumped at her temples as she shoved the photo in front of Trooper Hawke's face. "Look at this. The thick eyebrows, the blue eyes, and that chin. He raped his own daughter." She shuddered and thanked whoever killed the man.

"Do you have a photo of Betz? I don't remember

what he looked like." The trooper took the photo. His face didn't show any emotion, but his eyes blazed. "How wouldn't his wife have known about this? From the little I got from Mrs. Laude, she said Eloise said it happened in the church. Do you know where?"

Rosa nodded. She'd been able to get a bit of information out of each victim. They had all wanted someone to believe them, and she had been there. Listening and not telling them they were making it up. She even attended workshops on how to help rape victims. She'd tried over and over again to get someone to listen. But the perverted pastor had spread his good-natured and giving persona all over the county and used the fact she believed in herbal remedies to sway people from believing her accusations. Of course, she didn't go about tossing her knowledge around freely.

No. She knew better than that. She needed the women to like her and trust her if they were to come to her for help with their births.

"I am hesitant to share my records with you. I have tried over the years and all my efforts at exposing the man have only been thrown back at me by his followers and law enforcement." She studied the trooper. He nodded. His brown eyes held sorrow. For what she didn't know. Perhaps the young women the pastor had raped or the fact his counterparts wouldn't listen to her.

"You also need to know that when I suggested to these girls and young women they should go to the police, they all started to pull away. I had to promise not to tell anyone to keep them coming to me for their mental stability. From the classes I've taken on helping rape victims to heal, I knew that if I didn't listen to them, they wouldn't have anyone."

"I'm sorry that no one in law enforcement would listen to you. From the little bit I've learned from Jayne, her grandmother, and you, I feel there could be a lot of people who could have set fire to the Lighted Path Church. *If* it was set on fire and not an accident." He quickly added.

Rosa smiled. "You don't think it was an accident. Otherwise, you wouldn't be here." She tapped a finger on the pile. "These are only the ones who came to me asking for help to get rid of the burden they carried. There are others, like Eloise, who went away and had the child. Most did give the children up for adoption. I believe Eloise kept the baby to hopefully one day prove to her parents that she was indeed raped. But we will never know for sure."

The trooper cleared his throat. "I have reason to believe Jayne may have set the fire."

Rosa's heart rammed into her ribs, remembering the angry woman's words about making Pastor Betz pay. "You can't believe she came to kill him, do you?"

"I don't know how she and her car became jammed between trees on Starvation Ridge. But she reeked of smoke and had scorch marks on her clothing. It's enough to have me wondering if she was in the church when the fire started." Hawke counted the files. Seventeen. That added up to a lot of young women who were violated by someone they should have been able to trust. It also gave him a lot more suspects. He shook his head. Damn, he wished Rosa had come to him sooner. He would have backed her up when she went to see the sheriff and chief. "Do you know if he was still raping young women? How long has he been a pastor here?"

"I gave my cleansing tea to someone three months ago. Her family has been going to the Lighted Path Church for decades. As for how long he and Diane have been here…" She dug to the bottom of the pile and pulled out a file. "I'm not sure if this was his first victim, but she was the first one to come to me and tell me the truth. I believe Gordon and Diane arrived in the county around forty years ago. He was fresh out of college and newly married." Rosa opened the file and set it in front of Hawke.

He read the name. Marcia Grady, fifteen. "Does she still live around here?"

Rosa shook her head, tears glittering in her eyes. "I'm afraid you'll find her in the Winslow Cemetery. Her mother is Merrilee Grady. She owns the Rusty Nail."

Hawke wrenched his gaze from the file to the woman's face. "Did Merrilee know about the rape?" He couldn't see the feisty seventy-plus woman who dished out sarcasm and barbs letting a pastor get away with raping her daughter. But this was a long time after the fact for her to have decided to take matters into her own hands.

"I don't think so. I'm pretty sure Pastor Betz would have been strung up and castrated if she'd known." A smile curved the woman's lips, deepening the wrinkles around her eyes and mouth.

"You didn't tell her?" Hawke wondered at the woman having this information and not taking it to the family members. Surely if she had come forward enough families would have banded together and shown the man for what he was.

"Every woman who comes here, whether they go to full term or not, knows I will keep everything we do and say in confidence. I couldn't go running to the parents with this information. If I had, I wouldn't have had another teenager come to me when they needed help." Rosa started pulling all the files up into a neat stack.

"But if you had taken this to the parents, there would have been fewer women raped by Betz." He studied the woman. How could she have kept all of this a secret?

She glared at him. "Do not blame this on me. I tried to get the police involved without naming names. They wouldn't listen to me. This is on them, not me. I did my best by the women who came to me. It was law enforcement who let them down."

Chapter Six

Hawke drove home thinking about all he'd learned from Rosa. Why hadn't the past sheriffs and police chiefs taken Rosa's complaint seriously? He'd ask the present counterparts tomorrow.

Driving up the lane to the house he and Dani purchased, Hawke was joined by Dog. The brown and gray mutt ran alongside the pickup. Once the vehicle stopped and Hawke opened the door, Dog put his paws on the opening and sniffed up and down Hawke's pant leg.

"I haven't been spending time with another dog. I've had a busy day." Hawke scratched the dog's ears before gently nudging him out of the way. "Did you check on the boys today?" Hawke asked, closing the door and locking the vehicle before striding from the parking area to the barn.

He unlatched the large barn doors, pulled them

open, and walked through to the other side where a small corral opened out onto a pasture. Hawke used his fingers and whistled three short shrill tweets.

The sound of pounding hooves made him smile.

He pulled open the door to the feed storage and put a scoop of rolled oats into three plastic feed troughs.

Snorting and anxious hoof stomping meant the two geldings and mule were at the gate waiting for their nightly ration of grain.

Hawke walked over and hooked the troughs over the metal panels. Then he scratched each animal around the ears and asked them how their day was. There was nothing better than to end his day inhaling the scent of a sweaty horse, grass, and dusty wood.

When he and Dani had talked about purchasing a place together, he'd been single for a lot of years after his first short marriage. He'd been hesitant to share his life or be responsible for a house and land. But now, he wouldn't change a thing. He was enjoying having a house to roam around in on his days off and land that furnished grass and hay for his horses and Dani's string of horses that would soon be going up to the lodge to give rides all summer long.

He appreciated coming home and letting his work worries dissolve for a few hours while he made some time for himself. Something he hadn't done enough of the last fifteen years.

《》《》《》

Rosa smiled at the nurse on duty as she passed the nurse's station. It was an hour after visiting hours, but all the hospital staff knew she was a midwife and allowed her access to the building whenever she wanted. She wasn't treated as well as a doctor but she wasn't turned away.

She knocked quietly on the door of room 17 before pushing it open and peeking in.

Jayne was rolled on her side, facing the window.

"Would you like some company?" Rosa asked, walking over to the side of the bed by the window.

The young woman rolled onto her back and stared at Rosa for a long time, studying her face. "Do I know you?" she finally asked, sitting up.

"Trooper Hawke said you'd lost your memory, but I was under the impression you had regained it." Rosa held out her hand. "I'm Rosa Towman. You came to my house Sunday night. The bright yellow one on the end of Elm Street."

Jayne closed her eyelids. The eyeballs under the thin skin moved rapidly as if the woman was reliving everything in her life.

Rosa lowered her hand and in a soft voice said, "You visited me because you knew your mother, Eloise, had come to me after she was raped."

The young woman's eyelids flew up and she stared wide-eyed at Rosa. "The midwife mom told me to visit."

"Yes. You and I visited Sunday night. Can you remember what you did when you left my house?" Rosa hadn't believed when Jayne had threatened Pastor Betz that she would go through with it. Her intuition said this young woman had only wanted to face the man and accuse him.

Jayne plucked at the thin blanket covering her. "I think I went to my motel room. But I couldn't sleep. I came up with a way to find out who the preacher was. Monday, I sat in a café and asked people about my grandparents and learned what church they attended. After I discovered that, I drove around until I found the church. The one where mom said she'd been raped. I-I wanted to see it. She never blamed me or treated me as if I'd ruined her life, but that day, when he raped her, he'd ruined her life. She left the one person she truly loved—"

"Wade Archer," Rosa said quietly.

The woman sat up straight. "You know the name of the boy she wanted to marry?"

Rosa nodded. "The whole county expected the two to marry. Then Eloise came to me. I announced she was pregnant thinking she would be happy, but she cried. And told me the baby wasn't Wade's and he'd never marry her if he knew what had happened. I tried to tell her she was early enough that I could terminate the pregnancy with herbs. But your grandfather and grandmother sent her off to a relative and that was the last I saw of her." Rosa had always wondered what happened to Eloise. She'd been an intelligent girl with goodness in her heart. Until it had been ripped out by the one person who should have been helping light that goodness.

"Does he still live here?" Jayne asked.

"He teaches at the Alder High School and is the girls basketball coach. I think he also coaches the track team." Rosa held up a hand as if to stop the woman from springing out of the bed. "He has a wife and three kids. Don't contact him yourself. If you would like to visit with him, let me set it up. Take the shock out of your meeting."

Jayne nodded. "I understand. I don't want to hurt him, only learn more about my mom before…you know."

"I do understand. I imagine your mom didn't say very much about her life before you." Rosa noted the slight shake of Jayne's head.

"She never spoke of anything before me other than her mom and dad sent her away when she was pregnant with me." Jayne peered into her eyes. "I told Trooper Hawke about how we came here when I was small. Mom wanted me to have family. But it didn't go well. She stormed out of the house, picked me up, and we never came back." Tears glistened in the young woman's eyes. "Not that I needed family, but it hurt Mom even more, whatever they said to her. She never talked about them again. It was her last hour before cancer took her life that she told me about being raped and how her own parents hadn't believed her."

Jayne sucked in a breath. "I think their failure to believe her was what hurt her more than anything else. That her own parents would take the word of a preacher over her." She put a hand with ragged nails up to her mouth and her eyes widened. She continued, "That's why she never allowed me to go into a church or talk about the things I heard about church and the bible. That preacher robbed her of anything that could have helped her through the whole cancer ordeal. He robbed her of her life."

Rosa stood and wrapped her arms around the young woman. "She had you. At least she had your love until the end. That's more than I can say for your grandparents. They have both become bitter and hard to get along with. But they brought it upon themselves." She patted Jayne's back and released her.

"I believe in my heart that you didn't kill Pastor Betz. But Trooper Hawke said you mentioned standing in a church. Do you remember that at all?" She handed Jayne a tissue.

The young woman blew her nose and stared down at the crumpled tissue. "I have flashes of standing in a church. A man walked out of the back room." She shuddered. "The smile and look in his eyes gave me the creeps. He had bushy white eyebrows and blue eyes." She sucked in air and let it out in a rush of words. "Oh, my God! I was staring at the man who raped my mom, wasn't I?"

Rosa nodded slowly. "That is a pretty good description of Pastor Betz. What did he say?"

Jayne shook her head. "Nothing. He glanced over my shoulder and that's all I remember before I woke up in my car with Trooper Hawke knocking on my window."

This was information Rosa would use when she talked to Diane. While there were many women in the county who had wished a thousand deaths on the pastor, Rosa couldn't see his wife not knowing what he'd been doing all these years. She was active in many organizations and would have known about the pregnancies. Anyone, no matter the age, would have their pregnancy commented on. All anyone had to do was take a good look at several of the adults and children living in the community and they would soon see the resemblance to the deceased pastor.

Specifically, those that still attended the Lighted Path Church.

"The only person you can tell that to is Trooper Hawke. After seeing my decades of files on the women that the pastor had raped, Trooper Hawke believes me and knows there are more people than just you who had reason to kill him."

"Me? Is that what the police think?" Jayne's face drained of color.

Rosa patted the hand closest to her. "Trooper Hawke doesn't believe it. You're lucky he is the one who stumbled over you at Starvation Ridge. He has an excellent track record of finding the people who commit murders. If he is on the case, he will find the killer. That's what makes him a good cop. He digs into the truth and finds the answers." She stood. But she would have to make sure no one was hurt by his digging. "Get a good night's sleep. Call me when they say you can leave. You can stay with me until you're ready to go home."

"Thank you, Mrs. Towman."

"It's Rosa to my friends." She smiled and left the room as the night nurse walked down the hall toward her.

"That patient isn't pregnant. What are you doing talking to her?" Bev Archer asked.

"Her mother was my patient years ago. She doesn't have anyone close, and I'm being a friend when she needs one." Rosa studied the woman. Bev had a long brown braid that hung down her back. Her hazel eyes peered at Rosa over a long thin nose and thin glossy lips.

"Her mother? Who was that?"

"Don't go asking her questions about her mom. She's confused right now." Rosa started to walk away and then spun on her heel. "What time does Wade go to school in the morning?"

"Why do you want to know?" Bev crossed her arms and glared at Rosa.

"Never mind." As she walked out of the hospital, she fished her phone out of her purse. She'd let Trooper Hawke deal with Wade. She was going to visit Diane Betz in the morning.

Chapter Seven

Hawke finished up his chores before heading to work. As he stepped out onto the porch, his phone buzzed. A glance told him it was a text from a number he didn't know. Opening the screen and reading, he realized who was contacting him.

I saw Jayne last night. She said Pastor Betz looked at something over her shoulder before everything went black. I'm going to visit Diane Betz this morning. You should speak to Wade Archer before Jayne does.

He called the number rather than text his disapproval.

"Hello?"

"Rosa, leave the investigation to me and the city police. You could say the wrong thing to the right person and you'll be the next body we find." He believed she could get herself mixed up in trouble. He'd dealt with enough murderers to know when they were backed in a corner, they would kill again, just like a wild animal caught in a metal trap would chew off their leg to get away.

"I'm just going to see how Diane is doing. I won't bring up Jayne or the rapes. I just want to see if she is truly grieving." Rosa's cheery voice didn't fool Hawke. She planned to ask about more than how the pastor's wife was doing. She was on a fishing trip.

"Stay away from Diane Betz. I'll be speaking with her later. Why should I run interference between Jayne and Wade Archer?" He didn't see what the man would have to say to Jayne that would be a problem or vice versa.

"He's going to be in shock when Jayne shows up and tells him who she is. I just thought you might be able to let him in on what we know and that Jayne is in the area." Again, the lilt of her voice sounded too happy.

"Jayne is in the hospital."

"She is getting out today and I've offered to have her stay with me."

"Then *you* can keep her from seeing Archer. I have leads to follow up." He walked to his work vehicle and unlocked the door.

"I won't stop her from learning what she needs to know about her mother. She wants to know what her mother was like before her innocence and family were taken away from her." The call ended.

"Shit!" Hawke slid into his pickup and turned the engine over. There was nothing he liked about this investigation. No matter who he talked to, he was going to upset someone. It wasn't his fault, but he knew he would be the one who took the brunt of the anger.

Instead of picking up speed and heading to Winslow, where the Wallowa County branch of the state police resided, to do some info digging, he turned into his neighbor and ex-landlord's lane. He was always in awe of the white farmhouse that had been built by Herb Trembley's grandfather when he'd homesteaded in the valley.

Before he stepped out of the vehicle, Dog arrived, his tongue hanging out.

"Boy, I'm only visiting. You'll have to go home when I leave," Hawke said, patting the animal on the head.

Darlene Trembley stepped out onto the front porch. "Hawke, I haven't seen you in ages. Do you have time for a cup of coffee?"

"I wouldn't mind a cup. I have some questions for you and Herb. Is he around?" Hawke had used their knowledge of the county history on more than one occasion. They knew nearly everyone in the county and if they didn't know them, they knew someone who did.

"He's just down feeding the calf. One of the cows died giving birth so he has a bottle baby to care for." Darlene led the way into the cheery kitchen. She and Herb were ten years older than Hawke but had become his closest friends, even if they had been his landlords for over fifteen years.

Hawke sniffed appreciatively. "You don't happen to have fresh apple pie, do you?"

Darlene turned with a steaming cup of coffee in her hand. "I do. Would you like a piece?"

"Only if you didn't bake it to take somewhere."

Hawke's mouth watered thinking about Darlene's baking skills.

"I can spare one piece. Polly and her kids are coming over for dinner tonight."

"Are you sure you don't need it? The last time I saw Polly's son, he'd grown a lot." Hawke hoped he sounded more gracious than he felt. Dani wasn't much of a cook, and definitely not a baker. One of the things he missed most about not living over the Trembley's arena was Darlene's baking and cooking.

"Here you go. Enjoy." Darlene sat down with her own cup of coffee.

Hawke cut off the tip of the slice and forked it into his mouth. As the flavors delighted his tongue, he wondered if the rare treat of Darlene's baking made the pie taste so good or if she'd perfected yet another champion ribbon winner.

Herb stepped through the door, glanced at Hawke, and smiled. "You miss us, don't you?"

Hawke picked up his coffee, took a drink, and nodded. "I miss your wife's cooking."

Herb laughed and walked over to the coffee pot. "I knew you were going to miss her cooking when you left. Is this a neighborly call?" He put his hand on the pie plate and Darlene shot to her feet.

"None for you. The rest is dessert tonight when Polly and the kids are here." She pulled the pie from Herb's hands and placed it in a cupboard.

Herb sat down across from Hawke. His gaze lingered on what little was left of the slice of pie.

"Did you hear about The Lighted Path Church burning down?" Hawke put his fork down and picked up his coffee cup.

"Yes. That's awful. And the preacher was burned up inside. Was it arson?" Darlene asked.

"We won't know until Wes can take a look at it." Hawke studied the couple. "Did either of you know Pastor Betz or his wife?"

Herb shook his head. "Not the kind of church we like."

Hawke swept his gaze to the man. "What didn't you like about it?"

"We never attended, but from what Darlene told me about the gossip, I decided it wasn't for us." Herb shrugged and settled his gaze on his wife.

"What kind of gossip?" Hawke shifted his focus to Darlene.

"Just that he was against contraceptive practices and felt every family should have many children, whether they could afford them or not. And from what I gathered from one woman, he liked to spend a lot of time with young women in the congregation."

Hawke set his cup down. "Doing what?"

Darlene glanced over at Herb. "Talking to them about their wifely duties."

"And no one questioned the man about it?" Hawke asked, getting angry with the congregation that let this man prey on their daughters.

"Mrs. Daniels said that Diane was in the room when he talked to the girls. And when she asked Mrs. Betz what they talked about, she said, obeying your husband, keeping his house clean, making his dinner." Darlene's nose wrinkled in disgust. "This day and age it is a fifty-fifty partnership, not the woman doing all the domestic chores, unless she likes it."

"Have you ever met Mrs. Betz?" Hawke asked.

"Yes. She is the superintendent of the handicrafts section at the fair. She donates lap robes to the senior center and helps with the Sunday Supper and Bingo at the Senior Center once a month." Darlene refilled the mugs. "Everyone likes her. She's not full of herself like her husband."

Hawke decided the first person he was going to talk to was Mrs. Betz. "Thank you. If you hear anything else about the pastor, please let me know." He knew having asked Herb and Darlene about the church and pastor, they would now be asking everyone they knew about The Lighted Path congregation.

«»«»«»

On the way to Alder, Hawke called Sergeant Spruel to update him on what he'd learned so far. "I'll be spending the morning questioning people. After that, I'll head out north to check for shed hunters on the refuge since we can't do any more until Wes tells us what caused the fire."

"I appreciate you keeping me in the loop. Just try to do your Fish and Wildlife job every day for a few hours." Spruel ended the call.

Hawke grinned. The man had been his superior for the last seven years and understood his need to find answers. Coming across Jayne on Starvation Ridge was a puzzle that needed to be solved.

As the Alder city limits came into sight, Hawke dialed Officer Herold.

"Hawke, what's up?" the city officer answered.

"I'm en route to question Mrs. Betz. Want to be

part of the interview?"

"Yeah, I can meet you at Mrs. Larsen's, that's where Mrs. Betz is staying," Herold said.

"I'll be there in ten."

"Copy."

Hawke ended the call and drove through downtown Alder before making a right and heading toward the burnt church. He knew that Mrs. Larsen was a neighbor. The buildings on either side of the church were the pastor's house on one side and a building they used to sell donated items on the other. The Larsen house must have been on the other side of that building.

Turning the corner onto Burl Street, he noticed the city car sitting in front of a house three houses down and across the street from the church. He pulled in behind the car and Herold stepped out.

Hawke joined Herold. "This is where Mrs. Larsen lives?"

"Yes." Herold studied him. "Why?"

"Something had me thinking she lived on the same side of the street as the church." Hawke couldn't shake the feeling the woman had arrived from the opposite direction the day before when she gave aid to Mrs. Betz.

"Nope. This is the house. She's a widow. Her husband passed about three years ago." Herold walked up to the door and rang the bell.

They waited thirty seconds and the door opened. An average-sized woman with gray-streaked brown hair, cut blunt at chin length, peered out at them through the screen door.

"Are you here to talk to Diane?" she asked.

"Yes, we are," Herold said. "May we come in?"

The woman opened the screen, and they followed her into a small dining room bright with sunshine from the tall narrow windows circling half the room.

Mrs. Betz sat at the table. She held a pretty cup halfway to her mouth. She was also of average height. Hawke could see she was a good twenty to thirty pounds heavier than her neighbor. Her hair was silver with dark streaks throughout. Her long hair was braided, hanging down her back.

"Diane, these officers would like to ask you some questions." Mrs. Larsen sat, then stood back up. "Would you like some coffee?"

"No thank you, we're good," Herold said.

Hawke nodded.

The woman sat back down. Then she jumped back up. "Do you want me in here? I know Diane would prefer it, but on television, they always try to separate people when they talk to them."

"You can stay," Hawke said. "We're only here asking questions about the fire and where the Pastor and Mrs. Betz were when it started."

The flighty woman sat back down on the chair like a bird alighting on a branch.

"Mrs. Betz, were you the one who called in the fire yesterday morning?" Hawke asked.

The woman took a sip of her drink, placed the cup on the saucer, and shook her head. "No. I don't know who called it in. I was in the house when I smelled the smoke. I looked out and ran to see if Gordon had returned from a visit to the hospital. Mr. Neuman took a turn for the worst the night before."

"Was the back of the building already burning when you arrived at the church?" Hawke asked, thankful Herold was letting him ask the questions since he was the first on the scene.

"No, I was able to go in the back door. I called out to Gordon but he didn't reply. The smoke was terrible, I could barely see. I tried the office door but it was locked. The smoke was seeping in through the transit window on top."

"What did you do next?" he asked.

"I called and pounded on the door until I couldn't breathe and then I ran out to the front of the church hoping someone would see me." She glanced at Hawke. "I told you Gordon was still in the church."

He nodded. "When I went around the back the flames were leaping out of the windows and the door was on fire. There wasn't a way in." He glanced at the notepad where Herold was taking notes. "Could you tell where the fire started?"

"There was smoke and flames everywhere. I'm not sure." Mrs. Betz wiped her nose with a tissue.

"Before the fire, you said you thought your husband might still be at the hospital. Did he have any calls that morning or the night before from anyone other than the Neuman family?" Hawke wanted to see if the woman would mention Jayne's visit.

"Not that I know of. He was out in his office in the church when I went to bed. He was working on a sermon." She picked up her cup and sipped.

"Did he work late often?" Hawke asked.

"Only when he was having trouble deciding what subject he wanted to preach about." She flicked a glance at Mrs. Larsen.

"Did the Neumans call you or your husband about needing him at the hospital?"

Mrs. Betz stared at him. "What does this have to do with my husband and the church burning up?"

"I was just curious who took the call from the Neumans." Hawke opened his hands palm up as if to say it wasn't a big thing.

"I took the call and I told him when he came to bed." She picked up her cup, holding it in front of her face, elbows on the table.

"Thank you." He turned his attention to Mrs. Larsen. "How did you learn about the fire?"

She put her cup down and folded her hands on her lap. "I saw the smoke and followed it back to the area of the church. I started over and that's when I heard all the sirens getting louder."

"Were you out at all the night before?" Hawke asked.

"Out? What do you mean?" She flicked a glance at Mrs. Betz.

"Just out in your yard or coming home from somewhere. Did you happen to notice a car parked in front of the church at any time?" Hawke needed to find someone to say Jayne's car had been parked near the church. Not that he wanted to find her guilty, but more to find the truth to the story she told of standing in the church one minute and waking in her car at Starvation Ridge.

"No, I didn't see…" Her gaze dropped to the cup in her hands. "There was a blue smaller car in the parking lot yesterday evening. I thought maybe it was just someone needing a few minutes of privacy in the church." She glanced up at him.

"Do you see that a lot?" Hawke asked.

Mrs. Larsen nodded. "People visit the church at all hours of the day and night."

"Gordon thought the church and God should be available to whomever whenever they needed guidance." Mrs. Betz sipped her drink and added, "He kept the church unlocked but locked the office."

Hawke studied her. He wondered at the way she said the last bit. Almost as if she found it ironic. "Why did he lock his office?"

Mrs. Betz picked up her empty cup, looked in it, and shrugged. "He did keep the money we raised and charitable donations in the office."

Chapter Eight

Hawke felt Herold shifting as if he thought they were done questioning Mrs. Betz. But the question Hawke wanted to ask wasn't easy to spit out. The man was dead and he wanted to know if he'd been a serial rapist, something he hadn't discussed with Herold yet. He'd wait to ask the harder questions until he'd updated the other law enforcement personnel about what he knew.

"Thank you for your answers. They have been a big help." Hawke stood. Herold closed his notepad and thanked the women.

"Follow me to City Hall," Hawke said to Herold when they were standing on the sidewalk. "I have information for Browning and you need to hear it. It could be important to this investigation."

Herold nodded and strode to his vehicle.

Hawke slid into his pickup and headed to City

Hall. As he walked up the steps to enter the building his phone buzzed. It was Rosa.

I'm picking Jayne up in an hour.

Bring her to the City Police station. He replied.

Not if you will arrest her. She attached a red angry face emoji.

We need her statement for the accident report. They needed her statement for her insurance purposes. They also required documentation of her relationship to the deceased and an explanation of her smoke-scented and charred clothing.

We'll be there at 11.

Copy.

Hawke stepped into City Hall and found Herold waiting for him at the entrance to the police section of the building.

"Want me to gather up the chief and meet you in the conference room?" Herold asked, striding down the hall.

"That works. Jayne Laude, the woman I found at Starvation Ridge, will be in here at eleven to give a statement about the car and we can ask her other questions."

Herold stopped at a door and waved for Hawke to enter. "Browning says you found her smelling of smoke with charred clothes. But I didn't get anyone yesterday to say they saw a vehicle hurrying away from the church before they noticed the fire."

"Yeah, that's what puzzles me. Get Browning." Hawke helped himself to a bottle of water from a fridge in the corner of the room.

Herold returned with Browning. Both men entered

the room.

"Good news the Laude woman is coming in," Browning said, taking a seat with a cup of coffee in his hand.

"Yeah. About that." Hawke drank some water and slowly screwed the cap on the bottle as he formed his thoughts peering at Browning. He gave Herold a glance before holding his gaze on the senior officer. "I want to know why your predecessors, and I'm thinking you, since Rosa Towman told me that she had brought up Betz raping young women of his congregation to everyone who has been chief since the first girl told her what had happened, didn't do anything about it."

Browning squirmed in his seat not meeting Hawke's gaze. He'd ignored the information when Hawke had told him his suspicions of Betz the day before. "Are you saying she was telling the truth?"

"She has seventeen files of young women and girls who came to her because they were raped by the good Pastor Betz." Hawke stared into Browning's eyes. "Those are just the ones who came to her."

"When I took over there was a file sitting on my desk. In it were the names of the people who my predecessors had deemed unworthy of their time. Rosa Towman was on the list. When she came in, I gave her the same song and dance, I'm sure every chief she'd talked to had given her." Browning shook his head. "But you say she has proof?"

Hawke glanced at Herold. "Is there a photo of Betz in the file about the fire?"

The officer shook his head but pulled out his phone and messed with it.

"The daughter of one of his victims will be showing up here at eleven this morning. Her mother told her the truth just before she died. I told you yesterday that Mrs. Laude said her daughter had accused Pastor Betz of raping her but she thought it was Wade Archer who got her pregnant."

Browning leaned back in his chair. "When did you dig up all this evidence?"

"After talking to Rosa last night. She invited me to her house to see the files. She even had a photo of one of his teenage victims who looked like him, with bushy eyebrows and blue eyes." Hawke shuddered at the thought the man was so perverted he'd raped his daughter. "He caused several young women to commit suicide."

"Rosa has all of this documented?" Browning asked.

Hawke nodded.

"Why didn't she bring it with her when she came to see me?" Browning stood up and paced the room.

"Because she feared if she named the women, they would stop coming to her for help. If she couldn't stop the rapist, she could at least help the victims." Hawke saw her logic to a point. But if one or two had had family backing them, they might have been willing to come forward. If Eloise had been backed up by her parents, she would have been strong enough to have convinced law enforcement and a jury.

"Did his wife know?" Browning asked.

Hawke glanced at Herold.

"That's why you acted like you had something else you wanted to ask her this morning," Herold said, pulling out his notepad.

"Yeah. I decided I needed to bring it to the attention of your chief and the sheriff before I asked her." Hawke leaned back in his chair. "That's where I'm going after we question Ms. Laude."

"You saw Diane Betz coming out of the church when you drove up," Browning said.

"Yes. She said she saw the smoke from the house and went to see if her husband had come back from visiting someone at the hospital." Hawke picked up the water bottle.

"A Mr. Neuman," Herold added. "According to Mrs. Betz, the family called Monday night and asked for the pastor to call on him."

Hawke pointed at Herold. "Those are the first people you need to contact. Find out when they called and when Betz arrived and left the hospital."

Herold nodded.

"Mrs. Betz said her husband didn't have any visitors at the church and he was working on his sermon the night before the fire. Ms. Laude told me she was standing in a church, in front of Betz when everything went dark." Hawke put the lid back on the empty water bottle. "I'm hoping she can tell us what time she was standing in the church."

"But Mrs. Larsen did say she saw a blue car in front of the church last evening," Herold said.

"Which is the car that I found Ms. Laude in, stuck between two trees at Starvation Ridge,"
Hawke added.

Browning ran a hand over his face and stood. "It's late but I'm going to have a talk with Rosa Towman."

"She's the one bringing Ms. Laude in. You can talk to her while Craig and I question Ms. Laude." Hawke glanced at his watch. "They should be here in fifteen minutes." Hawke nodded to Herold. "While we wait you can contact the Neuman family."

Herold grabbed his notepad, stood, and left the room.

Hawke studied Browning. "Rosa is adamant that people's lives not be shattered by her telling us about all the rapes."

Browning ran a hand over his face and sighed. "I'll let her know we don't plan on having it splashed in the headlines but we do need the names so we can talk to them about alibis."

"That's what I told her. She feels compelled to make sure no one gets hurt. I hope we can do that, but this is a decades-old problem that won't be easy to hide."

"I agree." Browning stood. "I'll be in my office when Rosa and Ms. Laude arrive."

Hawke nodded and pulled out his phone. He stood and headed to the entrance of the building to make his calls outside, where he could pace.

Stepping back into City Hall, Hawke found Jayne and Rosa sitting in the waiting area.

"Come on back with me," he said, leading the way down the hall and into the room where he, Browning, and Herold had sat that morning. "Have a seat. I'll go find Chief Browning."

The two women sat and Hawke headed for the chief's office. He found both Browning and Herold in the room.

"Ms. Laude and Rosa Towman are here," Hawke said.

The two men stood and followed him back to the conference/breakroom.

"Mrs. Towman, it's been a while, I'm Chief Browning." The chief held out a hand.

"I know who you are. One of the people who wouldn't listen to me." She remained seated.

"I'd like to talk to you about that in my office," Browning said, dropping his arm.

"We want to get justice for everyone," Hawke said.

"I told you I don't want women to think what they tell me isn't confidential. And the man is dead, what difference does it make now?" Rosa didn't sound as angry as she had the night before.

"It might get women to counseling if they need it." Hawke now wondered if the woman was backing off because she might also be giving them the names of the person who set fire to the church.

Rosa glared at Browning and then Hawke. "I'm not naming any names until I get both of you to understand I don't want any of this to come out publicly. Some of these women have finally come to terms with what happened to them and their actions afterward. I don't want them to lose the confidence they've gained or to have people looking at them as if they brought the trouble to themselves. Believe me, if you heard each woman's story, you wouldn't be asking me to give you their names." Rosa crossed her arms.

"We understand that these women have gone through hell at the hands of someone they should have been asking guidance from." Browning waved a hand toward the hall. "I promise, we will only ask them their whereabouts during the time period the Medical Examiner determines to be the time of death."

"They aren't stupid. They'll know you are trying to see if they killed him." Rosa stood her ground.

"If they didn't kill him then they shouldn't be worried." Browning waved again. "Mrs. Towman, Rosa, come with me while Trooper Hawke and Officer Herold talk to Ms. Laude."

"Please, go with the chief, while we talk with Jayne." Hawke grasped the woman's elbow and maneuvered her out into the hall. Chief Browning followed, closing the door behind him.

Chapter Nine

"Jayne, this is Alder City Officer Herold. He'll be taking notes while I talk to you." Hawke took a seat across from the woman. She had more color today. Her head still had a bandage. "How's the head?" he asked.

She touched the bandage. "It doesn't hurt as much. But the doctor said I can't wash my hair for a week so the stitches don't dissolve too soon."

Hawke made a mental note to see if the ER doctor could tell from the cut what might have caused it. He hadn't seen anything in the car that would have struck her in the head during the impact of the car into the trees.

"Ms. Laude, we're going to record your statement," Herold said, putting a small tape recorder on the table.

"Is that necessary?" she asked, her eyes widening like a frightened animal.

"That way we get everything down in your words. Taking notes can lose words and meanings." Herold clicked the button on the recorder. "I'm Alder City Officer Craig Herold with OSP Senior Trooper Hawke we're here to take a statement from…" He pushed the button stopping the device. "When I push the button state your name, please." He clicked the button.

"Jayne Elise Laude."

"Jayne, would you please tell us what happened leading up to when I found you in your car at Starvation Ridge?" Hawke asked.

"I'm unsure what happened," she said, her gaze flicking back and forth between Hawke and the man sitting next to him.

"Start with why you came to Wallowa County," Hawke suggested.

"My mother passed away last year. About a month before she passed, she told me the truth about how I was conceived." Her gaze dropped to her hands on the table, the fingers woven together. "She had never talked about my father and I figured I was a one-night fling. But when she told me…I-I didn't know how to react. I kept asking her why she kept me. She said because she knew after what had happened, she could never trust or tolerate a man touching her. I was her chance to be a mother. And she gave me all her love." She tipped her tear-stained face up and peered into Hawke's eyes. "She may have hated how I was conceived but she loved me."

"Yes, it sounds like she did. What made you decide to come here?" Hawke asked softly. He felt for the young woman who had learned the hard truth in a harsh way.

"Mom asked me to come see my grandparents and

show them that she hadn't lied." Jayne studied him with confusion in her eyes. "I didn't understand how they would know."

"Until you stood in the church looking at the man who had raped your mother." Hawke waited for her to compose herself.

"Yes. After I talked to Rosa the day I arrived in town—"

"When was that?" Hawke interrupted her.

"Sunday evening. She verified that my mom had been raped by the preacher of her family's church. I spent Monday sitting in cafes and visiting with people. I asked if anyone knew the Laude family. Then asked if they attended the same church."

"Why didn't you go talk to your grandparents? They could have told you," Hawke asked, thinking about how resourceful the woman had been to find the answers she wanted.

"I wasn't ready to meet them. I wanted to stare the man who'd forced himself on my mom in the face." Anger deepened the color in her cheeks.

"When did you go to the church?" Hawke asked.

"Monday evening. It was about seven, I think. After I discovered the church, I drove past it half a dozen times trying to get up the courage to face the man." She wiped her hands on her pant legs as if just thinking about it was making her nervous all over again.

"You parked in the parking lot and walked into the church?" Hawke asked.

"I parked in front of the church. The sign on the door said if it was after seven to knock at the house next door." Her gaze met his. "So, it must have been after seven. I went to the house and knocked on the door. No one answered." She shrugged. "I went back to the church and tried the door. It wasn't locked so I walked in. There was a light shining at the back of the building. I walked in that direction. A man stepped out of a back room. He walked closer to me." She shuddered. "The look in his eyes and the creepy smile. Before I could say anything, he looked over my shoulder and things went black."

"Then what happened?" Hawke asked her.

"I woke up in my car with you tapping on the window." She untwisted her fingers and peered at him.

"How did your clothes get smokey and charred?" he asked.

She shook her head. "I don't know. I wasn't anywhere near a fire."

Hawke glanced at Herold. He was studying the woman. The woman's account sounded sincere. But the fact she was found in the morning with smoky charred clothes after the church burned, had him wondering if there wasn't more to the story. There were twelve hours unaccounted for from Monday evening to Tuesday morning at eight when the fire started.

His phone buzzed. A glance at the name had him standing. "Let Ms. Laude wait for Rosa in the waiting area." Hawke strode out of the room and down the hall as he answered his phone.

"Wes, are you back in town?" Hawke asked the Fire Marshal.

"I'm back and I just finished checking out The Lighted Path Church remains. It was arson. It started in the back southeast corner of the building."

Hawke stared at Jayne's back as she walked down the hall in the opposite direction. "Can you tell if it was set right away or had some method of making it start later?"

"How did you know that?" Wes asked.

"Just a hunch."

"I believe a delayed device was used. I could tell there had been an accelerant in the middle of the back corner room."

"The one where the body was found," Hawke added.

"Yes, that room. I can give you more information after I have the samples I picked up studied."

"Thanks, Wes. I'd like to know what we're looking for." Hawke ended the call as Rosa came out of Browning's office. She looked up and down the hall, spotted Hawke, and walked toward him.

"You'll find Jayne waiting for you out front," Hawke said.

The woman's face looked older. Her wrinkles had deepened and her skin didn't look as pink.

"Bringing all of this up is going to wreck marriages and pull families apart." Her voice didn't hold the steam and anger it had before.

"We won't have to bring it up if the person who murdered him isn't one of his victims." Hawke knew it was a small chance it wasn't a rape victim. Though it could be a family member who finally had enough and took care of things.

"I wish you had tried harder and the police had listened to you when it first started," Hawke said. But he knew as well as anyone that you couldn't dwell on what should have happened. "Take Jayne home and keep an eye on her. She's a person of interest in this case."

Rosa studied him. The trooper thought Jayne was capable of burning down the church. "You heard her side of things. I'd say whoever bashed her over the head and left her out at Starvation Ridge to die is the killer, not Jayne." She glared at the trooper and stomped down the hall toward the waiting area. Not for one minute did she believe Jayne would set fire to a church and kill the man she came here to publicly accuse of raping her sixteen-year-old mother.

Jayne sat on a chair, clutching her purse to her just as she had Sunday night when they'd visited. Rosa saw hurt, confusion, and sadness, but not a killer.

"Come on, let's go to my house and have a bowl of ice cream and compare notes." She motioned for the young woman to stand.

Jayne stood and walked slowly toward her. "How did your meeting go?" Jayne asked as they pushed out the City Hall doors into the warm spring afternoon.

Rosa drew in a deep breath to fill her lungs with fresh air and let it out slowly. "There are going to be a lot of women unhappy with me. I think it would be best for the two of us to stay at home."

"That bad, huh? At least you aren't a suspect in a murder." Jayne opened the passenger door.

"No, but I hope I'm not the next victim," Rosa said as a joke but her spine tingled. A sure sign something bad was about to happen.

Chapter Ten

Hawke had discussed with Browning and Herold that they would keep the information about the rapes between them until they needed to reveal that aspect of the investigation. It was the best way to keep Rosa helping them and to avoid angry civilians storming law enforcement for not doing something to stop the man.

He grabbed a cheeseburger and vanilla shake at the Shake Shack drive-through and now sat in the church parking lot studying the charred building as he ate.

His phone buzzed. A glance at the screen told him it was Dr. Vance.

"Dr. Vance, what did you find out?" Hawke answered.

"I discovered a crack in the skull that didn't happen during the fire," Dr. Vance said. "I'm pretty sure when the state pathologist opens him up, she'll discover he didn't inhale any smoke."

"You're saying you think he was dead before the

fire started?" Hawke wasn't sure if he liked that. It could mean the fire was started to hide the fact the man was killed. He could think of two people who would want to keep the murder averted from them. They'd just left the City Police Station.

"Yes. His body wasn't as destroyed as I think the person wanted. But when Wes told me the fire started in the room where the body was found, I looked it over closer. That's when I noticed the cracked skull and started the chain of paperwork to send it to the state pathologist in Clackamas."

"Thank you. I'll continue working this as if it were a homicide." He ended the call, finished eating his hamburger, and thought about what he'd learned. The fire wasn't an accident. The pastor was most likely dead before the fire started. And either someone drove an unconscious Jayne to Starvation Ridge and lodged her car between trees or the woman took off in the middle of the night disoriented, possibly because she'd killed someone, and ended up on a dirt road going into the wilderness.

Hawke shook his head. The second scenario didn't feel right. No one, no matter how disoriented they were, would take the road out to Starvation Ridge. There were so many others out the north highway that would be more visible and look like good roads.

He finished his food and exited his vehicle. There was crime scene tape around the church property, even the house. He wasn't sure why the house was included, but it meant Mrs. Betz wasn't staying there. He ducked under the tape where it was wrapped around a tree and walked into the charred remains where the front door once stood.

It was evident the front of the church was the last to catch fire. Here and there were smoky, singed pieces of the building and fixtures. The farther into the burnt building he walked, Hawke encountered more ash and fewer pieces of boards and blackened furniture. The back corner where the body was found, had ashes and fragments of metal objects that hadn't burned.

Hawke crouched near what looked like a bust of the Virgin Mary. The foot-long and six-inch wide rendition of the mother of God appeared to be made of bronze. It would make a good heavy object to bash someone's head in. Having been left in the fire, he doubted there would be any traces of fingerprints or blood. He made a note to bring back an evidence bag large enough for the sculpture.

He kicked around ash as the sound of vehicles crunched the gravel in the parking lot. Hawke glanced in that direction and stopped kicking. The vehicles had state plates.

"What are you doing walking around in the crime scene?" a man in his forties called out as he ducked under the crime scene tape.

Hawke strode toward the man. "I'm Senior Trooper Hawke. I'm working the homicide along with City Officer Herold." He held out his hand.

The man, who was followed by a woman and a younger man, ignored Hawke's outstretched hand. "We're from the State Major Crime Task Force. The fire marshal said this was arson and that a man was killed. We're here to take over the investigation."

Hawke settled his hand on his utility belt and

studied the group. "You're a forensic team here to sift through the ashes for evidence?" He'd heard the man say "Take over the investigation" but he wasn't giving it up.

"That's what these two do. Kate and Gage get your suits on and start looking." The other man continued to stare at Hawke.

"I've been questioning people and have learned the man who was killed has a history that would make him a target." Hawke crossed his arms, watching the man. "That means you'll be dealing with a lot of people who don't usually talk much to strangers, let alone talk about things they want to keep hidden."

"You're telling me as a local, you can get by with digging in people's dirty laundry?" The man put a hand inside his jacket and pulled out a cell phone.

"Yeah. I'll get more information and upset fewer people if I do the digging and not some outsider." Hawke had no idea who the man was calling to back him up.

"Hello, is Lieutenant Keller available?" the man asked. "Tell her it's Ed Goodwin from Major Crimes."

Hawke grinned at the man. Carol Keller went through the academy with Hawke. They had also worked on a case together when a young woman went missing at the Umatilla Reservation and Hawke's mom had called him to help look for her. His mother had feared the worse and it was. The young mother had been kidnapped for human trafficking and the sex slave industry. Luckily Hawke and FBI Special Agent Quinn Pierce had been able to find the woman before she and a dozen other women were shipped to other countries.

They had also retrieved, with the help of Dani and a young woman who worked security at the Spotted Pony Casino on the reservation, another young woman who had already been transported to Dubai.

"Lt. Keller, it's Ed. Yes, I'm in Alder. Kate and Gage have started searching through the remains." He listened and scowled at Hawke. "He happens to be standing right here." He held the phone out, "She wants to talk to you."

Hawke took the phone. "Hi, Carol."

"Hawke, how did you know I'd send a Major Crime team over there," she asked.

"I didn't. I was here trying to make sense of things when they arrived and Goodwin told me he was taking over the case." Hawke gave the man a pointed stare.

"What have you learned so far?" she asked.

Hawke walked away from Goodwin and told her about the actions of the deceased pastor and how a midwife had all the information about his indiscretions. "I promised the midwife I'd use as much discretion as I can so she would give us the names to question the women about their alibis." He also told her about Jayne. "I don't have to tell you how these people are going to join together to protect those who have been violated. I think it would be best if the investigation stayed local. People will open up better."

"I have no doubt you will put those you question at ease. Sergeant Goodwin is a bit abrasive. I'll have him only deal with evidence. You question the residents."

"Thanks, Carol." Hawke was relieved he could continue with the investigation. It would make the locals feel more at ease, but it would also allow him to keep an eye on Jayne and Rosa.

"You're welcome. How's your mom?" Carol asked.

Hawke walked back to a scowling Goodwin. "Doing well. My sister moved back home earlier this year."

"That's wonderful! I know your mom really missed her."

"Yeah. It's been good for both of them." Hawke wasn't going to tell Carol the whole story of how Marion had been accused of murdering her fiancé, and he had gone to Montana to prove her innocent.

"Put Sergeant Goodwin back on the phone. Good luck."

"Thanks." Hawke smiled and handed the phone to Goodwin.

He walked over to the two digging through the ashes as Goodwin tried to convince Lt. Keller that he would be less biased considering the circumstances. Hawke pointed out the brass Virgin Mary and suggested they send it to the lab as it would crack a skull. When he walked back by Goodwin the man scowled and headed toward his techs. Hawke figured Goodwin wanted to know what he'd said to them.

Hawke still had a lot of daylight left to head out to Wenaha and make sure no one was sneaking onto the Elk Refuge looking for sheds. There wasn't anything more he could do here today until they had more forensic information. He'd let Ed and his team dig around and hope the pathologist would have more to go on the next couple of days.

《》《》《》

Rosa stood with Jayne outside the fence surrounding the high school football field and track. She'd pointed out Wade Archer when they'd arrived. He was walking all over the track field talking to the students as they practiced running and throwing things. She'd never understood what pleasure anyone could get out of running. But she would have been good at throwing things.

"Should I wait until the practice is over?" Jayne asked. The young woman had been watching the man ever since they'd arrived. She had both hands gripping the chain-link fence as she peered through the squares.

"I think that would be the best. When kids start leaving the field, we'll wander down to the entrance to the field." Rosa had spotted two of the pastor's offspring on the track. A boy and a girl. They had no idea they were half-brother and sister. Rosa wondered how many of these children growing up had dated. She shivered. Surely the pastor would have kept track and made sure they didn't carry their relations too far. But then, he had taken his own daughter and caused her to commit suicide. Rosa wondered if the child had known how she'd come into the world and who was forcing himself on her. She hoped not.

"They're starting to leave," Jayne said, releasing her grip on the chain-link fence. She took a step and glanced over her shoulder at Rosa. "How do I…"

"I'll introduce you." Rosa walked alongside the nervous woman. "Just be natural. I'm sure he will be happy to meet you. I know he was heartbroken when your mother left." Rosa put a hand on Jayne's arm, slowing her as she watched Wade walking with two young men and talking.

When the three came out of the gate, Rosa called out, "Wade, could I speak with you?"

The tall, broad-shouldered man with dark blond hair walked over to Rosa, a smile on his face. "I didn't take you for a track fan, Rosa."

She smiled and said, "I'm not. I don't see the need to run unless you are being chased by a wild animal."

Wade laughed as his gaze wandered to Jayne. His brow furrowed as his gaze traveled over her face. "Have we met?"

Jayne shook her head.

"You aren't related to one of the kids? You look familiar." Wade continued to study her.

Rosa wondered if it was because he'd had several of her half-siblings on his teams or if he recognized the traits she'd received from her mother.

"Wade, this is Jayne Laude."

His eyebrows went up.

Rosa continued, "Eloise's daughter. She wanted to meet you. Her mom talked about you a lot."

Wade held out a hand.

Jayne clasped it and shook.

Rosa saw how the young woman trembled.

"How is Eloise?" Wade asked.

"S-she died about a year ago. Cancer," Jayne said.

Wade released her hand. "I'm sorry to hear that. I've always wondered why she took off."

"If you have the time, we'd like to talk to you about that," Rosa said, motioning to the stands.

"Not here. I live just a few blocks from here." Wade motioned to his right.

"Is Bev okay with us talking about your first love?" Rosa asked.

"She has swing shift, she won't be home for a couple more hours." He stopped beside a pickup. "Want to hop in or follow me?"

"We'll follow." Rosa led Jayne over to her car and drove behind Wade's pickup the two blocks to his house.

"What about his kids? Do any of them still live at home?" Jayne asked.

"They are off at college or out on their own. It's just Bev and Wade now." Rosa parked on the street and they followed Wade into the two-story older home.

"Would you like something to drink? I can make coffee, tea, or we have water or juice." Wade dropped a backpack by the door and walked across the living room to a doorway.

"If it's not any trouble I'll have coffee. Jayne will have hot tea. Thank you, Wade," Rosa said, maneuvering Jayne to the couch and they both sat.

Jayne's gaze moved about the room. "Are those photos of his kids?" she whispered.

"Yes." Rosa patted the fisted hand Jayne rested on her leg.

Wade walked back in carrying a tray. It held the two hot drinks and a glass of juice as well as a plate of cookies. "These new one-cup brewers are nice." He placed the hot drinks on the coffee table in front of Rosa and Jayne and then picked up the glass of juice and two cookies and sat in a chair across from them. "Now tell me all about Eloise. She obviously married."

Jayne's face grew red and tears glistened in her

eyes. Rosa squeezed her hand.

"Did I say something wrong?" Wade asked.

"Did you ever find out why Eloise left?" Rosa asked.

"Not really. She came to me and said, she couldn't ruin my life but wouldn't tell me what she was talking about. Then there was some rumor going around she left to have a baby. I knew it wasn't mine, we never went that far, but I also knew she didn't go out with anyone else." His eyes narrowed and he peered at Jayne. "Are you that baby?"

She nodded. "I was conceived from my mother being raped."

Wade slammed back against the cushion of the chair and spilled his juice down the front of him but he didn't seem to notice. "Who? Why didn't she tell me?"

"Because her parents didn't believe her. They said you must have gotten her pregnant." Jayne spit out the words.

"I would have married her after I cut off the jerk's dick." Wade's eyes blazed. "I loved your mom. We'd made plans to marry after we'd gone off to college. She didn't want her parents trying to talk her out of it. They sent her to Pastor Betz for counseling when we started dating. She hated it. After one time there she asked me to take her on drives the days she was supposed to be at the counseling."

Rosa could see Jayne was about to unleash on this man who knew nothing. "Stay calm," she said to Jayne. "Drink your tea. I'll do the talking." She shifted her gaze to Wade. "It was Pastor Betz who raped her under the auspices of showing her what it was like to have a relationship."

Jayne blurted, "He is my father."

Wade stood, pacing back and forth. "And she told her parents this?"

Rosa nodded. "They didn't believe her. Said a pastor wouldn't do that. The sad thing is, I knew and tried to get the police to do something about him. No one would listen, and he would tell them stories about me." She studied him when he stopped in front of her. "He has been doing this for thirty years. You have taught many of his children and rape victims. I know because they come to me to help them through the direction they want to take. But he also caused several suicides."

"I'm glad he burned in that damn church," Wade said. He turned a sad face to Jayne. "I'm so sorry your mom thought she had to run away from me. She could have told me the truth and I would have believed her. I would have helped her. Did she ever marry? Find love?"

"No. She felt she was ruined for anyone. But she talked of you often and how happy she'd been before, you know." Jayne picked up the cup of tea. "She talked a lot about you her last month. And she'd smile. You were what got her through. I wanted you to know that." Tears ran down Jayne's cheeks. "She said you and I were the best things in her short life."

Wade sat down on the couch next to Jayne and put his arm around her. "I wish she would have told me. We all three could have had the best life together."

Rosa took Jayne's cup away from her as the young woman folded into Wade's arms and cried.

Chapter Eleven

Hawke backed out of the viewpoint where he had sat studying the refuge below him with binoculars. He'd checked all the areas around the elk refuge where people parked to walk in and look for shed antlers. There weren't any fresh tracks. But he wanted to make sure someone hadn't hiked in from another direction.

Finding sheds wasn't against the law, but traipsing about in the elk refuge was. It disturbed the elk and they stayed away.

As he drove around, he'd contemplated how to go about talking to the women in Rosa's files to ask them where they were Tuesday morning when the fire broke out at the church. Most were going to be upset that he knew about what happened to them, but he had to get the victims to see it was the only way to bring a killer to justice.

His phone rang. He didn't know the number but answered it anyway.

"Hawke."

"It's Ed Goodwin. Kate and Gage are still sifting through the ashes. Where are you? I thought you could get me up to speed on this case." The man's voice didn't sound like he really wanted to be caught up but more wanted to know it all and take over.

"I'm out Wenaha. It's fifty-plus miles north of Alder. You're welcome to come find me." Hawke grinned as he sipped the coffee he'd poured from a thermos while sitting and watching the refuge.

"When will you be back?" Irritation grated in Goodwin's voice.

"I'd say close to six. But I plan to make my way down through Promise and end up in Eagle. I can meet you at the Rusty Nail Café in Winslow at seven."

"I'll be there." Goodwin ended the call.

Hawke wound his way out of the Wenaha area traveling south until he hit Promise Road. As he drew closer to Eagle, he enjoyed seeing the farm ground coming to life after the long winter.

Waiting to pull onto the highway west of Eagle, a car with tinted windows raced by well over the speed limit.

Hawke shot out into the lane behind the low-slung sports car. The driver was headed into Minam Canyon. Not a good place to be traveling at high speeds.

Flipping on the dash camera, Hawke grasped the mic on his shoulder. "Dispatch, this is Hawke. I need information on Oregon plate five-five-six, delta, hotel, kilo, a new Dodge charger, green and black. It's headed out Minam Grade at a high speed." He released the mic and used both hands as he slowed to take the corner.

His pickup didn't take corners as well as the sports car he followed and he didn't want to end up in the river.

The radio crackled and dispatch said, "The car belongs to Raymond Mellon. There's a warrant for him out of Multnomah County."

"Copy." Hawke switched on his lights and called for backup at the upper end of the grade.

He lost sight of the vehicle as he slowed to go around a 30 mph corner. When he came out of the 270 degree turn, he didn't see the car. The sportscar couldn't have raced out of sight that quickly. Hawke slowed down and turned around. Driving back toward the tight corner, he noticed skid marks in the gravel and grass alongside the road.

Following the tire trail, Hawke spotted the car in the middle of the river. It was spring with snow melt that caused the river to run fuller than usual. The car wasn't in any danger of going under as the river wasn't that deep, but deep enough to fill the vehicle with icy cold water.

Hawke called in for assistance. They would need a tow truck, paramedics, and another officer to help with traffic.

He parked his vehicle off the side of the road and tried to determine through the tinted windows how many people were in the car. A door opened. The force of the water spun the car to face Hawke with the river crashing against the side of the vehicle.

"Shit!" Hawke shoved open his door. As soon as his feet hit the ground, he opened the toolbox behind the cab and pulled out a rope. It had been a while since he'd roped anything.

He tied one end of the rope to a tree close to the side of the river and made a loop in the other end.

"Can you hear me?" he shouted over the rushing of the water.

A hand appeared out of the open door with a thumb up.

"Are you alone in the vehicle?" he shouted, swinging the loop above his head.

"No!" came a shrill cry from what sounded like a woman.

"Catch this rope and tie it to the steering column. Then the car can't travel downriver," Hawke yelled. When there wasn't a sign from anyone, he added, "Did you hear me?"

A thumb appeared again.

Hawke threw the rope upstream of the vehicle and hoped it would float down to the open car door. The loop floated past the car door too far out for the driver to grasp.

Hawke pulled the rope in, swung the wet loop over his head, and let it go, tossing it well behind the vehicle. This time the rope was within reach, but the man didn't lean out of the car far enough.

Grumbling, Hawke pulled the rope back in, swung the water-drenched loop above his head, and let it loose. It landed a little farther over and this time when the sodden line floated near the car, the man grabbed it.

Hawke released his hold on the rope to give the man the slack needed to wrap the rope over the steering wheel.

Sirens grew louder as the firetruck from Eagle and a sheriff's vehicle arrived.

Bert Mackey, the fire chief of the volunteers in Eagle, walked over to Hawke. "Looks like someone was driving too fast."

Hawke nodded. "I managed to get the car tied to a tree but I'm not sure how long that will hold the way the water's pounding the side of the car."

"John and Cole are suiting up. They can attach a cable. How many people are in there?"

"As far as I can tell, a male driver and a female passenger." Hawke hoped that was all. "The driver has a warrant in Multnomah."

"I'll be sure my guys know that." Bert walked away as Deputy Novak approached.

"Heard there's a warrant on the person in the car," Novak said.

"Yeah. From the way he took off after seeing me, I'm pretty sure he doesn't want to be caught. I hope he doesn't do something stupid." Hawke continued to stare at the vehicle wishing he could see inside, but the tinted windows prevented them from knowing if the person had a weapon or planned to harm the woman with him.

Hawke's phone buzzed as John and Cole, dressed in diving suits, waded into the river holding onto the rope connected to the car. Each one had a cable attached to a harness they wore.

Glancing at his phone, Hawke groaned. It was Goodwin. He was probably sitting at the Rusty Nail.

"Bad news?" Novak asked.

"I was supposed to meet someone." Hawke swiped his finger across the screen. "I'm not going to make it. There's a vehicle in the Wallowa River and we're trying to get the people out."

Goodwin scoffed. "You never planned to meet with me, did you?"

"I did. You can talk to Deputy Novak if you don't believe we're at the scene of an accident." The man just lost even more credibility with Hawke for calling him a liar. "I'll catch up with you tomorrow." Hawke ended the call.

"What was that about?" Novak asked as they both watched the firemen battle the water to stay on their feet and get to the Charger.

"They sent in a crime task force to work on The Lighted Path church case. The asshole running the task force thinks I'm not meeting with him because he wants to lead the investigation." Hawke's body relaxed as the two men reached the vehicle in the middle of the river.

"I heard you were the lead," Novak said, also watching the progress of the firemen.

"I am. Lt. Keller even told Goodwin that I was the lead. I guess Goodwin had it in his head that he was more qualified." Hawke watched as Cole, the smaller of the two firemen, started back toward the shore with a woman on his back. A glance at the Charger and Hawke's stomach knotted. It appeared the driver would rather bide his time in the river than be brought to shore. John was trying to pull the man from the vehicle.

"That doesn't look good," Hawke said.

The car started rocking and the water pushed it forward. John was upstream of the rope and vehicle. He jumped back and the car floated downstream as far as the rope would stretch. John let the current take him down to the car. Just as he was about to reach the door, a man stepped out and was carried downstream.

Novak ran to his car and took off with a spray of gravel.

During the rescue, the paramedics arrived. Hawke walked over to where Roxie, one of the paramedics, was checking a young woman's pulse.

"I'm Trooper Hawke. I need your name and the name of the driver." He pulled out his notebook.

The young woman peered up at him with large green eyes. Her teeth chattered as she parted her blueish lips and said, "Clara Barnes. That jerk is Raymond Mellon. He didn't tell me he was wanted by the police until after he landed us in the river."

"How did you meet Mr. Mellon?" Hawke asked.

"At High Mountain Brewery. We started talking the other night and I mentioned I had been trying to find a ride to California and he said he was headed that direction."

Hawke thought she was a fool for hitching a ride with someone she barely knew. "How is she?" he asked Roxie.

"She needs warmed up. I'll take her to the hospital and they can keep an eye on her until she's thawed." Roxie took the woman by the arm and led her to the ambulance.

Hawke walked to his vehicle and called a tow truck to pull the car out of the river. If Mellon didn't wash up on a bank before the road started up the side of the canyon, he wouldn't have anyone to pick him up and get him warm. Hawke called Novak on his cell phone.

"I'm keeping an eye on him," Novak said. "He could have gotten out once, but he saw me and shoved back into the river. He must be wanted for something pretty bad to prefer freezing to death to getting picked up by the law."

"How far are you from where the road leaves the river?" Hawke asked.

"About a mile. I think I'll sit here and then drive that direction in about thirty minutes. If he doesn't see me, he might get out and then I'll pick him up."

"Sounds like a plan. I'll wait here until the tow truck shows up then I'm off until tomorrow."

"Let me know if you need any help with the church fire investigation."

"Thanks." Hawke ended the call and dialed the Rusty Nail.

"Rusty Nail, Justine."

"Hi Justine, it's Hawke. Is there a grouchy-looking man still waiting for me?"

His friend laughed. "He *is* special. No, after he made a phone call, he stomped out of here."

Hawke chuckled. "That call was me. I wasn't able to meet him because a car went into the river in the canyon. Can you put up an order for chicken, mashed potatoes, and coleslaw? I should be by in an hour to pick it up."

"I'll put it up so it's hot when you get here."

"Thanks." He thought of Merrilee's daughter and how it was part of his investigation. "Is Merrilee cooking tonight?"

"No, she only stays around until after the lunch rush anymore. Did you need to talk to her?"

"Yeah. But I don't want to do it when she's busy. Do you think she'd mind if I popped in on her this evening?" He admired how the older woman had bought the restaurant and made a living off of it after her husband ran off leaving her with two children to raise. She had a lot of grit and sass. She was also cantankerous as she grew older.

"She gets up early to get in here and get everything ready for the day. I'd say if you want to get her in a good mood, come here before the restaurant opens and talk to her as she's prepping."

"Good advice. Here comes the tow truck," he said, watching the truck drive off the road and lumber in his direction.

"I'll put your order up."

The call ended and Hawke stepped out of his vehicle.

Dylan Gordon handled every accident. He stepped out of his truck and held out a hand. "Trooper Hawke. What do we have?"

Hawke shook hands and walked to the river bank. "I don't know if the rope will hold for you to pull the car close enough to hook onto it, or not."

Dylan scratched his head, studying the car and the river. "I guess if it doesn't hold, I'll just find it downstream somewhere."

"I'll leave you to it. Call dispatch when you get it retrieved and they'll let you know where to take it." Hawke returned to his vehicle and headed to Winslow to pick up his dinner.

《》《》《》

Hawke parked in front of the Rusty Nail as Justine was turning off the "Open" sign. He walked in, spotting a bag sitting on the counter. "This must be mine," he motioned to the sack before pulling his wallet out of his pocket.

"It is. I wondered how long I'd have to wait for you to pick it up." Justine walked over to the cash register. "I can't count this out until you pay."

"I didn't mean to keep you from getting home to your dogs." Hawke had met Justine when he'd first moved to the county for his fish and wildlife job. She raised hunting dogs and took in strays. After a conversation at the restaurant where Hawke talked about getting a dog to take in the mountains with him, Justine told Hawke she had a dog for him. He still wondered about how intuitive the woman was to have picked the correct dog for him.

"They'll be fine until I get there." She took his money, counted back the change, and started pulling money out of the till. "You should bring Dog by to visit."

"When I'm not so busy, I'll try. I know Dani would like to see your place. She's been thinking about getting a dog to stay with her up at the lodge." Hawke felt a little guilty saying that. Dani had only mentioned once that she liked it when Dog was at the lodge. It was nice having someone always on the lookout.

"I'll give her a call the next time I get one in that I think will be a good guard dog but also good with her guests." Justine glanced at the door. "I'll lock that behind you." She walked around the end of the counter.

"I'll come by tomorrow morning to see Merrilee." Hawke walked to the door, exited, and waited for Justine to click the lock in place before he slid into his vehicle. It had been a long day and would only be longer tomorrow as he began questioning Betz's victims to see who didn't have an alibi for the time of the pastor's murder.

Chapter Twelve

Hawke knocked on the back door of the Rusty Nail at 5 a.m. Thursday morning. The restaurant opened at six and he wanted to talk to Merrilee before anyone else arrived.

"Come in!" shouted Merrilee.

Hawke pulled the door open and stepped into a small kitchen emitting wonderful aromas. Merrilee stood at a stainless-steel table kneading dough.

She glanced up and frowned. "What are you doin' comin' in here before we open?"

"I had some questions for you and wanted to talk to you alone." Hawke nodded to a brick of cheese and shredder sitting on the opposite end of the table from where the old woman worked. "Need help while we talk?"

"Wash your hands and you can grate the cheese for the omelets." She continued working the dough. "What do you need to talk to me about? I heard you were questioning people about the fire at the church."

"The fire and the murder of the pastor of the church." Hawke dried his hands watching the woman.

She sucked in her bottom lip before blowing out a rush of air. "I suppose you learned that my daughter and I went to that church years ago. But I don't know what I could tell you about now. Since losing Marcia, I don't go to any church. Can't stomach how the Lord would let my husband run away and then take my daughter."

Hawke grabbed a sharp knife from where it hung on a magnetic strip and cut open the cheese wrapper. "It's your daughter I want to talk about."

Merrilee's small pointed chin rose and she met his gaze across the length of the table. "Why do you want to talk about Marcia?"

"How did she die?" Hawke asked, not meeting the woman's eyes as he grated the chunk of cheddar cheese he'd cut off the block.

"What do you need to know that for?" She stopped kneading the dough, punched it once, and turned it over before placing an upside-down bowl over it.

"Your daughter's death may have a bearing on the investigation." He glanced up and made eye contact with her.

The woman was in her seventies. Hawke wondered how old she was when she lost her daughter. If Betz had been impregnating teenage girls for thirty years or more, she would have been in her forties possibly fifties when it happened. That was a long time to outlive your child.

"Do you think one of Pastor Betz's parishioners killed him?" She began measuring flour into another bowl. "I said I quit going there twenty-seven years ago."

"Tell me about the church back then. Did lots of families attend? Did you feel Betz's sermons were useful to the congregation or did he preach to his own needs?" Hawke didn't want to sway the woman but he needed to know if the pastor had played his congregation into turning their young women over into his hands.

Merrilee put the lid back on the large canister of flour and stared into the bowl where she'd just measured the white powder. "He preached a lot about how the woman should take care of the man and do things that pleased him. I had a hard time taking that in considering the state my husband left me and the kids in."

"Did Marcia ever visit the church without you?" Hawke continued grating the cheese as if his question didn't matter that much even though his muscles were tense waiting to hear her answer.

"He did ask her several times to come by after school and he'd help her with a solo she was set to sing for the Christmas Eve service." Merrilee picked up a can of something and spooned it into the flour. "I didn't push her to practice. She was a natural and didn't plan on going off and being a singer."

"But she did go alone at least once?" Hawke pursued.

"Yes." Merrilee studied him. "And she never wanted to go to church or sing at the Christmas service."

Hawke figured he needed to go all the way with what he wanted to know. "And how soon after that did you realize she was pregnant?"

Merrilee's face grew red as she narrowed her faded blue eyes and glared at him. "How did you? Rosa. Why would she tell you now?"

"Because she has multiple files of young girls from Betz's church who became pregnant by him." Hawke put the cheese and grater down. "Merrilee, Betz has been preying on young women from his parishioners for as long as he's been here. When Marcia went to Rosa, she told the midwife everything."

"Why didn't she come tell me?"

"Marcia?" Hawke thought that was obvious. The teenager would have thought her mother wouldn't believe her.

"No, Rosa! That woman has known all along and never told me?"

"She tried to tell the police and no one would listen. Betz had them believing Rosa was a crank." It still made his stomach churn to think the police didn't dig any further than asking Betz what Rosa was talking about. "And she feared if she told parents the young girls who needed help wouldn't come to her."

"My Marcia died in childbirth. Did you know that? I couldn't blame Rosa. She did all she could. I didn't know Marcia was in labor and having problems until I went into her room. She was so ashamed of being pregnant that she spent the last five months of her pregnancy hiding in her room. I went up to tell her to come down to dinner and there she was white as a sheet lying in a pool of blood. The baby was too big and she'd not gone for help. Part of me always felt she'd hoped the baby would die if she didn't get help. I don't think she realized it could be her." Merrilee swiped at a tear trickling down her gaunt cheek.

"How can I help expose that sinner?" Merrilee asked.

"Did Marcia leave any diaries that she might have mentioned how she became pregnant?" Hawke moved back to his end of the table and returned to grating cheese.

"I boxed everything up in her room, except her clothes, and stuck it in the attic. I gave the clothes to the church clothing pantry. Come by after three this afternoon and you can go through the boxes." Merrilee added sugar, eggs, and buttermilk to the flour and started whipping it by hand. "I wish I'd have known about that man sooner. I would have allowed Rosa to wash his seed out of Marcia and sicced the law after him, after I'd castrated him."

Hawke finished grating the cheese, washed his hands, and told Merrilee he'd see her at three at her house before he walked out the back door and settled behind the steering wheel of his vehicle.

Picking up the mic, he called dispatch and let them know he was on duty and headed toward Alder. He'd grab breakfast at the bakery. One of the women on the list Rosa gave Browning worked there.

Hawke had spent a restless night thinking about how he would talk to Merrilee about her daughter and how to go about talking to each of the women on the list Rosa had provided. The more he sloshed the idea of keeping the women's past safe around in his mind, he agreed. There was no sense in bringing up a horrendous event that wasn't of their choosing if he could help it.

His drive to Alder was slowed when he came upon an old battered pickup sitting alongside the highway with its hood in the air. Hawke pulled in behind the vehicle. About once a month someone in law enforcement found Lewis Overton's pickup alongside a road with the hood up. Hawke approached the vehicle and found the owner sleeping across the seat. Rapping on the window woke the man.

Lewis was in his eighties, lived alone since his wife died ten years earlier, and was forever forgetting to put fuel in his 1964 Ford pickup. He pushed his body up off the seat and grabbed the steering wheel.

Hawke rapped on the window again. The man jolted and whipped his head to the side to peer out the window. Hawke made the motion of rolling down the window.

Lewis rolled down the manual window and smacked his lips before saying. "Our taxes must not be goin' for our protection. I been sittin' here all night waiting for one of you to come along and assist me."

"There must have been someone who stopped to assist you." Hawke pulled open the door.

"Some hooligans stopped and asked if I had any beer. Then threw their empties in the back of my pickup. That nice Lacie, her and her man own Al's Café, she stopped but I told her a policeman would be along soon."

"Do you want me to take you to a station in Alder or call your son?" Hawke asked.

"Can't you just give me a couple of gallons of gas to get me to town? I don't want to bother you or Jr."

Hawke knew Junior would lecture his father on spending all his money on the lottery instead of gas. "How about I take you to Herb Trembley's. He could give you a couple of gallons and a ride back to your vehicle." Hawke knew from stories he'd heard that Mrs. Overton had been the motivation in their marriage.

"That would be nice. Maybe Darlene will have something good baked up." Lewis's eyes brightened at the thought.

"Come on." Hawke led the man to his vehicle and put him in the passenger side. On his way to the driver's side, he called Herb to tell him what he was doing. When he was settled in his vehicle, he radioed dispatch to let them know he was helping a stranded driver.

He made a U-turn in the highway and drove the three miles back to the Trembleys. Maybe he'd just stop at his house and get some breakfast. He could always stop in at the bakery later in the day or tomorrow.

"It's nice of you to take me to Herb's. You know Junior hasn't been too tolerable of me lately." Lewis sat forward as Hawke parked in front of Herb's house.

"I'm sure Herb won't mind."

As they exited the law enforcement vehicle, Herb walked toward them from the barn with a calf bottle in one hand.

"I thought I heard a vehicle crunching the gravel," he said by way of greeting. "I haven't seen you in a while, Lewis."

The older man shuffled his feet and peered at

Hawke. "This here trooper said you might be able to give me a couple gallons of gas to get me to town."

Before Hawke could elaborate, Herb said, "No problem. Why don't you come in and have some breakfast first? Then I'll take you and some gas to your pickup."

Hawke smiled at Herb. His friend had figured out it was more than gas the older man needed. He was also in need of friends and someone to talk to.

"Thanks, Herb." Hawke spun to get back in his vehicle.

"You're welcome to join us for breakfast too," Herb said.

Hawke stopped with his hand on the handle of the pickup door. He'd love a good breakfast but he would rather talk with Herb and Darlene when there wasn't someone else around. "I'll take a raincheck on that. I'm late for a meeting." He slid into his vehicle and drove out of the driveway and over to his house.

His stomach grumbled the whole time he made toast and scrambled eggs and even while he ate them, knowing it had missed out on better grub.

Chapter Thirteen

While he ate, Hawke called Sergeant Spruel to fill him in on what he'd learned. They discussed the matter of keeping the man's activities with the women of his congregation to just the officers working the case. It would be easier to discover if someone took justice into their own hands if the man's deeds weren't all over the county. Hawke liked the idea of not making the women feel as if they were being targeted again. As Rosa had commented, there was a reason the young girls and women had come to her rather than a local physician. They knew she wouldn't give out their names. He patted the paper in his shirt pocket. Rosa had given him the names. And he was the only one who would talk with them.

He called Browning and Herold to set up a strategy meeting. They agreed to meet him at the City Police Station.

Hawke found the number for Goodwin of Major Crimes. His finger tensed as he pressed the call button.

"Where and when do you want to meet?" Goodwin asked instead of answering the phone politely.

"I'm headed to Alder now. We can meet at the City Hall. That's where the City Police Station is located," Hawke said, picking up his dishes and carrying them to the sink. Dog's toenails clicked along the floor behind him.

"How long will it take you to get there?"

"Twenty minutes." Hawke led Dog outside, closed and locked the door behind him, and walked to his vehicle.

"I'll be there." Goodwin ended the call.

"I can see why Lt. Keller thought I'd have better luck with people," Hawke said to Dog. "Take care of the boys and I'll see you tonight."

He closed the vehicle door and turned the key. As much as he didn't like telling the women's secrets to Goodwin, he had no choice if the two were going to work together on the Betz homicide.

《》《》《》

Rosa was indecisive if she should take Jayne with her when she visited with Diane Betz. She doubted the pastor's wife would know who Jayne was, but she would definitely see the young woman's resemblance to her dead husband. Rosa didn't know if that would be good or bad. She opted with having Jayne stay home.

"I'll come get you when I've finished talking to Diane. I've set up a meeting with a number of the women who came to me after the pastor talked them into having sex with him and they became pregnant."

She knew Hawke would want to talk to the women, but she wanted to let them know how she had tried over the years to stop Pastor Betz while trying to keep their names out of it.

"Are you sure they won't mind me being there?" Jayne asked.

"You are as much a victim as they are. They won't mind when I tell them who you are, if they don't figure it out by looking at you." Rosa touched the young woman's hair. It was like her mother's as was her delicate frame and heart-shaped mouth. "Wait here. I should be back in an hour. Possibly an hour and a half."

Jayne nodded and picked up the book she'd been reading.

Rosa grabbed her purse and car keys and headed to the garage. At the time the building was built it had been a carport at the side of the hospital for bringing in injured people. Over the years someone had made it into a garage. She was appreciative of the addition in the wintertime when she had to go out in a storm to take care of a patient.

Once she left her neighborhood, Rosa began to feel her nerves skittering under her skin. She had rehearsed what she wanted to say to Diane until the early morning, getting little sleep. But she wanted to be sure she worded things correctly so she didn't upset the recent widow.

Arriving at Suzanne Larsen's house, Rosa had more doubts about the encounter but believed Diane Betz deserved to know about her husband from Rosa before it was spread all over the county. She walked up to the front door and rang the doorbell. Suzanne's house was a newer one like this neighborhood. Ten years ago, all that had sat here were the church and pastor's home. But now the street was lined with houses. A short boon of housing and an influx of residents. But since then, things had stayed the same.

She rang the doorbell again, noting Suzanne's car sat outside of her garage. The two women must be here. Rosa spun and stared down the street. She spotted two women walking toward the burned church. From the back, they appeared to be Suzanne and Diane.

Rosa walked down the sidewalk and into the street, headed to find out what the two women were doing. She stopped at the sidewalk as they ducked under the crime scene tape and entered the house. Diane must have needed some of her clothing or other items.

Did she cross the police tape and talk to the woman in her own home or return to her car and wait?

As she stood trying to make up her mind a black SUV turned the corner and drove slowly by her, parking in the church parking lot. A woman and man stepped out of the vehicle and donned light blue jumpsuits and booties before ducking under the crime scene tape and walking into the remains of the burned church.

Rosa walked back to her car sitting in Suzanne's driveway and waited.

《》《》《》

Hawke walked into City Hall and found Goodwin pacing. "You could have asked to see Chief Browning instead of pacing," Hawke said, passing by Goodwin and heading to the conference room down the hall from the Chief's office.

"I wanted to make sure you showed up before I sat in some room for hours waiting." Goodwin's attitude didn't seem to have chilled any overnight.

Stopping at the door to the conference room, Hawke waved a hand. "Take a seat. I'll go grab Chief Browning."

Goodwin scowled but walked into the small room.

Hawke spun on his heel and headed to Browning's office. Both Herold and the Chief were waiting for him. Hawke tipped his head toward the hall. "I have Mr. Pessimist in the conference room. Goodwin is from major crimes and wants to know what we know. I told him we'd get him up to date."

"Are they taking over?" Browning asked.

"I received the go-ahead from Lt. Keller to be the lead. He's supposed to help but he doesn't like not being the top dog." Hawke stepped into the hall and led the two down to the conference room.

Once inside, Hawke made the introductions and they all sat.

"Before we start looking at files, I want us to be in agreement that the names of the women who were Betz's victims won't be mentioned outside of the four of us, and I'll do all the questioning with Rosa present. The women trust her and with her vouching for me, I'm hoping they will open up to me."

"I don't think you should be using a possible suspect to help you gather information," Goodwin said.

"Have you ever heard of the saying, 'Keep your friends close and your enemies closer?'" Hawke asked.

"Yeah, but that has nothing—" Goodwin started.

"It has everything to do with this case." Hawke

studied the outsider. "Having Rosa there will make the others more comfortable to possibly say something, like, their husband, boyfriend, brother knew what had happened. And it will give me a chance to see how badly the midwife had wanted the pastor dead." Hawke saw it as a way to watch and evaluate the midwife as well as the possible suspects.

"It makes sense to me," Browning said, opening up a folder and telling Goodwin what they had learned from the fire marshal and the local medical examiner.

Goodwin shifted his gaze to Hawke. "You found a suspect in a car fleeing the scene?"

Hawke shook his head. "I don't know if she was fleeing the scene. I found her twenty-three miles from town with her vehicle stuck between trees and unconscious. From the tracks, the car had to have been driven into the grove of trees before the frozen ground thawed, which means she couldn't have been in Alder at the time the fire started."

"But she smelled of smoke and had charred clothing," Goodwin said in an accusing tone.

"Yes. But the facts are she couldn't have ended up where she did after starting the fire. Not without leaving visible tracks. And there was no reason for her to drive off the road and end up in the trees. However, the path of the vehicle through the trees was executed deftly, as if someone placed the car where it was found, not some random accident."

"Why are you defending the suspect?" Goodwin asked.

"I'm not defending her, I'm following the evidence, which says she couldn't have set the fire."

Goodwin smiled. "Couldn't have set the fire, but could have killed the victim. Your M.E. said that the skull had been split before the fire took place."

Hawke nodded solemnly. "Yes, the woman you are calling a suspect, does remember confronting the man before she blacked out. And she states he was alive at that point."

"I want to interview this woman," Goodwin said, peering at each man at the table as if he expected them to bow to his demand.

"We have already questioned the woman. Until we have more evidence, there is no need to bring her back in," Browning said.

"How do I know you asked all the right questions?" Goodwin asked.

"We made a recording. You can listen to that," Herold stated.

Hawke hid the smile that twitched the corners of his mouth. It was clear Goodwin hadn't won over Browning or Herold with his pushy attitude.

Hawke's phone buzzed. He glanced at the number. Rosa. Why would she be calling? He stood. "Excuse me. I need to take this call."

Hawke stepped out in the hall and answered, "Rosa, what's wrong?"

"I've been sitting outside of Suzanne Larsen's house for an hour waiting for her and Diane to come back from Diane's house. What could be keeping them in that house for an hour?"

"Why are you waiting for them?" he asked, stepping back into the conference room.

"I wanted to give Diane my condolences and let

her know her husband's dance with the devil was being investigated." Rosa's voice had a defiant ring to it.

"Go home. I'll head over and see what is going on. I'll break the news to Mrs. Betz myself." Hawke ended the call and settled his gaze on the three men staring at him. "The victim's wife and her neighbor crossed the crime scene tape and have been in the Betz house for over an hour." He shifted his gaze to Herold. "Let's go see what they are doing."

Goodwin stood. "I'm going too. Why didn't Kate and Gage stop them?"

"Maybe their backs were turned when the women entered the house." Hawke didn't care that the forensic team didn't see the women. What he cared about was why they were in the house for so long. It didn't take the woman that long to grab some clothes and she'd been told to call the police and ask to be let in the house when she needed anything.

Chapter Fourteen

Hawke led the way to the crime scene. Goodwin followed close behind in his SUV and Herold followed in a city patrol car.

When Hawke spotted Rosa's car still sitting in the Larsen's driveway, he inwardly groaned. He had hoped the midwife had listened to his instructions and gone home. Parking in the church parking lot, he expected Goodwin to talk to his forensic team. Instead, Goodwin started for the house.

Hawke caught up to the man and stopped him. "We aren't storming in there. Just step back and let out some of that gas that seems to be making you cranky." He heard a chuckle from Herold but ignored the growl from Goodwin.

Stopping on the front steps, Hawke knocked on the door. When no one answered, he turned the knob and eased the door open. "Mrs. Betz, Mrs. Larsen, we know you're in here. This is still part of a crime scene. You need to leave the house."

A shuffling sound from the back of the house caught their attention. Hawke couldn't tell if it came from a room in the back or upstairs. He motioned for Herold to check the downstairs rooms and Goodwin to stay put while Hawke started up the stairs.

On the second floor, Hawke made his way down the hallway. The weight of his Glock in his hand as he crept down the hall was reassuring. At each door, he held his breath and slowly turned the knob, inching the doors open to check the rooms. A bedroom and bathroom appeared unused. The covers on the bed were neat and not a personal item was in sight. The bathroom fixtures were shiny, and the towels were all clean and crisp. The last door at the end of the hall was locked. There was only one reason the door would be locked.

"Mrs. Betz, open the door. You aren't to be in here until we've finished collecting evidence." He holstered his weapon. "By locking yourself in your room it leads me to believe you are tampering with evidence. I could take you to jail for that."

The lock clicked and the door opened. Mrs. Larsen peeked through the narrow opening.
"Diane is just gathering some more clothes and toiletries," she said.

Hawke studied the woman. Her face was pale and her voice quivered.

"She didn't need to hide in here and lock the door if that was all she was doing. You know you were supposed to call the city police and they would have escorted her over here and let her get what she needed."

Which wouldn't have taken an hour, he thought to himself.

"We didn't know it was you. It could have been whoever set fire to the church." Mrs. Larsen's eyes widened. "We were afraid. That's why we locked the door."

Hawke shook his head. "By locking yourselves in an upstairs room, you would have been killed if the person had set the house on fire." He waved at the door. "Open the door and let Mrs. Betz come out."

When the woman continued to stare at him, he said gruffly, "Now!"

The door swung open and Mrs. Betz walked through the opening with a suitcase. "Trooper Hawke, I'm sorry I didn't call. It seemed like an inconvenience to have a policeman come down here to wait for me to get my things."

"Officer Herold!" Hawke called out.

Stomping on the stairs and Herold arrived at the top of the stairway. "Yes?"

"Escort Mrs. Betz and Mrs. Larsen back to Mrs. Larsen's house, please." Hawke watched the two women, one short and plump and the other tall and thin walk down the hall to the stairs. They weren't good actresses. He could tell they had been up to something and he planned to find out what.

As soon as the two disappeared down the stairs, Hawke stepped into the bedroom and did a slow scan of the room, looking for anything out of place.

"What are you doing?" Goodwin's voice said from behind him.

"I'm trying to figure out what those two were

doing in this house for over an hour and why they had the door locked if they were the only ones here?" Hawke noticed a trail of insulation from what must have been the closet door.

He walked over and opened the door. It was a spacious closet. He flipped on the light. There was more insulation on the floor, underneath the opening for the attic crawl space. A quick glance and he found the ladder tucked behind a rack of dresses.

"What are you doing?" Goodwin asked, walking around in the closet, opening and closing drawers and shoving hanging clothes back and forth.

"I'm going to see if they left anything of interest up here." Hawke opened the ladder, climbed up, slid the door over, and then proceeded higher on the ladder to look into the attic.

It was dark and he could only make out some objects to the right. Reaching down to his duty belt, he grasped his flashlight and shined the light around. Two empty cardboard filing boxes lay on their sides. The lids were on the floor of the attic. He had a suspicion the suitcase Mrs. Betz had carried out of here hadn't held any clothes. But rather files she didn't want anyone finding. What kind of files? Had Betz kept a record of the women he'd impregnated and their offspring? The thought sickened him.

"What did you find?" Goodwin asked.

"Empty boxes." Hawke descended the ladder, flicked off his flashlight, and attached it to his duty belt.

"Empty boxes? Why would someone…?"

Hawke saw when the realization struck Goodwin.

"She took something out of those boxes." Goodwin

headed for the stairs.

Hawke put a hand on his arm stopping him. "I'll ask her about that when I ask her my other questions. You are to observe and keep quiet if you want to be a part of this investigation. Lt. Keller understands I know how these people react to law enforcement. They don't like talking to us and will be even less likely to talk to an outsider." Hawke passed Goodwin, taking the stairs two at a time, remembering Rosa was waiting for Mrs. Betz.

When Hawke reached the street and could see Mrs. Larsen's house, Mrs. Betz wasn't anywhere to be seen but Rosa and Suzanne were talking by Rosa's car and Herold stood at the front door of Mrs. Larsen's house.

As he drew nearer the two women by the car, he picked up snatches of their conversation.

"But I need to talk to her," Rosa insisted.

"Diane isn't in any shape to listen to what you might have to say." Mrs. Larsen spun to leave and Rosa caught her arm.

"If she's truly your friend, you'd want me to talk to her. She's going to be in a worse way when the truth comes out." Rosa held the woman's arm.

"Rosa, what are you doing?" Hawke asked, stopping several feet back from the two women staring at each other.

Rosa dropped her arm. "I'm trying to make Suzanne see that Diane needs to hear the truth from me before it starts hitting her from all directions." Rosa didn't take her gaze from the other woman.

Hawke crossed his arms, studying the women. It was true, if Mrs. Betz didn't know about her husband's statutory rape of his parishioners, she would be better off learning it from a reliable source than the whispers and rants.

Uncrossing his arms, Hawke said, "Mrs. Larsen, please allow Rosa, myself, and my two colleagues into your house so we may question Mrs. Betz." When the woman didn't make a move toward her house, he added, "Or I will have you arrested for obstruction of justice."

Mrs. Larsen shook herself and stared at him. "Why would you do that?"

"Because you are not allowing me to speak to a person with information about the recent death of Pastor Betz." Hawke motioned for the women to walk to the house. When Mrs. Larsen started walking in that direction with Rosa behind her, Hawke fell in behind the two women.

At the door, Mrs. Larsen stopped. "Let me tell Diane you are all coming in."

Hawke shook his head. "I'm done with your stalling. Open the door and let us in. Rosa can go find Mrs. Betz."

Reluctantly, Mrs. Larsen opened the door and stepped back so they could all enter her small living room. Rosa headed down the hallway in search of Mrs. Betz.

"Sit down, Mrs. Larsen," Hawke said, motioning to the couch. He wanted both women sitting where he could watch their reactions.

"What is this about?" Mrs. Betz asked as Rosa herded her into the living room. "Why are you all here?" Mrs. Betz asked as Hawke motioned for her to sit next to her friend.

"We have questions." Hawke grabbed a lightweight chair and placed it in front of the two. Rosa took the recliner in a row with the couch. Herold stood beside and slightly behind Hawke with his notepad ready. Hawke didn't see Goodwin but he heard him breathing heavily to his left.

"First, what did you haul out of your house in that suitcase?" he asked.

Mrs. Larsen's eyes widened.

Mrs. Betz's gaze lowered to the coffee table between them. "I wanted more of my things."

"What things?" Hawke asked.

The woman's gaze lifted to his. Her eyes blazed. "Women things. You wouldn't understand."

Hawke leaned back in the chair, holding her gaze. "I understand you took paperwork out of the attic."

Mrs. Larsen sucked in air and Mrs. Betz scowled.

"You left a trail of insulation. What was in those boxes that was so important you had to get it out of there? Did your husband have gambling debts?"

"That's ridiculous! He was a pastor for God's sake." Mrs. Betz didn't emphasize the word pastor.

"Not any more ridiculous than his getting underaged girls pregnant under the cover of teaching them what to expect from their husbands or boyfriends." Hawke peered into the woman's eyes. She knew what her husband had done.

Her body shook as her gaze lowered. "I didn't condone his actions but he was my husband and I couldn't give him what he wanted most. A child." She raised her head. "When he realized I would never be able to give him offspring, he started spending more and more time with the young women of the church. At first, I thought it was him being kind to the girls who had family problems. It was his way of being a father."

She clenched her hands. "Then one day I was looking for him. There was a call he'd been waiting for. I found the office locked and I could hear him talking. I pounded on the door and called out to him afraid he was being robbed." Mrs. Betz shook her head. "When the door opened a terrified, disheveled girl ran out of the room. My husband was putting himself back together. I hit him and told him he was horrid for doing that." She swallowed.

"Would everyone like something to drink?" Mrs. Larsen asked.

"Water please, Suzanne," Mrs. Betz said.

Everyone else declined anything.

When her friend left the room, Mrs. Betz continued, "When I threatened to go to the police, Gordon said he would tell them I had known all along and condoned his conduct. He said that would make me an accessory." She stared at Hawke. "He used the one thing I cared about the most, keeping up appearances to keep me from saying anything."

"That's pure bullshit!" Rosa said, breaking into the conversation. "The minute you knew you should have said something. I tried. But the police wouldn't listen to me and your husband, and I do believe you, spread rumors that I was crazy and made up the stories."

Suzanne entered the room at that moment. She handed Mrs. Betz a glass of water and sat down, putting a supportive arm around her friend.

"And you, Suzanne. You came to me to help you abort a fetus that I know you received after volunteering to be the church organist. You stopped volunteering shortly before you came to me." Rosa stared at the woman. "I have a feeling Pastor Betz gave you some story about how he could help you with your marriage."

The woman's chin dropped and her mouth hung open for only a split second.

"If you know so much, why didn't you do something?" Mrs. Betz threw the accusation at Rosa.

Hawke decided he'd learned enough from the women's verbal combat. "She did. The dickheads in charge didn't take the time to check up on it because your husband had them all believing he was an upstanding citizen." He leaned forward with his forearms on his thighs and peered into Mrs. Betz's eyes. "Tell me again about the night before the fire and when you realized the church was on fire."

"I already—"

He raised a hand stopping her words. "My colleague, Sergeant Goodwin, with the Major Crime Team hasn't heard it yet."

Chapter Fifteen

As Mrs. Betz started in with her version of what happened the night before and the day of the fire, Hawke paid close attention.

"Gordon was out in his office in the church writing up a sermon. I was in the house getting ready for bed when the phone rang. It was poor Annie Neuman, she wanted Gordon to come to the hospital and visit with her and her husband. She said he wasn't responding to the medicine and feared he wouldn't make it through the night."

Hawke stopped her. "When I questioned you yesterday you didn't remember who had called about Mr. Neuman. Now you are sure?"

The woman bristled. "When you asked me before I was in shock. But when Annie called to console me, she mentioned the call the night before. That's what made me remember it was her."

"Go on," Hawke said.

She gave him a scowl and continued, "I put the note on the corkboard by the phone and went to bed."

"Did your husband stay up late in the church a lot?" Hawke asked.

"He was working on a sermon. He would stay up at all hours to get it finished early enough in the week to be able to practice it."

Hawke studied the woman. "You didn't wake up and see he hadn't come to bed and go looking for him?"

"Why would I do that when I knew he was in his office in the church?" She gulped water and swallowed.

"Was he in the house when you woke the following morning?" Hawke asked.

She took another gulp of water, not looking at him, and then said, "I saw the clothes he'd worn the day before in the hamper but he wasn't in the house. I figured he'd left early to visit Mr. Neuman."

Hawke leaned back in the chair. "And yet, believing your husband was at the hospital you ran out into the burning church looking for him."

The woman stared at him.

"I'd called earlier in the morning and told Diane I'd seen Pastor Betz return," Mrs. Larsen blurted.

"That's how you knew your husband was in the church?" Hawke asked.

"Yes. I figured he'd gone back out to work some more on his sermon." Mrs. Betz finished the glass of water.

Rosa cleared her throat. "I have to go. I'm late for a meeting." She stood. "I said what I came to say. I'm not a bit sorry your husband is gone and wish you had come forward and saved the lives of the unborn, the girls who committed suicide, and the children who don't even know how they were conceived. I believe your husband was a monster." The midwife headed to the door with a heavy step.

Hawke felt the same as Rosa but as a law enforcement officer, he had to remain unbiased as he dug up all the evidence. "Now that Rosa is gone, I'd like to take a look in that suitcase you brought from your house."

Mrs. Betz huffed, heaved her body off the couch, and walked to the hallway.

While she was gone, Hawke peered at Mrs. Larsen. "You were one of the man's victims and yet, you didn't turn him in and are friends with his wife."

The woman's face paled and she gave a half-hearted shrug. "The Lord forgives all sinners."

Hawke continued to watch Mrs. Larsen. She squirmed until Mrs. Betz returned with a suitcase that could or couldn't be the one he'd watched her carry out of her house.

"Would you please set it on the table and open it?" Hawke asked.

The woman did as she was asked.

He stood and moved the contents around trying to see if the clothing was concealing anything. Like folders or papers.

"Are you going to handle all of my clothes?" the woman snapped.

"Diane, he's just doing his job." Mrs. Larsen put an arm around her friend's shoulders. "She's not been her usual self since—"

Mrs. Betz spun toward the taller woman and sobbed in her arms.

Hawke motioned for the other two men to head to the door. "I'm sorry this is upsetting. You should have known we would dig up his rotten side to find his killer." He followed the other two men out to the street.

Once outside he faced Herold. "Her story changed from the first one."

"It did," Herold agreed.

Contemplating what the woman or women were hiding, he noticed Rosa's car no longer sat in the driveway. That sent him wondering what kind of a meeting she'd hurried off to.

《》《》《》

Rosa walked into her house. Ten of the women in her files sat in the waiting area. Jayne was serving tea and coffee.

"Thank you," Rosa said as she walked by to put her purse and jacket in her room.

Back out in the waiting area, Rosa sat on the stool she'd brought into the room with her. She motioned for Jayne to pull up a chair beside her.

"You all know each other from living in the county. This is my friend Jayne. She came here following her mother's wishes." Rosa noted two of the women who were close to Eloise in age nodded. "Her mother was Eloise Laude."

"You said was. What happened to Eloise?" Madeleine asked.

Rosa nodded to Jayne.

"My mother died of cancer a year ago. In her last weeks, she told me about the man who raped her and made her pregnant with me." Jayne's hand shook as she sipped the water she held. "She told me to come visit with Rosa to learn more about my paternal side. Mom didn't want there to be any surprise medical issues crop up that could be avoided." Jayne glanced at Rosa.

"In case you hadn't already figured it out, Eloise was one of Pastor Betz's victims." Rosa made eye contact with every woman in the room. "While it has never been spoken, you all know you have something in common. You were his victims too."

She'd expected an outright blast of airing their dirty laundry. What she witnessed were furtive glances about the room as if each one was digesting what she'd said and wondering how the other women had been caught up in this. She'd had several in one group that met every other week. They had known the other women were raped but hadn't known they had the same abuser.

Olivia raised her hand. "You knew all of us had been assaulted by Pastor Betz and you didn't do anything?"

Rosa had expected this question. "I asked each one of you to come with me to the police to report it. You all said you preferred not to and not to tell anyone. And I did go to the sheriff and the chief every time there was one newly elected to try and make them see Pastor Betz was a fiend. But he would charm them and make me sound like a lunatic. I have tried over the years but without your help, I couldn't do much."

"Someone did the young girls a favor, just a decade or two too late," Hannah said, boldly looking around the room.

Rosa would make sure Hawke knew to talk to Hannah. She was one of the boldest in the group. Rosa had been surprised when the woman had balked at reporting Pastor Betz. But then later learned he had threatened her with doing the same to her younger sister if she said anything.

"I don't think the police have said anything publicly yet, but the fire that killed pastor Betz wasn't an accident. They are looking for someone with a grudge against the man."

Murmuring and clanking of tea cups on saucers filled the room.

Rosa raised her voice. "Oregon State Trooper Hawke is in charge of the investigation. He and I have been talking and I gave your names to him."

Voices rose tossing out accusing remarks.

"How could you!"

"What were you thinking!"

"You think we killed him?"

She stood, held her hands in the air, and slowly gained control of the room. "He isn't going to tell anyone about what happened. But he wants to talk to each one of you. So you don't have to go to the police station or have him come to your homes, I'm scheduling you to come back tomorrow and he'll talk to each one of you with me present."

"What if I don't want to talk to him?" Jordynn asked.

"Then he will be coming to find you at work or at home." Rosa was doing her best to do right by these women. They had to see that and come here to be questioned. Unless they wanted the whole county to know what had happened to them.

The women eventually calmed down and each one was given a time to return the next day. When the last woman walked out the door, Rosa breathed a sigh of relief.

"I thought they were going to string you up," Jayne said, placing the used cups on a tray.

"Every one of those women has more strength than they realize. They would have been able to hold their heads high if they had just gone with me to the police and reported that perverted pastor." Rosa glanced at Jayne. "Sorry. I forget he was your father."

Jayne shook her head. "Don't be. He was a reprehensible man and I will never think of him as my father. He will always be the man who ruined my mother's life."

Chapter Sixteen

Hawke followed Goodwin over to the burned church. Kate and Gage walked toward them in their blue suits. They were both carrying an evidence bag in their gloved hands.

"We were just taking what we found to the car," Gage said.

They stopped in front of Goodwin and Hawke.

"What do you have?" Hawke asked.

"We found what looks like something that could have been used as a timing device." Gage opened the bag and showed a piece of something smooth and green where it wasn't burned.

"What do you think that is?" Hawke studied the coloring and shape. It looked like a piece of pottery to him.

"It could be a piece of a mosquito spiral," Kate said. "We'll know for sure when the ashes I scraped up near the accelerant area are tested."

Hawke studied the two. "A mosquito spiral was

used to start a fire?"

"It's a delay device," Gage said. "We've run across it before. I can send you the website where there is a tutorial on using delay devices when burning something."

"I'd like to see that. It might give us an edge when we narrow down our suspects." Hawke made eye contact with each officer. "Good job." He faced Goodwin. "I suspect you'll take those to Pendleton. I'm headed to my office to read more of the reports and start digging into the women I'll be interviewing tomorrow. See you later."

Hawke ignored the scowl on Goodwin's face and headed to his vehicle. He planned to spend the rest of the afternoon in the office, digging up information. He had all the names of the women Rosa had given him. He wanted to learn more about each one before he talked to them the next day. All he could do until the forensic reports came back was to talk to everyone who had a grudge against the pastor.

《》《》《》

Walking into the Winslow Station his phone buzzed.

"Hawke," he answered.

"It's Rosa. I have ten women from the list who will be here starting at nine in the morning to talk with you."

"That's good to hear. Which ones won't be coming?" he was more interested in those now that he knew they didn't want to talk to him.

"Well, four of them, of course, have died. The three who didn't come to the meeting I set up live out of the county. I don't think they had anything to do with his murder. Once they left here they didn't want anything to drag them back." Rosa sighed. "I'm afraid they had parents much like Eloise's. When the girls tried to tell their families what happened they were called liars and all three ran away. None of them were pregnant that I know of."

Hawke thought it sounded like the women were better off left out of this. "I'll be at your house at eight-thirty tomorrow. I'll bring my own pickup so there isn't any sign that a policeman is talking to them." He'd talked on the phone the night before with his mom. She'd instilled in him that women who had been sexually assaulted had a harder time trusting men. And that he wasn't to accuse them or look at them as if they had done anything when he talked to them. Knowing his mom had dealt with these issues through her support of the Missing and Murdered Indigenous Women movement, he planned to be as neutral and open with the women as he had been with Dani when she'd told him of a sexual harassment charge she'd had to bring against an airman in the Air Force.

Hawke continued into the office. He waved at Spruel as he walked by the man's office. Once seated at his desk, Hawke turned on his computer and pulled up the documents that had been added to the Betz file. Instead of going with the verbal overview Browning gave that morning, Hawke read the Medical Examiner report from the first word to the last and then flipped to the report from the State Forensic lab. They had received reports back on Jayne's clothing.

He stopped at the wording, *carbon, calcium, potassium, and magnesium were found in the clothing sent to the lab. This is the compound for wood. There were no chemicals leading us to believe the clothing had been in a building fire.*

The clothing Jayne had been wearing hadn't been in the church fire. This only made matters more puzzling. If she wasn't in the church when it caught fire, why were her clothes smoked and charred?

He resisted the urge to jump up and drive to Rosa's place to try and sort this out with Jayne. If she hadn't been in the fire but remembered being in the church, she must have been there as she stated the night before the fire. He wondered if forensics could determine how long the pastor had been dead before the fire started.

Could they be looking for two people? One who hit Jayne and then killed the pastor and another who tried to cover up the murder in the morning by setting the church on fire.

Hawke finished reading the rest of the reports, not seeing anything else that puzzled him. He plucked the list of names Rosa gave him out of his pocket and started putting them into the Department of Motor Vehicles site to get addresses and phone numbers for them. Then he would start searching the police database to see if any had been in trouble with the law.

《》《》《》

Hawke leaned back in his chair and rubbed his eyes. He needed to get that prescription filled the optometrist gave him for glasses when he did computer work.

"Anything new come up?" Spruel asked, walking over with two cups of coffee. He placed one on Hawke's desk and pulled a small book out from under his arm where he'd had it tucked.

"Several things." Hawke went on to tell him about the possible delay device to start the fire, the results of Jayne's clothing, and he'd found two of the women he'd talk to tomorrow had been brought in for assault charges against men.

Spruel studied him, "Do you really think a woman did all of this?"

Hawke could tell by Spruel's face he didn't think so. "Women are stronger than you think, not physically maybe, but mentally. If they are pushed far enough, most women will crack- either in a mental breakdown or to the point of doing whatever they must to rid themselves of the problem." He knew this from watching the women on the reservation. Those that didn't take to booze and drugs would show unheralded strength of character and physical strength to take care of their family and themselves. His mother was an example. She'd withstood beatings from his stepfather to save her children from harm. Unless he put himself between her and the monster he never called dad. He shook that thought away.

"I am not going to rule out anyone."

"Does that include Jayne and Rosa?" Spruel raised one eyebrow.

"That includes them. Since they met the Sunday before the fire, I have to keep an open mind to the fact the two of them could be working together."

"I'll pass that along to Keller and she can assure Goodwin you aren't playing favorites." Spruel sipped his coffee.

Hawke shoved back from his desk. "Is that what

Goodwin told Carol? That I wasn't even looking at Jayne and Rosa?" He hadn't cared for the man when they first met but this was going to make working with him even harder.

"He said you are keeping him out of the investigation to keep him from finding evidence against those two."

Hawke paced back and forth. "He is so blinded by his need to be the lead he doesn't understand the need to not compromise the women who were the victims of Betz. He has the subtlety of a buffalo in rut. He wouldn't get anything out of the women the way he would treat them. That is why I sent him back to Pendleton with the evidence his team dug out of the ashes."

"That's what I figured and told Keller the same. She's going to keep Goodwin in Pendleton working on something else more suited now that they have gathered all the forensic evidence."

"Then maybe I can get something accomplished without having to hold back because he's snooping over my shoulder. Browning and Herold agreed to not say anything to anyone about Betz perverted bent. We'll try to keep it quiet for the victims' sake. Unless one of them is his murderer." Hawke hoped it wasn't one of the victims who'd committed murder. He had however known people who'd snap over trivial things. What these women went through wasn't trivial.

"I'm headed home. Keep me posted." Spruel held out the book he'd had under his arm. "Merrilee was by and left this for you."

Hawke glanced at his watch, it was nearly 6 pm.

He'd forgotten to go to Merrilee's and go through her daughter's boxes. She must have gone through them herself and found the diary. "Thanks. I was supposed to go by her house this afternoon."

"That's what she said. I won't say what she called you." Spruel smiled.

"I got sidetracked and forgot about the meeting or I would have called her." Hawke felt bad. She'd said he could go through the boxes. It had been evident the woman still couldn't bring herself to go through her daughter's things. He'd apologize the next time he saw her.

"Let me know if you learn anything new from that." Spruel pivoted and headed into the breakroom.

"I will," Hawke called after him and resisted the urge to start reading the book now. He put it beside his hat on his desk.

Hawke stretched and noticed a new document had been added to the Betz file. He opened the report. Herold had typed up his interview with the Neumans. Reading the interview, Hawke reached for his cell phone. Once he'd read to the bottom, he scrolled and found Herold's name. He punched the name as he read the sentence again. *Pastor Betz never arrived at the hospital.*

"Hawke, did you learn something new?" Herold answered his phone.

"I just read your interview with the Neumans. I saw where they said they called the house phone and no one answered, then they called the church and talked to Mrs. Betz. Did they say what time they made that call?" Hawke believed they had caught the victim's wife in a lie. She said she hadn't been in the church that evening. And that she'd taken the call in the house.

He heard Herold thumbing through his notebook. "They didn't mention a time. I can contact them and ask."

"Do that. Also, the pastor never came to the hospital. That means he never received the note or was dead when the call was taken."

"I wondered that when I was typing it up," Herold agreed.

"I'm going to reread our visit with Mrs. Betz then go home. I'll be at Rosa's tomorrow interviewing all of the victims she could round up. Call or text what you find out about the time of the call."

"Copy."

The call ended and Hawke picked up the notes he'd made on each woman and headed out to his vehicle. He had a feeling that Mrs. Betz hadn't been telling them the truth when they interviewed her.

Chapter Seventeen

Friday morning Hawke woke groggy from staying up late reading Marcia's diary. It was all in there, how Betz had groomed her by not touching, then barely touching, to massaging her shoulders to "loosen" her up and relax her to sing better, to taking her into his office and working on her song, where he continued to touch her a little more each time, until he told her she was beautiful and deserved to have her first time be with someone who could teach her how to be a good wife. Hawke had felt himself physically feeling sicker and sicker as he read Marcia's diary. It not only showed how the predator had perfected his approach to capturing his prey, it also showed him how the young women either felt honored at his attention or in the case of Marcia repugnant but didn't know how to tell him to leave her alone. After all, he was a clergyman. And she wrote of her fear that if she told her mom, she'd kill the man and Marcia would be left alone with a baby she didn't want.

The diary gave him more compassion for the women he would be interviewing today. He didn't put on his uniform to make the women more comfortable when they talked to him. When he walked into the kitchen, Dog started hopping around.

"No, I'm still going to work. I just need to look less threatening. I promise tomorrow we'll go for a ride on Dot." On his days off Hawke rode either Jack or Dot to keep his body in shape for the hours he spent in the saddle during the seasons he rode horseback for days on end checking hunting and fishing licenses in the mountains.

Dog walked over to his bed and lay down. His sad eyes watched Hawke as he made breakfast. After Hawke ate, he called Dog, "Come on, let's go give the boys a treat."

Dog popped up but wasn't as enthusiastic as normal.

"I know you miss hanging out with me." Hawke patted the dog on the head and walked to the barn. Inside, he picked out three alfalfa cubes and strode out to the gate leading into the pasture where his two horses and mule were eating grass.

"You three want a cube?" he called.

The animals' heads popped up at the same time. They saw him and came loping to the gate, putting their back feet in braking mode at the last minute.

"Whoa! You three could have wiped out the gate and me." He fed them each a cube and scratched their faces. "We're going to ride tomorrow," he told Dot, or Polka Dot as Kitree had named the horse, as he rubbed up and down between the appaloosa gelding's eyes. Darlene had found Dot as a four-year-old and thought he would make Hawke a good trail horse. It turned out she'd been correct. The gelding was turning into as good a trail horse as Jack who was in his mid-twenties and would soon not be making the long trips into the mountains.

He glanced down at Dog. "Tomorrow is Saturday. How about we see if Kitree would like to ride with us?" Dog's eyes brightened and his tail thumped at hearing Kitree's name. She and Dog had bonded when he and Hawke trailed her through the Eagle Cap Wilderness after her parents had been killed in the mountains. She was adopted by Dani's wrangler and his wife, who was the cook and housekeeper at the lodge.

Hawke pulled out his phone and called Sage Kimbal, Kitree's mom.

"Hawke, what are you calling me for? You can survive without Dani a few more days." The woman chuckled.

Hawke smiled. "Yeah, I can. I was calling to see if Kitree would like to trail ride tomorrow. She can ride Jack."

"She already left for school. I'll ask her when she comes home and let you know."

"Thank you. Have you heard from Tuck about how repairs are going up at the lodge?" He hadn't heard a word from Dani since she and Tuck flew in to start repairs on the buildings and fix anything the winter might have damaged.

"Tuck radioed last night that they expect to be home Monday or Tuesday. But there is still quite a bit of snow around," Sage added.

"Okay. I didn't expect to hear from Dani. She's not used to checking in with anyone." Which he understood being someone who only thought about checking in with Spruel for his job, but he had thought since they were living together, she might at least let him know when she planned to be home.

"From what Tuck says she's been crunching numbers when she isn't holding a hammer and saw. It sounds like she's trying to figure out how to add a couple more larger cabins for families to stay in."

"That's a good idea. But I doubt she'll get that done for this season." Though, he knew when she wanted something, Dani tended to push and make it happen. That's how she'd made her way up the ranks in the Air Force. "I have to go. I'll wait to hear from you if Kitree wants to ride."

"Sounds good. Have a good day." Sage ended the connection.

Hawke glanced at Dog sitting at his feet. "Come on. I'm using my vehicle, you might as well ride around with me, though I'll be in one place most of the day. Maybe Rosa has a backyard you can sniff around in."

Dog woofed and spun in a circle before trotting ahead of him toward his personal pickup.

《》《》《》

Rosa paced back and forth in the entryway. She hoped Trooper Hawke came before Hannah arrived. She wanted to make sure he knew to ease into the questions he really wanted to know.

"What are you so worried about?" Jayne asked, walking out of the kitchen carrying a tray.

"I want to make sure Trooper Hawke treats everyone well." Rosa liked Jayne. She was a smart interesting young woman. They planned to go see her grandparents this afternoon after Trooper Hawke spoke with Ava.

"From how he's treated me so far, I don't think you have anything to worry about." Jayne carried the carafe of coffee and three cups into the room Rosa used to visit with her clients.

Rosa had to agree with her. Hawke had treated Jayne well, given he still considered her a suspect. But Rosa hadn't mentioned that. She was pretty certain that Jayne hadn't killed the pastor. Not given she was hit over the head and left out at Starvation Ridge. No, it was more likely she arrived at the church at the same time as the person who killed Betz.

The sound of a car approaching pulled Rosa out of her thoughts. She peeked out the window high in her front door by standing on her tiptoes. It was Trooper Hawke, only he wasn't in his police vehicle or dressed in his uniform. She smiled. He was making sure the women felt at ease.

Rosa opened the door. "Good morning, Trooper Hawke. I see you are prepared to make the women feel comfortable with your questions."

"Please, just call me Hawke." He walked into the entryway as Jayne came out of the visiting room.

"Good morning," Jayne greeted the trooper.

"Morning, Jayne. I have some good news for you. Though it brings up more questions." The man motioned toward the kitchen. "May we visit in the kitchen?" he asked Rosa.

"You may, but I have the visiting room set up for meeting the women today." She walked toward the room where Jayne pivoted and reentered.

Hawke followed the two women into a small room that looked as if it had been the receiving area back when the building was a hospital. There were three stuffed chairs facing a small table that held a tray with cups, a coffee carafe, sugar, and creamer. "I'll take the chair facing the door," Hawke said when Jayne started to sit in the chair on the far side of the table.

She glanced at him and shifted to the next chair. "What good news do you have for me?" she asked.

Hawke waited for Rosa to sit in the other chair and focused on Jayne. "Forensics has determined that the smoke and char on your clothing wasn't made from the church fire. It is pure wood smoke. Like a campfire. Does that help you remember anything else?"

The young woman stared at him. "A campfire?" Her head rotated back and forth slowly. "I don't remember anything about a campfire. But how would my clothes…" Jayne glanced at Rosa. "Why can't I remember any of this?"

It was evident the two women had become close over the last few days. Hawke had another idea. "Do you know if the clothes I found you in were the same ones you were wearing when you went to the church? And where were your extra changes of clothes?"

"I only brought two changes of clothing. I had planned to only spend one night. After I went to the church I was heading back to Yakima." Jayne waved a hand down her body. "These clothes Rosa and I bought at the thrift store. The clothes I wore to the police station were ones that Rosa brought to the hospital for me to wear. I don't know where my second set of clothing went if it wasn't in my car."

Hawke pulled his notepad out of his t-shirt pocket. "What was the second set of clothing you brought with you? I need descriptions and sizes. And what did you pack them in?"

Jayne described her clothing and added, "I wore the extra set of clothes. All that was in my bag was my mom's diary and the information Rosa had given me Sunday. The dirty set of clothes, that are missing, I had in the motel dirty laundry bag that was in my room."

"Which motel?" Hawke asked.

"The Settler's Motel. I was surprised when I found the plastic bag in the closet. I put my dirty set of clothes in the bag, tied a knot in the end, and tossed it in the back seat of my car." Jayne said as a knock sounded at the front door.

"I'll get that," Rosa said standing. "It should be Hannah." She hurried out of the room and Jayne stood.

"I'll make myself scarce while you talk to these women. I hope they all have alibis. I think the pastor has ruined their lives enough." Jayne stood and left the room by a door Hawke hadn't noticed when they all entered the room.

Rosa herded a tall thin woman in her thirties into the room. She had long dark hair that hung evenly over both outside corners of her eyes. Her mouth was pinched as if she found the whole meeting distasteful.

"Hannah, this is Hawke. He has some questions for you," Rosa said, seating the woman directly across from him before taking the seat to the side of Hannah.

Rosa then poured coffee into the cups and passed them around.

"Hannah, thank you for coming this morning. I have promised Rosa that I won't reveal any names to anyone unless that person turns out to be the one who killed the pastor," Hawke said.

The woman had stared straight at him as he talked. Her eyes narrowed and her face flushed when he mentioned Betz.

"Could you tell me how old you were when the pastor assaulted you?" Hawke asked in a soft voice.

"I don't think that's any of your business!" Hannah shoved to her feet. "I've worked hard to put that out of my mind and here you are bringing it all back up."

"The man is dead and even though he wasn't a pleasant person, I still have to find out who killed him." Hawke remained calm, watching her over the cup of coffee he held ready to sip.

"Is that type of question necessary?" Rosa asked.

"I'll explain why I asked this question to you later. But it is important to frame of mind." Hawke sipped his coffee and said, "Take your time. I don't want or need details, just your age."

Hannah studied him for several minutes before picking up the cup in front of her. "Seventeen."

"And how old are you now?" Hawke asked in the same soft tone.

"Thirty-four."

"Do you have children?" He continued, sipping his coffee and acting as if this were a normal conversation.

"Two. I married when I was thirty. They are three and one." She seemed to relax as he talked about her life now.

"What were you doing Monday night?" Hawke asked. He saw Rosa stiffen out of the corner of his eye.

"Monday night? My husband and I put the children to bed, watched a movie, and went to bed. It was like every other night." She set the cup down. "Why did you ask that?"

"Both of you were home all night?" Hawke ignored her question.

"Yes. We went to bed together and woke up together." She frowned. "What are you getting at?"

"Nothing. Do you and your husband attend church?" Hawke asked.

Hannah glanced at Rosa and back at him. "What does that have to do with anything?"

"I'm trying to determine if the assault on you made you anti-church."

"When my mom didn't believe me and she told Pastor Betz about my accusation, they laughed about it. Laughed! The only person who believed me was Rosa. I was lucky. I didn't become pregnant like some of the others. But I swore that I would never set foot in church again. And I haven't. We were married at the lake by a justice of the peace."

Hawke nodded. He understood the woman's dislike of church after having a pastor rape her. "Does your husband know what happened when you were seventeen?"

The woman's face paled. "No! I've never said a word to him about it. Please don't say anything."

"I won't say a word. However, all honest relationships don't have secrets between them."

Hawke held out his hand.

Hannah hesitated then grasped it.

"Thank you for your bravery in talking with me. I won't be putting this in any records or documents. Your secret is safe with me."

She smiled weakly and Rosa escorted her out of the room.

When the midwife returned, she picked up the cup Hannah had used and headed for the door. She stopped and asked, "Why did you ask what age she was when Pastor Betz assaulted her?"

"To see her reaction, learn how young she was, and how long ago it happened. They all tell a story about the woman's emotions as she thinks about her answers."

"It's like a litmus test," Rosa said.

"Yes, it's a test. A way to gauge her reactions to other questions." Hawke finished off his cup of coffee. "When does the next woman arrive?"

"You have ten minutes before she comes. I'll be in the kitchen cleaning this cup for the next person."

Hawke pulled out his notebook and wrote down everything Hannah said. While he said it wouldn't go in any documents, he still wanted the answers and his impressions written in his book to use for reference.

Chapter Eighteen

The other nine women came and went throughout the day. Each one had their own tale of fear, shame, and anger. With each story and seeing how manipulative and vain the pastor was, Hawke's anger at the man and the county law enforcement for not listening to Rosa grew.

The only woman who didn't answer Hawke's questions in a civil tone was one of the younger women. Tinsley. She came in with a chip on her shoulder and it remained there no matter how hard Hawke tried to prove he wasn't out to hurt her. It was apparent the pastor's assault on her was fresh in her mind and her anger was barely being kept in check. But she was a frail-looking young woman who seemed to have all of her muscles in her mouth.

"That dirty old bastard tried to tell me I was special. That by letting him touch me, I would float to heaven as an angel. He raped me and laughed when I told him I'd tell my parents." Her face reddened.

"Why would he laugh at you mentioning your parents? Were they loyal to him?" Hawke asked.

"My parents didn't go to church. They don't believe in God or anything other than enough money to buy cigarettes and booze."

"If you feel this strongly about the pastor, why didn't you go to the police?" Hawke asked.

She stared down at her hands in her lap for several seconds, before her blazing gaze met his. "Because the police in this town have hauled my mother and my sister in for prostitution. Do you think they'd believe the good pastor raped me? They'd just think I was mad because he didn't pay me. But I'm not a whore! I don't want anything to do with my family. I wish to hell I could get out of here."

When Tinsley left, Hawke asked Rosa about her.

"Her family is rather colorful and not in a good way," Rosa began. "Her teachers told me that Tinsley always tried to do well in school and be a good person. But her family life was all about being put down and taught to do things illegally. When she started going to church, the families had her over to their homes for meals and bible study. And when Pastor Betz started taking a special interest in her, she bloomed. Until…"

She didn't have to say what happened. Hawke knew. "What happened then?"

"She left the church, started dressing slutty, and her mouth just keeps getting worse and worse. She came to me when she missed her period. Tinsley told me what happened and cried. She had been on the right path and that monster shoved her over the edge."

Hawke wondered… "Any chance she told her family and one of them took revenge on Betz?"

Rosa shook her head. "No. They wouldn't have cared one way or the other. I was surprised that Tinsley was a virgin until the Pastor got his claws into her. She didn't want to have the child. She was afraid her family would take it to sell."

Hawke stared at the woman to make sure he'd heard right. "Sell it?"

"Yes. That family will do anything for money that they squander on booze and drugs. I wish Tinsley would move away and start fresh. I tried to talk her into moving to a town where my sister lives. She would look after her and see that she gets a job and a place to stay. But she made excuses of why she couldn't go."

Hawke wondered if she didn't want to leave so she could hurt Pastor Betz. "Do you believe where she said she was on Monday night?"

When Rosa didn't reply, he knew the woman didn't believe it either.

He'd go talk to Desiree Halver. She worked at the High Mountain Brewery and would know if Tinsley was working there.

"Thank you for bringing the women together for me to talk with. I know they trust you and I hope I didn't ruin that trust." Hawke walked toward the door. He was ready for a hamburger and he'd get it at the brewery and talk to Desiree.

"You did fine. I think they might have a little more respect for policemen after this." Rosa stopped behind him at the door. "Do you think any of them are the killer?"

Hawke faced her. "At this point in the investigation, I don't know. A couple have shaky memories of their whereabouts but I don't see them killing anyone. Tinsley, I'm suspicious about but that doesn't make her a killer. I'll check her alibi now and then I'll start checking into the whereabouts of the spouses and family members."

"You really think it is one of the women or their spouse that killed the pastor? But why now?" Rosa studied him.

"Do you have any idea who his most recent victim was?" Hawke asked. That would be the person he needed to focus on. The other women had lots of years between the event and none of them seemed to be harboring a sense of revenge, just shame.

"There have been rumors Gemma Fowler is pregnant. She's nineteen and was in the Lighted Path choir." Rosa opened the door.

Hawke pulled out his notepad and wrote the name down. "Where can I find her?"

"She's in college at Eastern Oregon. She's studying to be a teacher."

"Thank you." Hawke walked out to his vehicle. Dog sat up, watching his approach. Once Hawke was seated, he patted Dog's head. "How was your walk with Jayne?"

The long tail thumped on the seat.

"That good, huh? I'm headed to get lunch at the brewery, I suppose you want a burger too?"

This time the tongue came out as the tail whapped the seat.

"I'll take that as a yes." Hawke started this pickup and drove to the High Mountain Brewery. The largest part of the back half of the building was a brewery, the front half was a restaurant and bar. They opened at eleven a.m. and closed at two a.m.

Hawke found a parking spot. He lowered the windows enough Dog could sniff and entertain himself. Walking up to the entrance, Hawke glanced at the area in the parking lot where the employees usually parked. He didn't notice Desiree's car. She usually worked the opening shift. If she wasn't there, he'd talk to the manager, Bud Dewey.

Inside the establishment, Hawke scanned the large open area. Of the twenty people, he knew half. He didn't see Desiree anywhere.

"Can I help you?" a man in his twenties, with a man bun and a sleeve tattoo, asked.

"Table for one and I'd like to speak to Bud, please." Hawke didn't recognize the young man. Since the county had become more about art and tourists than logging and farming, the citizens had become more bohemian.

The host led Hawke to a table by a window and placed a glass of water he'd picked up on the way over on the table. "Would you like something besides water to drink?"

"Coffee, please. Just black, no cream or sugar." Hawke responded, picking up the menu.

"I'll send Bud out before I get the coffee."

Hawke nodded and the man disappeared. He'd barely had a chance to read the special of the day when Bud arrived.

"Hawke, I didn't expect to see you." The short, balding man pulled out a chair across from Hawke and sat down. "It's been a busy morning. Had a big shipment go out and the temperatures were fluctuating."

The young man arrived with Hawke's coffee and a cup for Bud.

"Thanks, Steven," Bud said, before taking a sip.

"Have you decided?" Steven asked, watching Hawke.

"I'll have a deluxe cheeseburger for here and a plain burger, no fixings in a box to go."

"You must have Dog with you today," Bud said.

"I do. His tail started thumping fast when I said I'd bring him a burger." Hawke grinned as Steven glanced back and forth between him and Bud.

"Do you want fries with both burgers?" Steven asked.

"Only the one to go. I'll have potato salad with mine. Thanks." Hawke handed the young man his menu and shifted his attention to Bud. "Do you have a Tinsley Smith who works here in the evenings?"

"Is she in trouble?" Bud sat his coffee down and stared at Hawke.

"No. I'm just following up on something she told me."

"She does. My wife asked me to give her a job. She needs to make money to move away from her family. You know who they are, I'm sure." Bud glanced around and lowered his voice. "They're the lot out north that blew up their barn making meth and the boys are always caught stealing. Verna, my wife, says Tinsley has a chance at a good life if she can get away."

"I'd like to confirm Tinsley was working here on Monday night." Hawke leaned back as Steven brought him a plate with a burger and potato salad and a to-go bag.

"She was. She helps out in the kitchen and washes dishes."

Hawke couldn't see the mouthy young woman he'd talked with washing dishes, but it seemed there was a side to her that others saw. He nodded. "That's all I needed to know."

When Bud didn't stand to leave, Hawke raised his gaze from putting ketchup on his burger to the man's face. "Is there something else?"

Bud squirmed a bit. "There's rumors going around that Pastor Betz wasn't as wonderful as everyone made him out to be. Is that true?"

This was where it got sticky. Hawke preferred people knew the truth, and it might muddy the investigation if everyone started making things up. He'd only promised Rosa not to bring names into the investigation, but people would know who went to the church and who didn't.

"Let's just say, there is someone out there who put a stop to a man who believed he was above the law and his maker." Hawke picked up his burger and took a bite.

Bud got the message and left the table.

While chewing, Hawke texted Herold. *Two names to look up, please. Gemma Fowler, I want family names and everything you can find out about them and Tinsley Smith's family. I need to know if any of them, other than the two girls, went to The Lighted Path church. Thanks.*

Copy, Herold replied. *Any luck with the women at Rosa's?*

Tinsley is the only one who wasn't cooperative, but that is probably just her upbringing.

Herold replied with a thumbs-up emoji.

Hawke finished his meal, paid for it, and headed to his pickup where Dog was waiting patiently. As he fed Dog, Hawke flipped through the notes he'd made. The complexity of the homicide puzzled him. The victim was hit hard enough on the head to have killed him, yet the church was set on fire and Jayne who most likely arrived when the murder was about to take place, was hauled to Starvation Ridge and left in clothes that smelled of smoke.

If the smoke on her clothes was pure pine, the fire must have been out in the woods. He started his pickup. "Let's go hike around Starvation Ridge," he said to Dog and pulled out of the parking lot.

Chapter Nineteen

Out on Starvation Ridge, Hawke and Dog began their examination of the ground at the cluster of trees where the car and Jayne were found. They walked in a zigzag path back perpendicular to the road. Two hundred yards, give or take, he came across a circle of burned sticks. Doing a perimeter walk he crossed the path of two sets of tire tracks. The tread, width of the tires, and wheelbase led him to believe they were both cars. He snapped photos of partial treads and hoped to match one to Jayne's car.

He walked back to his vehicle and grabbed evidence bags and a pair of latex gloves from the duffel in his back seat, shoving them in his back pockets. Back at the fire, he put ash in one bag. He didn't know if forensics could determine what was burned or if the chemical composition would match that of the smoke and char on Jayne's clothing from that night, but it didn't hurt to have a sample.

To have the presence of mind to bring Jayne here,

the killer must have had prior knowledge of the area. As Hawke thought this, he pulled out his notebook and started a list of things he was learning about the killer.

He took photos of the blackened sticks and ground and made note of where he found them. Ready to leave, he looked around for Dog. The animal had his nose shoved into a bush about twenty feet from the burned circle. "Did you find something?" Hawke asked, walking up behind his friend.

Dog backed up.

Hawke's gaze landed on a syringe. "Good boy, this might have some fingerprints." He pulled an evidence bag out of his pocket and scooped the syringe into the bag. After sealing and labeling the bag, Hawke found a stick and poked around under the bush some more. Brushing away a pile of leaves with the stick, he spotted a plastic bag. He took photos of the bush with the bag showing.

"What have we found?" he asked Dog as he knelt, pulled a pair of gloves out of his pocket, and then lifted the bag out from under the leaves. Bold printing on the bag read *The Settler Motel*, Alder, Oregon. He untied the top of the bag, took a photo, and pulled out clothing that matched the description Jayne gave him of her missing clothes. The ones she had on the night she'd visited the church. He left the bag and clothing to retrieve two larger evidence bags. He kept a full evidence kit in his personal vehicle never knowing when he might come across something. Beside the kit was a duffel with hiking gear and several changes of clothing and a First Aid kit.

Back at the bush, he opened an evidence bag,

picked up the shirt, and spotted blood on the shoulder and sleeve before lowering it into the bag. He sealed and labeled the bag. Then he shoved the pants into the other bag and wrote the time, day, and location. Last, he put the plastic bag in an evidence bag. If the person hadn't had the forethought to put on gloves there might be fingerprints. Before carrying the bags back to the pickup, Hawke swirled the stick around through the leaves to see if he could find anything else. Jayne's clutch purse was still missing.

Satisfied he wouldn't find anything more, Hawke carried the evidence bags back to the vehicle and told Dog to load up. He scanned the area one last time to make sure he hadn't missed anything and he slid in behind the steering wheel. On the drive back to Alder he called Spruel to see if someone could meet a State Trooper in La Grande to take the evidence he'd found to Pendleton.

"If you can get it to Bisset, she can get it out to La Grande," Spruel said.

"I'll give her a call." Hawke ended his call and scrolled through his contacts for the newest member of the Wallowa County State Troopers. She was patrol, not part of Fish and Wildlife.

"Trooper Bisset," she answered her phone.

"Ivy, this is Hawke. I have evidence that needs to go to Pendleton. Spruel said if I gave it to you, you'd get it to La Grande."

"Hey, Hawke. I'm sitting between Winslow and Alder at the moment. An elderly white male ran out of gas."

Hawke chuckled. "You mean Lewis is lonely. I bet

he was happy to see you, someone new who doesn't know all of his stories."

Ivy chuckled. "I guess he's done this before."

"Yes. I was the lucky one to help him out earlier in the week. Call his son." Hawke gave her the son's name and number. "I'll meet you in Alder at the bakery."

"Copy."

Hawke ended the call as he entered Alder city limits. Sitting in front of the bakery he called Herold and asked if he could meet him at the bakery to catch him up. He agreed.

"Wait here, I'll bring you a treat," Hawke said, patting Dog on the head and exiting his vehicle.

Herold parked beside him and stepped out of his city cruiser. "Is this your day off?"

"No. I interviewed the women on Rosa's list. I didn't want to make them nervous." They walked into the bakery and up to the counter. Olivia, one of the women he'd interviewed that morning stood across the counter. Her eyes widened.

"Hello Olivia, I'd like two maple bars, a cake donut, and coffee. But put one of the maple bars in a separate bag, please." Hawke pulled out his wallet. "I'm getting what Officer Herold wants, too."

"Thanks!" Herold pointed to an apple fritter. "I'll take that and a coffee."

Olivia told Hawke the total and he paid. As they waited for their coffee and donuts, he spied Ivy parking on the other side of the city cruiser. This was really going to make Olivia nervous. Hawke nodded to the State Trooper standing by her vehicle. "I'll be right back," he said to Herold.

Hawke walked out of the bakery and over to his vehicle. "You made good time," he said, unlocking his door.

Ivy followed him over. "When I mentioned calling his son, Lewis asked me to bring him and a gas can into town. Said he'd find someone who stopped at the station to give him a ride back to his vehicle."

Hawke grabbed the evidence bags he'd filled. "Hand these directly to whoever is taking them to Pendleton. I don't want it to sit around at the La Grande office."

"Will do. Does this have anything to do with your burned church?" Ivy took the evidence bags and walked toward her vehicle.

Hawke followed. "Yeah. Stow those in your car. I have something for you for the road." He walked back into the bakery where Herold sat at a table eating his fritter. "I'll be right back." Hawke grabbed the bag with the maple bar and donut and walked up to his pickup. He fed the donut to Dog and strode over to Ivy, handing her the bag. "Something to keep you awake on the way out and back."

The young woman's face lit up when she peeked into the bag. "Thanks, Hawke." She slid into her vehicle as Hawke returned to the bakery.

"You made Bisset happy," Herold remarked.

"She's doing me a favor. I found Jayne's other set of clothing and a syringe shoved under a bush about two hundred yards from where the car was left. There had been a campfire built and two sets of tire tracks." Hawke pulled his phone out of his pocket and went to his photos. He showed Herold the photos he'd taken.

"You think Jayne was drugged and that's why she couldn't remember things?" Herold picked up his cup of coffee.

Hawke nodded and pulled his maple bar out of the bag. "I think someone set her up with the smoky clothes and not remembering more than she'd been to the church. Whoever killed Betz and set the church on fire had either been planning this for a while or can quickly problem solve."

"Or they don't get flustered under duress." Herold bit into his fritter.

Hawke thought about that. So far the only person he'd met who fit that description and was connected to this investigation was Rosa Towman.

«»«»«»

Rosa parked in the overgrown driveway. It had been years since she'd set foot on this land. She glanced over at Jayne. Her gaze was on the swing dangling by one rope.

"Come on. We aren't going to know how they will react until we see." Rosa patted Jayne's hand and opened her door.

"They live out here all alone?" Jayne asked.

"It's the way they want it. There are a few neighbors who look after them, making purchases for them in town and dropping them off. They use the local shuttle when they have doctor's appointments." Rosa waved to the empty carport. "Neither one is able to drive anymore."

"I feel bad for them even though they did this to themselves," Jayne said.

"Let's see how they react." Rosa stepped up to the

front door and knocked hard on the screen door. Peeling paint sprinkled down onto the porch.

She heard someone moving inside.

"Get the door, Anita!" yelled a hoarse male voice.

"I'm trying." The sound of wheels and metal clunking on wood approached the other side of the door.

The door swung open and the hunched-over woman twisted her head, to look up at them. "We aren't in need of a ride today." She grabbed the door to close it.

"Mrs. Laude, I'm Rosa Towman and this is Jayne, your granddaughter," Rosa said quickly.

Jayne stepped closer to the screen, peering down at her grandmother.

"Jayne?" The woman's eyes teared up. "Eloise's daughter?"

"Yes, I'm Eloise's daughter." Jayne opened the screen door and bent to put her face closer to the old woman's.

"Have you come to take care of us?" Anita asked.

Rosa studied Jayne as she straightened and stared at a woman she'd never met before.

"I have questions about my mom and her life before you called her a liar and pushed her away." Jayne's face reddened. "You owe me an explanation of why you wouldn't believe your own daughter and not reconcile when she tried to."

The woman's tears dried and she glared at Jayne. "You're just as stubborn and proud as your mother. She was a handful. Always questioning everything, arguing, telling us we didn't love her." Anita swayed.

Rosa grabbed the woman's arm and started to back her into the house.

"No! Don't go in there. It will only upset Jerome." She pointed to a chair on the porch. "Put me there."

"Who's out there, Anita?" Jerome called from inside the house.

"A neighbor," she called back and allowed Rosa to sit her in the chair.

Once seated, Anita waved a hand, motioning for them to sit on the porch. Jayne did, but Rosa pushed on a post and found it held. She leaned against it. This was Jayne's conversation, not hers.

"We had Eloise fifteen years into our marriage. Doctors told us we'd never conceive. Then oops, I was pregnant. We were set in our ways and hadn't been around children much. But we knew we had to keep a tight rein on her. When Pastor Betz and Diane came to the county it was like our prayers had been answered. They helped us through some tough times with Eloise. And the pastor, bless him, he started bible study with her."

Jayne rose to her feet and paced the porch. She stopped and bent to peer into the older woman's face. "Those bible study lessons are when he raped my mother."

"No, he wouldn't. It was Wade Archer," the old woman protested.

Jayne went down on her knees and pointed to her eyebrows. "Look at me. Who do these eyebrows remind you of? And my blue eyes? And..." She outlined her chin. "My chin? None of these came from Wade Archer. I know, I visited with him the other day. But the photos I've seen of Pastor Betz…These are all attributes I received from his genes. Not anyone else's. I am the illegitimate child of your wonderful pastor and my loving mother. I was conceived when he raped my mother. And you wouldn't listen to her."

Anita's eyes teared up again. "I couldn't believe the man who had been so helpful to us would do that to my daughter. He was so caring and loving. He helped so many people."

Rosa wanted to gag. The man had preyed on his flock.

"No, he didn't help people. He used them and preyed on their daughters. Mom wasn't the only young woman he raped. I've met over a dozen that man pushed himself on over the years. And you could have stopped him if you had believed your daughter." Jayne rose. "I want to go. I'm done."

Rosa pushed away from the post, she felt for Anita, but she understood Jayne. This woman was a stranger to her and one who had caused her mother a lot of pain. She owed the woman nothing. She and her husband had put themselves in the position they were in.

"Jayne, please, don't go," Anita said.

"I'm sorry, but I feel nothing but disgust for you. You don't want me around loathing you. Goodbye, Mrs. Laude." Jayne walked off the porch.

Rosa followed. They slipped into the car and drove away. She sent a furtive glance toward Jayne. A tear trickled down her cheek.

Chapter Twenty

It was dinner time and Hawke was still in Alder. He'd decided he wanted to talk to Gemma Fowler's parents. She might be the most recent victim and that put her family on the suspect list. He asked Herold for their address and information. Tom Fowler worked as a mechanic and Cathy, his wife, worked at the grocery store in Alder. Herold said the family was well-liked, had never been in trouble with the law, and led a quiet life.

Hawke parked in front of the small house and rolled the pickup windows down a few inches so Dog could enjoy the smells. Walking up to the front door, Hawke pulled his badge out from under his shirt by a chain. It was how he wore his badge when he wasn't wearing his uniform. Mostly when he wore plain clothes in the mountains.

At the door, he pressed the doorbell and waited.

A dog barked from inside.

A male voice yelled, "Quiet!"

The door opened. A woman in her late forties with dark hair pulled up into a ponytail stood staring at him. "Can I help you?"

"Mrs. Fowler?" Hawke asked.

"Yes. And you are?"

He held up his badge. "Oregon State Trooper Hawke. I have some questions I'd like to ask you and your husband."

Her brow wrinkled and fear flashed in her eyes as she stepped back to allow him in. "Has something happened to Gemma?"

"No. She's fine as far as I know."

"Oh, that's good to hear. I worry about her at college."

A tall, broad man with a buzz cut, dressed in a clean t-shirt and cargo pants walked into the living room. "Who are you?"

Hawke reintroduced himself. "I would like to ask you and your wife some questions. Have a seat."

The couple exchanged glances and sat together on the couch.

Hawke pulled a footstool over and took a seat across from them with a coffee table between him and the couple. "I'd like to know what the two of you were doing this past Monday night?" He started with.

They both stared at him.

"Why do you want to know that?" Mr. Fowler asked.

"I'll answer your question after you've answered mine." Hawke pulled his notebook and pen out of a pocket.

"I worked late Monday. One of the other checkers called in sick," Mrs. Fowler said. "I got home about ten-thirty?" She peered at her husband. "Tom was still up puttering around in the shop behind the house."

"Yeah, it was ten-thirty when Cathy got home. Since Gemma went off to college the house is too quiet when Cathy's gone. I go out and work on projects in my shop." Tom grasped his wife's hand.

"While your wife was at work, did you go out or talk to anyone?" Hawke asked Mr. Fowler.

"I talked to Will Edgars on the phone. I was working on a mower for him. I told him he needed to order some parts for it. But that's it."

"What time did you talk to him?" Hawke asked.

The man rose. "It should still be on my phone. It's in the kitchen. We were making dinner when you showed up." Mr. Fowler walked through the door he'd entered.

"What is this all about?" Mrs. Fowler asked.

"I'll let you know when your husband returns."

The man returned carrying a cell phone. "It says I talked to Will twenty minutes at seven-twenty-six."

Hawke wrote the information down. It was highly unlikely Mr. Fowler knocked out Jayne and did something with Betz.

"I understand your family went to The Lighted Path Church," Hawke said as an opening.

"Yes, until recently." Mrs. Fowler's voice was edged with anger.

"Why did you stop going?" Hawke pushed.

Mr. Fowler set his phone on the table and sat

beside his wife. "Because we believe that bastard raped our little girl."

"Did you take this to the police?" He knew they hadn't but wanted to find out why.

"No. Gemma didn't want everyone to know what had happened. She was so ashamed and upset. She told us what and how it happened." The woman made a disgusted face. "I tried to tell her she needed to say something, but she said he threatened to spread vicious rumors about her if she told anyone. That made her fearful of what people would say about us. To ease her fears, we sent her to stay with my sister in La Grande until school started." Mrs. Fowler's eyes filled with tears. "How could someone of his position do such a thing? Talk one way to the congregation and say things so vile and treat a young woman like that?"

"What did you do when your daughter told you?" Hawke studied Mr. Fowler.

"I went to the church and confronted him. I didn't want to drag my little girl through the scandal and he knew it. He just smiled that benevolent way he had and said, she should be honored that he chose her. Chose her! We thought he honestly saw talent in her organ playing. It turned out his lessons were so he could…" Mr. Fowler rubbed his hands over his face.

"Did you say anything to anyone else about his conduct?" Hawke asked.

Mrs. Fowler nodded. "I told every mother who had a teenage daughter to not allow him to be alone with them. They asked why not and I told them he made inappropriate advances to Gemma, and they tried to put it back on my daughter." The woman's cheeks reddened. "I have to admit when I heard the church had burned down, I thought good. He'll leave the valley. But then I heard he died in the fire and I thought it was fitting."

"Where were both of you Tuesday morning?" Hawke asked.

Husband and wife stared straight at him.

"I was headed to work. I saw the smoke billowing, drove toward it, and saw the church on fire." Mr. Fowler put an arm around his wife. "I called Cathy and said Gemma can come home now. The church and hopefully the pastor was gone."

"Did either one of you set the church on fire?" Hawke asked.

They both shook their heads.

"I had thought of doing a lot of things to the bastard, but I didn't come up with burning the church. I say give the person who did a medal." Mr. Fowler stood, drawing his wife up beside him. "We have dinner to make."

Hawke stood, thanked them for their time, and headed out to his vehicle. His gut said they didn't do it, but their attitudes made him wonder if his gut was off on this one.

《》《》《》

The next morning, Sage dropped Kitree off at Hawke's by eight. He was dressed, had breakfast, and had already saddled the horses and loaded them in the trailer.

"Hawke!" Kitree shouted and ran at him, hugging him around the waist.

He patted her back and tipped her straw hat back so

he could look into her face. "You keep growing like this and you're going to be taller than me."

She giggled. "I'm coming into my growth spurt stage, huh mom," Kitree said, addressing Sage.

The woman's cheeks blossomed pink and her eyes sparkled.

This was the first time Hawke had heard Kitree call her adopted parent by mom. It appeared it pleased Sage. She was a warm-hearted woman and deserved a loving daughter after having lost one to cancer.

"Yes, she is a teenager and that's when most people go through a fast-growing period." Sage held out a small pack. "I made her a snack and lunch. I wasn't sure where you were going."

"I thought we'd ride around Whiskey Creek. There's still too much snow and mud to go up in the mountains." Hawke motioned to his pickup. "You two load up."

Kitree and Dog, or Prince, as Kitree called him, ran to the vehicle.

"Thank you for taking her riding," Sage said.

"I've been meaning to do more with her but things just seem to always be busy." Hawke glanced at the pickup and smiled. Kitree and Dog were sitting in the front seat, her arm around the dog and his tongue hanging out happy as could be.

"I think Dog and I get tired of each other's company."

Sage chuckled. "I think you two miss Dani when she's at the lodge."

"That too." But he wouldn't admit that to anyone but Sage. "I'll drop her off when we're done."

"I'll be home all day. We have a horse that's supposed to foal and the rest of the family is off at a track meet." Sage walked over to her SUV. "Have fun!" she called and climbed in.

Hawke walked over to his pickup and climbed in. "It's supposed to be warm and nice all day. We picked a good day to go for a ride."

"I needed this. School has been hard and with Dad up at the lodge with Dani, Mom has been clingy."

Hawke laughed. "You're one to talk about clingy."

She punched him in the arm. Hawke laughed when Dog took her wrist in his mouth.

Once they left the pavement, the road was muddy and slick. Hawke stopped in the road and stared ahead. The roads were thawing and growing muddier.

"We don't have to go riding here. We could go back to your place," Kitree said.

As he started to agree with her, his phone buzzed. Goodwin.

"Hawke," he answered.

"We're back in Alder. Keller said something about you found a fire and clothing. We want to go over the area," Goodwin said.

Counting to three, Hawke drew in a breath and let it out slowly.

Kitree giggled.

He glanced at her and smiled. "Today is my day off and I gathered all that was there for evidence."

"How do you know until we go over it? Can we find the location if we drive in that direction?"

"No, you won't be able to find it." Hawk shrugged. It looked like they would be riding on Starvation Ridge.

"Take Highway three north out of Alder. Wait for me at Forest Road forty-six. I'll lead you from there." He ended the call and started backing up to a spot he didn't think he'd get stuck when he turned around. "Looks like we'll be riding out on Starvation Ridge."

"It's a good thing you packed a lunch."

Hawke glanced at Kitree.

"Starvation Ridge?" she said as if he wasn't very smart. "We won't starve because we have a lunch."

He chuckled and took the Whiskey Creek Road back to Leap Lane and then across to Hwy 3. He headed north knowing the major crime team would be waiting for him.

Chapter Twenty-one

Goodwin was pacing back and forth beside the SUV when Hawke pulled up beside the vehicle.

"What's with the horse trailer," Goodwin looked past him, "and the girl?"

"I said it was my day off. We were going for a ride. I'll show you the spot and we'll go up the ridge farther and ride." Hawke put his vehicle in gear and pulled onto the forest road.

"He's got an attitude," Kitree said.

Hawke chuckled and agreed. It was a slow drive since the road was now rutted from all the vehicles that had been in and out since Hawke found Jayne in her car. Seeing a good flat rocky spot where he could leave the pickup and trailer, Hawke pulled over.

"We'll unload and ride from here. You want to take the horses out while I show Sergeant Goodwin the spot he's looking for?" Hawke didn't wait for Kitree to answer. He knew she'd do what he'd asked.

Dog stayed with the horses and Kitree while

Hawke walked over to the waiting SUV. "It's just up the road a quarter of a mile." He got in the back seat and directed them to the area. "Park here on the road."

They all got out. Kate and Gage put on their white suits and each grabbed what looked like a toolbox and followed he and Goodwin over to the blackened ground.

"How do you know this fire had anything to do with the investigation?" Goodwin asked as the other two started taking samples of the ashes.

Hawke filled him in on the tire tracks, the extra set of clothing found in the motel bag, and the syringe.

Goodwin's eyes narrowed. "How did you know to look here?"

"I didn't. I started from where the car was jammed between the trees and worked my way this direction, figuring whoever brought Jayne up here had to have another vehicle. I hadn't expected to find a fire or the clothes. I was just following leads and trails."

He heard a horse snort and looked over. Kitree riding Jack and leading Dot stopped on the road next to the SUV. Dog trotted over to Hawke.

"Looks like my ride is here. Enjoy." Hawke smiled at Goodwin and walked over to Dot. He swung up into the saddle and said, "Lead the way," to Kitree.

《》《》《》

On the way back to the pickup and trailer, they passed the fire pit site. Goodwin and crew were gone. There wasn't much left to find after he'd turned all the evidence in. But maybe they would find something that would help them figure out who had killed the pastor and framed Jayne.

"Is this a crime scene?" Kitree asked.

"It might be. We won't know for sure until forensics can connect the items I found here to a death that occurred."

"Someone died here?" Kitree asked softly.

Hawke stopped and pulled Jack to stop beside him. He had found her in the Eagle Cap Wilderness after someone had killed her parents. She still had nightmares about it, Sage had told him. "No. No one was killed here. But someone was left here with incriminating evidence that made them a suspect."

Kitree peered into his eyes. "Did you find the person like you found me?"

"Kind of. She had been hit on the head and her car was jammed between two trees. I think whoever put her there started the fire that burned down the church in Alder. They wanted law enforcement to find her dead, to believe she had caused the fire."

"But you found her and saved her?" Kitree asked, a smile spreading across her face. "Just like you found me and saved me."

Hawke nodded. "Yeah, I found her and didn't understand why someone would be out here if they fled after setting a church on fire." Hawke squeezed his legs and Dot continued walking.

Kitree rode Jack alongside Hawke. "And you found more evidence where Sergeant Goodwin and his team looked earlier?"

"Yes. More evidence that explains how the woman I found got out here and why she didn't have any memory of the trip."

"Someone drugged her?" Kitree asked.

Hawke glanced over at the teenager. He'd known she was smart when she was hiding from him on the mountain, believing he was going to kill her. But her mind was quick to add situations up and come up with answers.

"Yes. And they'd held her clothes over the fire to make them smokey and even charred a bit." Before the church was set on fire, he thought to himself. Whoever had done this had planned to set the church on fire. Had Jayne walked in on the person setting up things for the fire? But she'd said Betz had walked out of the back. They couldn't have been setting things up in his office if he were in it.

"Hawke. Hawke!" Kitree's voice invaded his thoughts.

"What?" He twisted his head her direction and realized he'd kept them walking past the pickup and trailer.

"Are we riding more or did you not see the horse trailer?" Kitree giggled.

"I was thinking."

"It's a good thing Polka Dot is smart or you could walk right off a cliff when you're thinking." She giggled and he took a swing at her with his hat. She giggled more and trotted Jack over to the horse trailer.

Hawke smiled. This was exactly what he needed today.

《》《》《》

Sage was waiting for them on the front porch when Hawke drove up to the house to drop Kitree off.

Hawke got out to stretch his legs and walked up to Sage. "We had a good ride. Not where we wanted to go

185

but it turned out okay."

"We had to lead some police people to a place where they smoked some clothes," Kitree said, giving Sage a hug.

Sage smiled and hugged Kitree back and asked, "Where they smoked some clothes?"

"Kitree can tell you about it. I'm heading home. Thank you for going with me Kitree, it was what I needed after a stressful week."

"You're welcome!"

"Tuck radioed. They're coming down tomorrow. Something about they need more supplies." Sage smiled. "It will be good to have him home for a few days."

"Yeah. I've got some things I'd like to run by Dani. Thanks for the information."

"You're welcome. Have a good rest of your day."

"I plan on it." He whistled for Dog who had run off to play with the cattle dogs wandering around Tuck's family's ranch. It was where Tuck, Sage, and Kitree stayed when they weren't up at the lodge in the Eagle Cap Wilderness.

Back at his house, Hawke unloaded and unsaddled the horses, giving them both ample amounts of grain.

"Did you have a good ride today, too?" he asked, brushing them and enjoying the scent of horse sweat, dust, and the crunching as they ate.

Dog lay on a bale of hay, his head on his front legs, his eyes closed.

Horse stood at the pasture gate making irritated noises. He was unhappy he wasn't getting any grain. But he'd been allowed to stay behind and eat all the grass he'd wanted.

"Yep, this day couldn't get any better," Hawke said as he continued to brush them.

His phone buzzed. It was Carol. "Hi, are you having a good Saturday?" he asked.

"Sounds like you are," she replied.

"I went riding with a friend, and yes, we had a good time." He smiled, thinking about how easy it was to hang out with Kitree.

"Well, I don't know if this is good news, but the syringe had been used to inject ketamine. A drug that can produce amnesia."

"That's why Jayne didn't remember anything when I found her. Thanks. This is good news. I hadn't felt she had killed Betz or set the fire, but while her amnesia felt real, I was wondering if it was a way to throw suspicion off of herself."

"If she hasn't been your suspect, who has?" Carol asked.

"Anyone who is related to the pastor's victims. And there are a lot of them." This sobered his thoughts. "Thank you for the information. I'm going to do some digging on ketamine." He ended the call, put the horses back in the pasture with Horse, and went to the house. He washed his hands and poured a glass of iced tea before pulling out his laptop and typing ketamine in his browser.

《》《》《》

An hour later he had a list of uses for the drug that were legitimate and had circled, depression and bipolar. After more internet browsing, he discovered that the treatment is given by a physician in a safe environment.

So how else could a person get their hands on the drug?

He wondered if Jayne might suffer from depression or be bipolar. He dialed Rosa's number.

"Hello, Trooper Hawke. Have you learned something that will help you solve the murder?" the midwife answered.

"I did learn something interesting. But I have a couple of questions for Jayne. Is she with you?" Hawke raised his glass of tea and ice clanked against his mouth. He forgot he'd finished it off.

"Trooper Hawke?" Jayne asked.

"Yes. Jayne, do you suffer from depression?" he asked without preamble.

She sucked in air, and said, "No. Why do you ask?"

"Are you bipolar?"

The young woman laughed. "No, I'm not bipolar and I don't suffer from depression. Though it's a wonder considering I now know my father was crazy. Why else would he have done what he did?" The hurt and anger in her voice wasn't lost to Hawke.

"I heard from forensics today that the syringe I found on Starvation Ridge had a drug called ketamine in it. This drug is used for sedation in animals and can cause amnesia."

"Is that why I couldn't remember anything?" Jayne asked.

"I think so. Between the hit on the head and the drug, your memory was scrambled for a bit." Hawke asked for Jayne to give the phone back to Rosa.

"Yes, Trooper? I heard what you said. Where would someone get ketamine?" Rosa asked.

"That's what I wanted to ask you." With her access to the hospital, she could have taken it. But then why would she use it on Jayne?

"The most obvious answer would be the hospital. As far as I know only the head nurses of each shift have access to the drugs. It's also used on animals. I don't know how strict vet clinics are about keeping their drugs locked up."

"Thank you for your insights," Hawke said, getting ready to end the call.

"Did you ask Jayne those questions because you thought she had ketamine?" Rosa's tone insinuated he was crazy to have thought such a thing.

"Good night, Rosa." He ended the call and didn't let Rosa's attitude sway his judgement on the reason for his call. It made sense to see if his top suspect had access to the drug.

Hawke made a sandwich for his dinner, poured kibble into Dog's dish, then took his dinner to the kitchen table and opened up the file on the case. He reread the reports and interviews while eating. He noticed a new entry. It was Herold's follow-up on the Newman phone call.

When I asked what time the call was that Mrs. Betz answered at the church, they said 7:30 p.m.

Hawke pulled a notepad over and started a timeline of what they knew. If Mrs. Betz answered the church phone at 7:30 she had to have been in the church right after Jayne was hit over the head. Jayne said she'd gone to the house because it was after seven and no one answered. Hawke was beginning to believe Mrs. Betz was in the church preparing to kill her husband.

Chapter Twenty-two

Sunday morning Hawke was restless. He had
questions that he needed answers to. He had texted Dr.
Vance asking her where a person could get ahold of
ketamine other than the hospital or a veterinary clinic.
She'd yet to reply.

After his call to Jayne and Rosa, he didn't think
they had anything to do with the drug being used. That
left his next prime suspect. How would Mrs. Betz get
her hands on some? And who could have helped her? It
would take two people to drive Jayne's car out to
Starvation Ridge, leave the car, and return to town. Not
to mention the two sets of tire tracks he'd found at the
campfire.

Deciding to have breakfast at the Rusty Nail, he
and Dog hopped into the pickup after they'd checked
on the horses. His and Dani's. She'd be home today. It
would be nice to have someone to eat meals with and
bounce ideas off. Not to mention someone to hold as he

fell asleep. For her brusqueness, she had turned out to be a woman who loved to snuggle. Which suited him fine when they were alone.

At the Rusty Nail, Hawke was surprised to see Merrilee cooking. Weekends she usually stayed away from the restaurant.

"About time you dragged in here and had a decent meal," she called out to him when he sat at the counter.

Justine filled his cup with coffee. "She's been in rare form the last few days. It's as if a weight has been lifted from her shoulders."

Hawke smiled. "That's nice to hear. She deserves a little bit of peace." He wondered if it was because she'd learned the truth about her daughter and the man responsible was dead.

"I'll have my usual," he said.

Before Justine put the ticket up, Merrilee said, "I've got it halfway cooked, no need for the ticket."

Justine wadded the ticket and shoved it in her pocket. "It looks like you caught her in a really good mood."

Hawke smiled and did a scan of the café. He would have had more luck meeting Lighted Path Church members if he'd eaten in Alder but there were also those who traveled from Winslow and Eagle to attend the church in Alder.

He motioned for Justine to lean across the counter and in a quiet voice, he asked, "Do you happen to know if any of your patrons dwent to The Lighted Path Church?"

"I heard Merrilee did before I moved here," Justine whispered back.

"I know that already. Anyone else?" Hawke picked up his cup and sipped.

"Not that I know of, but you could ask Merrilee." She flicked her gaze toward the kitchen. "Unless you think it's going to put her in a foul mood. Then don't say anything. I like working with her when she isn't grouchy." Justine flipped her brown braid over her shoulder and added more coffee to his cup before walking out from behind the counter to replenish other patrons' cups.

Hawke studied the top of Merrilee's gray head moving around above the window between the kitchen and seating area. He stood and walked over to the door leading into the kitchen.

"May I come in and ask a question?" Hawke asked, standing in the doorway.

The older woman's rheumy eyes stared at him for three seconds before she nodded. "This have anything to do with what you told me the other day?"

Hawke took two steps into the kitchen. "In a way. Do you have any customers who went to The Lighted Path Church? I'd like to get some different opinions of Mrs. Betz from them." Hawke knew their voices wouldn't be heard in the seating area due to the noisy fan in the kitchen.

"Diane? She's a worker and she supported that arrogant twit of a husband." Merrilee handed him his plate with chicken fried steak, gravy, hashbrowns, and eggs. "But if you really want to know more about Diane, you should talk to Blythe Hugiley and Lorraine Dardnel. They were both on the charity committee and the thrift store staff."

Hawke lifted his plate as a salute. "Thanks for breakfast and the information. Have a great day."

"I am!" she replied and hollered, "Order up!" as Hawke stepped back to the counter and sat down to enjoy his meal.

《》《》《》

Hawke and Dog sat in the empty Winslow OSP office. On Sunday there were only the officers on patrol. The office staff, Spruel and a civilian who did secretarial chores, took the weekends off. After his computer booted up, Hawke went to the DMV records and typed in Blythe Hugiley. Her driver's license popped up and where she lived. A small mobile home court in Alder. He put in Lorraine Dardnel. She also lived in the same court. That would make it easy to get the two together and only have to use up an hour of his day instead of two.

He called Mrs. Hugiley.

"Hello?" a female voice with a quiver answered.

"Mrs. Hugiley?" Hawke asked.

"That would be my mother, but she's not with us anymore," the voice said matter-of-factly.

"I see. Are you Blythe Hugiley?" he asked.

"Yes, I am. Are you trying to sell me something?" she asked.

Hawke chuckled. "No, I'm Oregon State Trooper Hawke. I'm investigating the fire that burned down The Lighted Path Church and I understand you and Lorraine Dardnel knew a lot about the church and I thought I might come around today and visit with the two of you."

"Oh, yes! Lorraine and I worked on the committees

together for years. I could ask her to pop over in thirty minutes. Would that work for you, officer?"

"That would work fine for me," Hawke said, thinking these might be the two best people to help him understand The Lighted Path Church.

《》《》《》

Rosa and Jayne sat in the parlor sipping tea and checking off the names on Rosa's list of women she knew had been assaulted by Pastor Betz. "We still haven't visited with Brittany who works at a vet clinic," Rosa said.

"You think she took the ketamine to knock me out?" Jayne asked. Rosa shrugged. "If she didn't, she might know if any is missing and if any of the other women on this list had been to the clinic before the fire and murder."

"We should tell Trooper Hawke," Jayne said, setting her cup of tea on the table beside her chair. "It's his job to talk to suspects."

"The police don't have a very good record with following through on what I tell them." Rosa did think Hawke was trying to help but he was going about it wrong. Or at least she thought so. He was keeping true to his word on not dragging the women through publicity, but he was also going around talking to people that knew nothing about the pastor's violation of his female parishioners.

"We'll talk to Brittany tomorrow morning and then see what we can learn from Trooper Hawke," Rosa said, rising to her feet. "He's going to need our help if he plans to crack this any time soon."

《》《》《》

Thirty minutes later, Hawke sat in an overstuffed chair facing the two women in their 80s, sitting side by side on a small sofa, holding cups of coffee and smiling at him. They had both insisted he use their first names. It appeared Blythe was a spinster and Lorraine lost her husband fifteen years earlier and had moved to the mobile home court to be near her good friend Blythe.

"Now what did you want to know about the church?" Blythe asked, getting down to business.

"You are both aware that it burned down on Tuesday with Pastor Betz inside?" he asked.

The two women nodded their heads in unison.

"I'm looking into who would want to burn the church down and Merrilee Grady said you two would know the most about the church and the people who attended." He hoped that using Merrilee's name didn't put them off helping him. She could be offensive to some people.

They both smiled and nodded. "Merrilee is correct," Lorraine said. "She worked with us on the charity committee until that unfortunate incident with her daughter." The woman bowed her head as if praying.

"What can you tell me about the Betzs? Were they a solid couple, work hard together to keep the church full of people?" Hawke asked.

Blythe put a long, thin finger to her pale lips as if she were contemplating what to say. She removed her finger and said, "I don't believe they were a solid couple as you say. He had an eye for the ladies and she had an eye for the money."

"An eye for the ladies, how do you mean?" Hawke

hoped he could get clear information about the man fooling around.

"He liked to touch women. Always squeezing your shoulder, rubbing a hand up and down your back." Lorraine shivered. "My Dave lit into him after one of the services because he'd walked up to me and ran his hand up and down my back. Dave wanted to stop going to the church but I'd made friends with Blythe and liked the committee work, so I told him I would always step away from the pastor when he came near me. Because, well, I didn't like him touching me any more than Dave did."

Hawke had written this in his notebook. He glanced up. "Did he touch all women like that?"

Blythe nodded. "He could make you feel uncomfortable when you were alone with him. Oh, he'd praise you and make you feel good about your singing, or your work on a committee, but he used that as a way to get close to you."

Hawke stared at the two of them. "If his groping was so prevalent why didn't anyone do anything about it?"

"Because his praise made you feel so good and his sermons were so uplifting. Even the men would leave every Sunday feeling as if he'd been speaking to them directly. He was very charismatic with his preaching and just talking to you. Until he touched you." Lorraine shivered.

"And yet none of the women in the parish thought a thing about him giving the teenagers and young women private attention?" He didn't understand how the man's promiscuousness had gone on for so long without someone saying something to the authorities.

Blythe's cheeks reddened. "We talked to Diane about it. She said she'd talk to her husband. And she would be present when he tutored the women. He was never alone with them."

Hawke studied the woman. She thought that was so. The wife had let the man ruin so many lives. Why?

"Tell me about Mrs. Betz."

"She is so wonderful. She brings baskets of goodies to people when they are sick or bed-ridden. I've seen her give a family whatever they wanted from the thrift store because they couldn't pay for the items. And she helps at the monthly soup kitchen. She spends hours helping everyone. I don't know how she had time for herself," Lorraine said.

Blythe shook her head. "But she shouldn't be in charge of the charity funds. There were several times I found her tallies of what we'd made didn't match the receipts of the items we sold. She said it was because she gave so and so this or that from the store but I happened to mention it to one family and they said they hadn't received anything from the store." The old woman stared at Hawke from across the coffee table. "I think she was stealing money from the church."

Chapter Twenty-three

Hawke spent the rest of Sunday typing up what he'd learned and reviewing the reports as he waited for Dani to arrive. He'd purchased steaks to grill and packaged salad, after visiting with Blythe and Lorraine, before heading home. Dani could cook if she was in the mood, and he knew she wouldn't be after working the last two weeks up at the lodge.

Around three in the afternoon, tires crunched on the gravel and Dog walked to the front door. "Is Dani here?" Hawke asked Dog, stretching and standing.

"Woof!" Dog barked and his tail started wagging.

The door opened and the tired face he'd been waiting for appeared. Dani dropped her duffel bag to the side of the door and pointed a thumb over her shoulder. "I brought all the bedding back to wash and put in totes. We have a critter in the lodge that Tuck and I haven't been able to catch."

Hawke chuckled and pulled her into his arms. "I'll take care of it. I bet you'd like a warm shower."

Her head moved against his shoulder. "Yeah, I take quick ones when the water is cold."

They released and he peered down into her face. "You must have been working long hours, you look exhausted."

"It seemed like there were twice as many repairs needed after this past winter. And the critter messing everything up doesn't help. If we leave tools or supplies out during the night, they disappear. I think it's a pack rat but until we have a sighting, I'm not sure."

"You should see if someone has a couple cats you could take up there." Hawke massaged her shoulders.

"We thought of that. Tuck is going to ask around. They need to be adult cats if it's a pack rat." She stepped back, "I'll go get that shower."

Hawke dipped down and kissed her lips. "Welcome home." He straightened and headed out to get the laundry.

《 》《 》《 》

As they sat eating dinner, Hawke told Dani about the fire, the murder, and the multiple suspects.

"I don't think you have that many suspects," Dani said. "If those poor women didn't rally together and go to the police with their charges, I can't see one of them having the courage to kill him."

Hawke had the same thoughts. "Which leaves us with Jayne who had just found out the truth and could have come here for revenge and who admitted she was in the church, also Rosa, the midwife, who had been trying to get him arrested for years without luck. I could see her coming up with the plan of giving Jayne an alibi, being unconscious in the car while the church burned. She would also have access to the drug that was used on Jayne." As much as he didn't want it to be either Jayne or Rosa, there was a very strong possibility it was either or both of them.

"Then there are the parents of the last girl you say the pastor raped. It is very fresh in their minds." Dani shoved her plate to the middle of the table. The steak bone was the only thing left on the plate. She picked it up and handed it to Dog. He sniffed, licked his lips, and sunk his teeth into the bone, before taking his prize to the dog bed in the corner of the kitchen.

Hawke nodded. "Yes. The father was pretty tweaked about the whole thing happening and his daughter not wanting to go to the police for fear everyone would know."

Dani stared at her beer. "It takes a lot of guts to talk to a man about what another man did to you." Her gaze rose and met his. "Especially when it is fresh in your mind. Even though there are those who say 'She shouldn't be surprised that happened the way she's dressed or the way she acts.' It doesn't matter if a woman walks down the sidewalk naked, no man has the right to take her body without her permission." Anger darkened her cheeks.

Hawke knew this was a sore spot with Dani. She'd been assaulted in the Air Force and had been shunned when she'd reported the incident. But she'd stopped her superior from assaulting other women.

"And when they have rank or think they are superior to others, they seem to prey on the women even more," she added. "I'm sure as a pastor he had the full attention of his parishioners and loved it."

"He used his charismatic personality to sway the men and get closer to the women. But I still don't understand, with so many people knowing he was lecherous, why they allowed their girls to be with him alone." That's what had been plaguing Hawke's mind all day. Everyone he talked to said that Mrs. Betz was present when the young girls were with the pastor. But surely, she wouldn't watch him take the women. If so, she was as depraved as he was. Yet, everyone said she was wonderful and giving.

"I'm sure this is one that you are having problems with because you feel justice has been served with the man who preyed on women dead, but you still have to find who killed him." Dani stood and picked up the dishes.

"Yeah, it's tough in that respect. And I like the two women who most likely killed him."

《 》《 》《 》

First thing Monday morning, Hawke and Herold headed to the hospital to ask whether any ketamine was missing. He was surprised to see one of the young women he'd interviewed sitting behind a desk in the receiving area.

"Madison, I didn't know you worked here," he said, by way of making his presence known.

She looked up from the pile of files she'd been rearranging. "Trooper Hawke." She glanced around, her eyes widening at the sight of Herold in uniform behind him.

"Are you a nurse?" he asked.

Her cheek color brightened. "No. I wish. But I don't have the money to go to school for nursing. I work here in receiving, filing things, and making appointments for people who see the traveling doctors as well as admitting patients."

"Do you ever go farther into the hospital with your duties?" he asked.

She frowned. "What do you mean?"

"Do you have access to areas where medicines are stored?" He watched her.

Her eyes glanced from him to Herold and back to Hawke. "No. Nurses or aids come up and escort the patients to where they need to be. My duties are here. I even take my lunch behind that wall." She pointed to a wall behind a printer and bank of cupboards.

"I'd like to talk to the head nurse. Where might I find her or him?" Hawke asked.

"Keith is at the nurse's station. Go through the doors to the left and walk down the hall. You can't miss the station." She pointed to double doors just beyond her office area.

Hawke walked over to the doors. He pushed on the button to open the doors as Herold caught up to him. "Where'd you go?" Hawke asked.

"My grandma was brought in yesterday. I was asking for her room number." Herold said, still holding his notepad.

"You can visit her while I talk to the nurse," Hawke said, never one to deny a person time to spend with an elder.

"I'll go see her when we finish."

They walked up to a U-shaped counter with charts,

chairs, and machines filling the area inside the space.

A man, and the nurse he'd met the day he found Jayne, sat at computers typing. Both wore scrubs.

"We're looking for the head nurse," Hawke said.

Both heads raised at the sound of his voice. The male nurse stood. "I'm the head nurse. What can I do for you officers?"

"Could we have your name for the record?" Herold asked.

"Keith Powell." He glanced back at the other nurse. "Do you need Vicky's name?"

Hawke smiled at the woman, "We met the other day."

She returned his smile. "Are you here about the Jane Doe?"

"In a way. We'd like to know if you've had any ketamine missing?" Hawke asked, his gaze traveling over both nurses.

They both shook their heads. "Not that I'm aware of," Keith said. "But I can go make a count and see if it is the same as the records."

"Please, if you don't mind," Hawke said. When the head nurse left, Hawke asked, "Have you seen anyone in here that isn't family visiting?"

"No. But Bev Archer thought it was odd that the other night she found Rosa Towman in the hospital after hours. There wasn't anyone in the maternity ward." Vicky snapped her fingers. "Rosa is who picked up Jane Doe when she was released." Her gaze settled on Hawke. "Is that why she didn't have a memory? Someone gave her ketamine?"

"We have reason to believe she was given the drug

to make her forget something she saw." Hawke studied the woman. She seemed curious but not as if it bothered her that they knew about the drug.

Keith returned. He sat down at his computer and clicked the keys. "All the numbers check out. And it would have had to be someone with a key card to the pharmacy to be able to get away with the drug."

"Who has access to the pharmacy?" Hawke asked.

"Myself and the night nurse."

"Who is that?"

"Bev Archer."

"Thank you. You've been helpful." Hawke and Herold went their separate ways.

Out at his vehicle, Hawke decided to check out the three veterinarians in the county. Since he was in Alder, he'd start with Dr. Ashley.

Pulling into the parking lot at the veterinarian's, Hawke spotted Rosa's car. She didn't have any pets. He would have noticed when he'd been to her house the three times. What was she doing here?

He walked into the clinic and found Rosa and Jayne sitting in the reception area. Their eyes widened and both opened their mouths at the same time.

He held up a hand and motioned for them to follow him outside. When they were all three standing by Rosa's car, he asked, "What are you two doing here? And don't say you brought a pet because I know you don't own a pet." He placed his hands on his duty belt and glanced back and forth between them, waiting for a response.

"I said we should call you," Jayne blurted.

Rosa sighed. "Brittany, one of the women you

talked to, works here. We were going to ask her if there had been any ketamine go missing and see how she reacted."

He glared at Rosa and softened his gaze when he turned his attention to Jayne. "I understand your not being able to dissuade Rosa. You could have called me without her knowing."

The younger woman sent a furtive glance toward Rosa. "I thought about it."

Rosa humphed.

"This isn't a game," Hawke said, facing Rosa. "You ask the wrong person something and they might think you know more than you do and you could become their next victim."

She didn't look sorry, but she nodded.

"You two go back to Rosa's. I'm following up the ketamine lead. I'll let you know what I learn." He moved to let the women walk to the doors of the vehicle.

"Are you getting any closer?" Rosa asked.

"I'm checking off names. That's something." He headed to the door of the clinic wondering how Brittany would react to seeing him at her place of work.

Reentering the building, he was greeted by a smiling woman with gray streaks in her dark hair and emerging lines on her face. He guessed her to be close to his age of nearing sixty.

"How can I help you?" she asked, her gaze scanning around him as if searching for something.

"I'd like to talk to Dr. Ashley and Brittany, please."

Her gaze landed on his face. "You don't have an

animal in need of care?"

"No. I'm here to ask them questions." He didn't want to say what about.

"I'll send Dr. Ashley out and find Brittany. She should be cleaning the pens out back." The woman disappeared into a hallway where whimpering and yowls drifted from.

In less than a minute Dr. Ashley appeared. "Hawke, is this a social or business visit?"

"Business. Has your vet clinic come up short in ketamine lately?" he asked, studying the young woman who had grown up in Wallowa County and returned to start up her practice. He'd heard nothing but good things about her and how she handled animals.

"Not that I'm aware of. But I do an inventory the second Saturday of every month and send out an order for what I need." Worry lines wrinkled her forehead below her dark curly hair.

"I'd appreciate it if you could do a check of how much you've used and how much is left. We believe ketamine was used on a person. The hospital's is all accounted for so I'm going to the vet clinics now." He shrugged to let her know he hadn't come straight to her clinic. Even though it was the most likely with one of the pastor's victims working here.

Brittany walked down the hall with the receptionist and stopped when she saw him.

"I'll visit with Brittany while you go check on that," he said, motioning for Dr. Ashley to go. When she was headed out of the room, Hawke said, "Brittany, you and I can step outside and have a visit." He smiled, to show both the young woman and the receptionist he wasn't here to take her in.

Brittany nodded and walked to the door. She stepped outside and turned to him. "Why are you here? No one knows anything."

Hawke motioned for her to walk over to a cement wall. He sat and patted the cement next to him. "Have a seat. I'm only here to ask if you took any ketamine from the drugs here?"

Her eyes widened. "Someone stole ketamine? It wasn't me. Why would I want that?"

He believed her shocked tone. "Has anyone from your victim's group been in to the clinic?"

She stared at the ground and shook her head. "No, not recently. Tinsley brought her cat in a couple of weeks ago."

"Was she ever left alone near the drug cabinet?" Hawke asked.

"I'm not sure. I went on lunch when she showed up. Gail's the vet tech and receptionist. She'd know more about that than I do." Her gaze shot to the door as it opened.

"Hawke, my numbers all match," Dr. Ashley said.

"Thank you for checking." Hawke stood. "Thank you for talking to me Brittany." He smiled at the young woman, waved at the vet, and walked over to his car. Two more clinics to check.

Chapter Twenty-four

The vet clinic in Prairie Creek wasn't missing any ketamine. Hawke drove back through Alder, headed to Winslow. Ajax Macklin, a vet who specialized in large animals but also did small animals for his clients, lived outside of town.

Entering Winslow, Hawke passed the Rusty Nail and OSP office, when the highway curved out of town, he continued straight onto Warnock Road. Macklin had a farm and small clinic about a quarter of a mile from town.

Spotting the vet's vehicle in front of the building he used as a clinic, Hawke pulled up alongside and stepped out.

The door to the building opened and Macklin emerged with a teenage boy carrying a bucket.

"Trooper, what can I do for you? I'm on my way to help with a delivery." Macklin stopped in front of Hawke.

"Is there someone else here who could check your records and see if you're missing any ketamine?" Hawke asked.

Macklin pulled off his cap and ran a hand over his shiny head. "Did you catch someone with it?"

Hawke thought that sounded like he was missing some of the drug. "No, we found a syringe at a crime scene that tested for ketamine. Did some go missing?"

"Yeah, about a week ago. I keep the stuff locked up, but I went to get something else out and the door wasn't locked. I did inventory and a vial of it was missing. At first, I thought maybe I just forgot to record using it, but after going over my procedures from the time I restocked to then, I wouldn't have used it enough times."

Hawke nodded to the building. "Is this locked up when you're out on calls?"

"Most of the time, but not always. If a farmer calls needing something and I'm going to be out, I leave the door unlocked so they can get what they need. However, the drug cabinet is always locked, unless I'm getting drugs out. When I found it unlocked, I knew something wasn't right."

"But you didn't report it was missing," Hawke said, pulling out his notebook. "What was the date you noticed the cabinet unlocked?"

The vet's phone buzzed. He glanced at it. "It's Adam Marks, his milk cow is having problems." He handed the phone to the teenager. "Tell him we'll be there in thirty." Macklin's face reddened as he looked at Hawke. "You didn't hear that."

For Macklin to get from here to the Marks' farm it

would take him nearly an hour. That was why the man had seemed upset about saying thirty minutes in front of Hawke.

"I would think when you are headed to assist an animal it's like a human emergency. But keep the speed under seventy." Hawke grinned at the vet as the man realized Hawke was giving him permission to drive over the speed limit.

As the teenager talked on the phone, Macklin led Hawke into the building and over to a messy desk. He dug out a date book and flipped back a couple of pages. "That day. I circled it because of finding the cabinet unlocked."

Hawke jotted down the date. "Is there anyone here when you're out on a call?"

"Not during the week. My wife works at the county courthouse." Macklin walked to the door. "I really need to go."

"Do you mind if I look around, see if I can find anything to tell us who might have taken the drug?" Hawke added. "I can lock it up when I'm finished."

"You can look around. But don't lock it. Bruce Hornsby will be coming by to grab some stuff while I'm gone."

Hawke nodded.

Macklin hurried out the door. A vehicle revved to life and gravel pelleted the building when it took off. Hawke hoped the vet didn't get a ticket on his way to the emergency.

First, he had to find the cabinet that held the medicine. The building consisted of the front room with a desk, a bookcase with medical and animal books, pamphlets, and posters. The room behind had an examination table, cupboards with basic tools of the trade, bandages, dog treats, and a scale. There was also a wooden door, up shoulder height with a lock in it. No wording, nothing that said it was a medicine cabinet other than the lock.

Hawke fumbled with his duty belt and pulled out his lockpicking set. Less than a minute he had the door open and stared at the drugs. He spotted the vials of ketamine. They weren't hard to find.

He closed the door, locked it with the pick set, and finished checking out the building. Out in his vehicle, he jotted in his notebook about being able to pick the lock on the cabinet with ease. Only whoever picked it to get in, didn't have the knowledge to lock it or hadn't cared if it was discovered unlocked.

His stomach rumbled as he headed back to Winslow. It was after one and he hadn't had lunch. Hawke decided to grab lunch at the Rusty Nail and then go to the office and type up all his notes on the investigation.

At the café, Justine greeted him and nodded to a table in the corner. Dani and Darlene were chatting. It appeared they'd finished their meal. He picked up the iced tea Justine had poured and walked over to the table.

"Mind if I join you?" he asked, sitting down.

"I guess not," Dani said, sarcastically. "I didn't expect to see you until tonight."

"I was surprised to see two of my favorite women in here as well." He didn't miss the grin on Darlene's face. "What are you up to?" he asked, studying them both.

"Just catching up on the gossip," Dani said.

Hawke choked on the sip of tea. When he regained his breathing, he said, "When have you cared about gossip?"

"When it comes to you." She raised her eyebrows.

"Me? What gossip is going around about me?" Hawke glanced from woman to woman and landed on Darlene. "What have you heard?"

"Well, someone has started a rumor that you and Rosa Towman are seeing a lot of each other." Darlene glanced at Dani. "We know it's for the investigation you're doing right now, but it is kind of funny." Both women chuckled.

Hawke rolled his eyes as Justine delivered his lunch.

"Dani, do you want me to keep an eye on him while you're up at the lodge?" the waitress asked Dani.

The two had become friends since Dani bought the lodge and moved to the county. And they called themselves members of the Hawke club.

"There is no need for that. I'm a one-woman man. Why would I want to deal with the drama of more than one?"

Dani cleared her throat. "Drama? You think you deal with drama from me?"

"No, that's not what I meant." Hawke held up both his hands. "I meant there would be drama if I had to deal with two women. Not that you are drama."

The three women laughed and he set to eating his food.

Dani and Darlene left the café before he finished

eating. Dani said she'd have dinner ready at seven.

Justine came by to clear away the plates. "Have you had any luck on the pastor's murder?"

"I'm working on it but it's hard to catch someone when all the evidence is burned. It's more about catching someone up on an alibi or discovering something that could incriminate them."

Justine glanced around and slid into a chair near Hawke. "I heard that the pastor had been molesting the young women. Is that true?"

"Where did you hear that?" Hawke asked, wondering if his investigation would finally bring to light the horrendous acts the man had done under the pretense of his position.

"Yesterday, I overheard a group of women saying something about it and then this morning, there were different women in here whispering, but I caught bits of it when I refilled their coffee."

Hawke pulled out his notebook, "Can you give me names?"

She leaned back and studied him. "So, it is true?"

"There is an investigation into the pastor's life and we are discovering he did like the young women in his congregation. That's as much as I can say."

"No wonder you are running all over the place. You have a lot of suspects."

Hawke agreed and asked for the names.

Justine recited the women's names. "They won't know that I told you, will they? You know I pride myself on not gossiping but this sounded like something you needed to know."

"They won't know where I received this

information. Your reputation will be intact." He smiled at one of his oldest friends in the county.

She returned the smile and went back to work.

Hawke drove to the office and entered the building. Spruel wasn't in his office. Hawke had wanted to catch his superior up on what he'd learned. Sitting down at his desk, Hawke pounded out the reports for what he'd learned the last couple of days. If he was lucky there might be more forensic reports in the file.

While he clicked through to where the files on the case were logged in, he noticed an email from the State Medical Examiner's Office. He read through the email, taking notes. When he finished writing, he studied his notes: *No soot in air passages. Was dead before the fire started. Presume the blow to the head caused death. From food in the stomach, he died no more than 2-3 hours after eating dinner. Roast, bread, green beans.*

Hawke returned to the reports from the interviews with Mrs. Betz. She said he'd had dinner and his dirty clothes from the day before were in the hamper. They had no proof of that but he could ask her what he had for dinner.

《 》《 》《 》

When Hawke finished adding his information to the reports and sending a message to Herold to meet him at Mrs. Larsen's for some follow-up questions with Mrs. Betz, he turned off the computer and stood.

"When did you sneak in?" Spruel asked from behind him. "Did you get any patrolling done today?"

Hawke groaned inwardly. As usual, he'd become obsessed with discovering what happened to the fire victim to the detriment of the Fish and Wildlife side of his job. "I came in to catch up the report on the Betz homicide and read the pathologist's report. According to the stomach contents they figure he was dead two to three hours after he had dinner. That's a long way from the time the fire broke out Tuesday morning."

"The forensics don't lie, unless he had his dinner for breakfast," Spruel said. "What about the patrolling?"

His boss was more lenient this time of year when there was less hunting and fishing going on and fewer officers wanting vacations.

"I'll do a drive around tomorrow. Right now, I need to get to Alder and ask Mrs. Betz what they had for dinner the night before the church burned and then get home. Dani is cooking up something special."

Spruel studied him a minute then broke into a grin. "I'm glad to see you are like all the rest of us now and catering to a woman in your life."

"It's that or have her beat me up." Hawke chuckled and Spruel laughed.

"I can't have you coming in with a black eye from your woman. Just get out and patrol tomorrow."

"Copy." Hawke placed his hat on his head and hurried out of the building before someone else wanted to start up a conversation.

Chapter Twenty-five

Herold sat in his cruiser when Hawke parked on the street in front of Mrs. Larsen's house. By the time Hawke had slid out of his vehicle and headed to the sidewalk, Herold met him.

"Did you read the report from the pathologist?" Herold asked.

"That's why we're here. To find out what they had for dinner and when." Hawke strode up the walk to the front door. He rang the bell and they waited.

Several minutes passed with Hawke ringing the bell again before Mrs. Larsen answered the door. She was flustered and looked as if she'd been sweeping cobwebs out of the attic.

"Trooper Hawke and Officer Herold, what can I do for you?" The woman swiped at a cobweb hanging from her glasses.

"We have some questions for Mrs. Betz," Hawke

said, taking a step as if to enter the house.

"She's not here. She left this afternoon to stay with a sister in California. I was tidying up from having someone in my house."

"How did she leave?" Hawke asked.

The woman blinked several times, before saying, "She went by the community bus to La Grande and then was going to get a bus to her sister's."

"Where does her sister live?" Hawke asked.

"I don't know, she just said California." Mrs. Larsen wrung her hands. "She's not been herself since the fire, and, you know. I'm kind of glad she's gone. We were friends before this all happened because she was so nice and kind, but since, she's become hard to please."

Hawke studied the woman. Something was off, but he couldn't tell what. "Do you have the number for her cell phone?"

"She doesn't have one. Pastor Betz thought they were evil because people seemed in a trance when they were on them."

Hawke pulled out one of his cards. "If you hear from her, get a phone number or the name of her sister, please, and let me know."

Mrs. Larsen grasped the card, glanced at it, and nodded.

As they walked back to their vehicles Hawke said, "Can you see if Mrs. Betz was on the bus that left this afternoon? And I'll see if I can dig up information about her sister."

"I'll go talk to Carter at the bus shed." Herold took off his hat and slipped into his car.

Hawke settled behind the steering wheel of his pickup and headed home. He could dig around on his computer after dinner.

Driving home his mind went over the conversation with Mrs. Larsen. The whole thing felt off. There wouldn't have been that many cobwebs from having a houseguest. She was hiding something. What he wasn't sure.

《》《》《》

After dinner, Hawke and Dani pulled out their respective computers and settled on the couch next to each other. Dani looked up the timetable for the local transit bus and the connections it made in La Grande. Hawke tried digging into Mrs. Betz background and family. After two hours they both closed their computers.

Hawke's phone buzzed. It was Herold.

"What did you learn?" Hawke asked by way of answering.

"There was a bus that left this afternoon at one for La Grande. But Carter doesn't remember anyone fitting Mrs. Betz description getting on the bus. He said only three people traveled out to La Grande. An old man and a mother with a teenage daughter. Why did Mrs. Larsen lie to us?" Herold asked.

"Good question. I've been wondering about the way she looked. She'd been in the attic or a cellar. But why?" Hawke thought out loud.

"Do you think she had anything to do with the fire and now Mrs. Betz being missing? She seems too timid," Herold added.

"Let's dig into her tomorrow. Ask around and find

218

out if she's as timid as she's been acting."

"Copy." Herold ended the call.

Hawke picked up the hot tea Dani had made while he was speaking to Herold.

"Did you find a sister to the missing woman?" she asked.

"Nope. I'm beginning to think I've been following the evidence all wrong." Hawke sipped his tea and ran all that he knew over in his mind.

《》《》《》

Tuesday morning, Hawke stopped by Herb and Darlene's on his way to work. He wanted to know more about Mrs. Larsen.

Darlene invited him in for coffee and hot from-the-oven coffee cake. The house smelled of cinnamon and coffee. Hawke inhaled deeply as he entered the kitchen. Herb sat at the table already digging into a piece of the cake.

"I bet you smelled this clear over at your place," Herb said, grinning.

"No, but I'm glad I needed to talk with you two. It smells delicious." Hawke sat down where Darlene had placed a cup of coffee and a plate of cake.

"What did you want to talk to us about?" Darlene asked, sitting down with her coffee and cake.

"Do you know much about Mrs. Larsen?" Hawke forked a bite of the cake into his mouth and savored the sweetness of apple chunks and cinnamon.

"She was on a couple of committees with me. He had an old-fashioned sense his wife was to stay home and cook and clean while he made the money and doled it out only as she needed for food, clothing, and household things. They never had children that I know of. But then I could never see him having sex unless he was sure it would make them money." Darlene picked up her coffee and sipped.

Hawke stared at her. "You think he didn't want children?"

"I'm sure of it. He felt they could barely make enough money for Suzanne and himself. She was very open about how she couldn't afford to do anything because he didn't give her any money other than for the groceries and clothes."

"How did he die?" Hawke asked.

Darlene glanced at Herb. "I'm not sure. Do you know?"

Herb shook his head. "I haven't a clue."

"Did she seem timid at the meetings?" Hawke asked.

"Timid? No, I wouldn't say timid. Reserved, yes. But if she thought a suggestion was good, she would get behind it and help persuade the others it was for the good of whatever we were doing."

Hawke finished eating his cake while deep in thought.

"More coffee?" Darlene asked, pulling him from his thoughts.

"No, thank you. I need to get going. Thank you for the coffee, cake, and information. I need to get to work." He stood and left the house, still mulling over the information he'd gathered.

In his vehicle, he called in he was on duty and headed toward Eagle to head out to Promise. A day of driving around in the north country would give him a chance to puzzle through everything he'd learned so far.

«»«»«»

Rosa and Jayne sat in the Rusty Nail waiting for breakfast and Geri Macklin. Rosa knew that Trooper Hawke had talked to all of the vets and the hospital about the ketamine. She was also told by a hospital employee that Bev Archer was trying to say, she, Rosa, had been sneaking around the hospital when she didn't have any patients there. Rosa was pretty sure Bev was mad that she'd brought Jayne into Wade's life. Bev had been ready to grab Wade when Eloise left the county.

Jealousy was a fickle emotion.

"Why did you want to talk to Geri?" Jayne asked.

"Her husband has a vet clinic outside of town. I just want to know if she's ever heard her husband mention Diane Betz being at his clinic." Rosa leaned back as the waitress placed their meals in front of them. They weren't waiting on Geri as she was just going to pop in on her way to work.

The bell over the door tinkled and Geri strode over to where they sat.

Rosa made introductions.

"I was surprised to get your call," Geri said as the waitress placed a cup of coffee in front of her and offered her a menu. "Only coffee, thanks."

"We're trying to piece some things together and wondered if Diane Betz ever came to your husband's clinic," Rosa said without preamble.

The cup Geri lifted to her lips stopped halfway. "Why would you be interested in that?"

Rosa leaned close to the woman. "We think Mrs.

Betz killed her husband."

Geri leaned back nearly dropping her cup on the table. "No? Really?"

"We have our suspicions. Has she ever been to the clinic?" Rosa pressed.

"No. I'm sure if she had my husband or son would have mentioned it."

Rosa took a bite of her French toast and chewed. She swallowed and asked the question swirling in her head. "What about Suzanne Larsen?"

"Suzanne? She could have come by and picked up medicine for her brother. Paul has sheep and seems to always be having trouble with foot rot. I know Suzanne has come by and picked up antibiotics for him. Her signature was on the invoice I used to bill him."

Rosa glanced at Jayne.

"I have a phone call to make," Jayne said, standing and walking out of the café.

《》《》《》

Hawke's phone rang just before he'd be out of service. He noticed it was Jayne.

"Hawke," he answered.

"This is Jayne. Rosa and I were talking to Geri Macklin and she said that Suzanne Larsen would come get medicine for her brother's sheep."

He stared ahead of him as he pushed on the brake, stopping on the gravel road before he lost the signal. "Why were you talking to her?"

The sigh on the other end of the conversation made him grin. Rosa was digging where she shouldn't be, but she had come up with something that could point at Mrs. Larsen stealing the ketamine.

"Rosa knew that you were talking to the vet clinics and she happened to be Geri's midwife and asked her to stop by the Rusty Nail and have coffee with us. Then she brought up whether or not Mrs. Betz had ever been to the clinic and Geri offered that she hadn't. Then Rosa asked about Suzanne."

"Where are you two right now?" Hawke didn't want Rosa dragging Jayne into trouble.

"We're at the Rusty Nail in Winslow."

"I want you both to stay there until I arrive to get this down in my notes."

"I'll tell Rosa."

Hawke said with authority, "I mean it. Don't let Rosa go anywhere. She could put you both in danger."

"I understand."

Hawke ended the conversation and found a place to turn around and head back to Winslow.

Chapter Twenty-six

On his way to the Rusty Nail, Hawke called Herold and asked him to write up a warrant for Suzanne Larsen's phone records and phone. He also asked him to get a warrant to search her house since a prime suspect, Mrs. Betz, had been staying there and may have left some evidence.

Parking in front of the Rusty Nail, Hawke exited his vehicle and walked into the restaurant. He found Merrilee sitting at the table with Rosa and Jayne. He caught Justine's eye and motioned to bring him coffee.

Hawke took the empty seat between Merrilee and Jayne. "Morning ladies."

Jayne blushed and fiddled with her napkin. Rosa and Merrilee stared at him.

Justine delivered his coffee and went back to the counter.

"Merrilee has something to tell you," Rosa started

the conversation.

Hawke turned his attention to the restaurant owner. She held her head high, her dull blue eyes peering at him.

"When you came in here asking me questions about my Marcia, you didn't tell me everything," Merrilee started. Her usual glower was back as she studied him.

"I didn't for one minute think you'd killed him," Hawke started.

"But you think Jayne or I have," Rosa said.

"Not Jayne. Forensic evidence has more or less put her in the clear." Hawke shifted his gaze to Rosa. "However, I've not found anything to clear you."

The woman humphed. "I know you still suspect me. Why do you think I've been doing so much of your work to help prove I'm innocent?"

Hawke's gut said the woman hadn't killed the man even though she was thrilled he was dead. "Tell me what you want to say, Merrilee, and then I need to know everything the two of you know about Suzanne Larsen." He rotated his head looking from Merrilee to Rosa and back to Merrilee.

"Suzanne Larsen?" Merrilee said. "She has been a member of the church from the time Pastor Betz moved here. Only then she was Suzanne Booth. She was only married to her husband for about fifteen years before he died. The whole county was surprised when she married him. Everett was a scrooge, but he believed every word that came out of Pastor Betz's mouth. And Suzanne doted on the pastor."

Hawke latched onto the last. "Do you think she

thought his touching and advances toward her meant he loved her?"

Rosa nodded. "I would think so. Everett was a cold fish and stingy. I would think the pastor showing her attention would have given her the idea he cared for her."

"And yet, she and Mrs. Betz were friends," Hawke said, knowing he would never figure out what went on in women's minds.

"Diane is a nice woman who takes in anyone whether their needs are spiritual, physical, or loneliness," Merrilee said. "I remember when my husband left and when Marcia died, she came to the house and listened as I ranted and cried. She has a good heart."

"Do either of you know about Mrs. Betz having a sister in California?" Hawke asked.

Rosa and Merrilee both shook their heads.

"She never talked about family," Merrilee said.

Rosa nodded. "I don't think either she or the pastor had family. I never heard them speak of any."

"And you say Mrs. Larsen has a brother?"

Rosa nodded. "He raises sheep near Eagle. Suzanne took care of him before she married. But I think she discovered that the hard work at the farm was better than the cold husband she'd married."

"Why do you say that?" Hawke asked.

"Because she would go out to the farm a couple times a week and help. She'd stop in here for lunch on her way home," Merrilee said.

Hawke studied the woman waiting for her to say more.

"She would visit with me. Extolling the virtues of Pastor Betz and talking about her brother and the farm. She never said anything about her husband or marriage." Merrilee picked up her coffee and drank.

"An unhappy marriage and a fixation on the pastor." Hawke's gaze landed on Rosa. "If Mrs. Larsen was in love with Betz, do you think he would lead her on or only go after the young women?"

Rosa shrugged. "All the pregnant victims that came to me were mid-twenties and younger. But that doesn't mean he didn't dally with an older woman who couldn't get pregnant."

"Do you mean Mrs. Larsen couldn't have had children if she'd wanted to?" Hawke asked.

"I'm saying he seemed to want to impregnate the young fertile women. You saw how varied they were in their looks. It didn't seem to matter if they were blonde or brunette or skinny or curvy. He just wanted them young." Rosa wrinkled her face in disgust.

Merrilee's eyes sparked with anger.

Hawke glanced at Jayne. Her face was also distorted in revulsion.

Hawke's phone buzzed. He answered it.

"I have the warrants," Herold said.

"I'll be there in fifteen." Hawke ended the call and smiled. "Thank you for the information. I have to run."

He walked out of the restaurant leaving the three women without an answer to their question of where he was going.

《》《》《》

Hawke parked in front of Mrs. Larsen's house. Herold stood by his cruiser talking to Chief Browning.

They were both watching the house.

Walking up to the men, Hawke noticed the car that had been in the driveway the other days he'd been here was gone. He motioned to the emptiness. "Was she gone when you arrived?"

"Yeah, the car was gone. We haven't knocked on the door yet," Browning said.

The three walked up to the front door. Hawke rang the bell and knocked loudly.

Not a sound came from inside the house.

"Check around for a key to get inside," he said.

Browning and Herold tipped flower pots and turned over rocks in the flower beds next to the house. There wasn't a key.

"Let's check around back. Maybe she hides a key back there," Hawke suggested.

"Or leaves the back door unlocked. That's what my grandma does," Herold offered.

They walked around to the backyard. Hawke knew of a time when everyone in the county never locked a door. But with the rise in crime and newcomers bringing in more drugs, most everyone locked their doors now.

He tried the door first. The knob didn't turn. They started looking under items on her back patio. Hawke shifted his attention from the back of the house to the backyard. There was a small shed. He walked over and tried the door. It was unlocked. The place smelled of sulfur and he found a package of mosquito coils with two missing. He pulled out his phone and took photos.

"Over here!" he called to Browning and Herold.

They hurried over and studied the inside of the

building.

"The forensic team that was here said they thought a mosquito coil was used to delay the start of the fire," Herold said.

"Yeah, that's why I thought this might be interesting." Hawke pocketed his phone and headed to the back door. The evidence he just found in the shed was even more proof the house needed to be searched.

He pulled out his pick set and went to work on the lock. By the time Browning and Herold joined him, the door was open.

"I'm glad you're on our side of the law," Browning said.

Hawke grinned. "I could have gone either way. But I only used lock picking to get into my own home when I was a child and in cases like this." He put the picks back in his duty belt and walked into the kitchen. It was neat and tidy.

"I'm going to look for a spot where there would be a lot of cobwebs. She was up to something yesterday when we came by." Hawke moved about the kitchen to see if there was a stairway to a basement. He didn't see one. That would mean the attic.

He left the other two going through drawers and cupboards in the kitchen and walked into the living room. It was also neat and tidy. He wandered down the hall opening doors. The first door was a guest bedroom. It looked as if a tornado had landed. The bedding was disheveled, a woman's shoe lay on its side, the lamp was knocked off the bedside table. But the one thing that was out of place…the closet door was neatly shut. He grasped the handles and pulled the folding doors open. The clothing in the closet was shoved apart and a ladder sat underneath an attic crawl space opening.

Hawke stepped back and took a photo, then climbed up two steps on the ladder and pushed up on the cover to the crawl space. He tried to set it to the right but something wouldn't let him set it that direction. He tried the left and it disappeared. Moving up two more steps to put his head through the hole, he smelled excrement as his light landed on a body. To the right of the hole, he found Mrs. Betz. Her hands and ankles were bound with duct tape, as well as her mouth. He felt her wrist. There was a weak pulse.

"Browning, Herold!" he shouted as he took photos. The woman flinched.

The two came running.

"One of you call for an ambulance, the other help me get her down."

Hawke pulled the tape off the woman's mouth. She whimpered but remained listless.

"Mrs. Betz, it's Trooper Hawke. Officer Herold and I are going to get you down out of here. It might be a bit uncomfortable, but it's the best we can do." He wasn't sure if she heard him. However, he had no choice but to climb up into the attic and manhandle the woman down through the hole to Herold and Browning.

They placed her on the bed, and Hawke took more photos as Browning removed the tape.

"Get her some water," Hawke said, as he went back up the ladder to see if anything else had been shoved up there. He knew why Mrs. Larsen had cobwebs in her hair when she met them at the door the day before.

Hawke used his flashlight to shine around the attic. He didn't find anything else. He wondered at the strength of the woman to have put Mrs. Betz, a good twenty, possibly thirty pounds heavier than Mrs. Larsen, up in the attic.

While they waited for the ambulance, they continued their search of the premises. Hawke opened the door to the other bedroom. It was tidy, smelled of roses, and had pink frilly curtains and bedspread. He pulled out the drawers, finding only clothing. Moving to the nightstand, he opened the drawer and found a diary.

Hawke sat on the bed and flipped back to the page dated the day Jayne visited the church.

I saw a young woman, Gordon's type, walk into the church. I'm going over and see what they are up to. He turned the page and nothing. It was as if she'd walked away or forgot about the journal. He flipped through the pages before her last entry. She'd written something down every day up until Jayne arrived at the church.

The sound of the EMTs brought him out of his thoughts. He closed the book and walked down the hall.

Bonnie and Roxie were lifting Mrs. Betz onto the gurney. Hawke motioned for Browning and Herold to follow him.

In the kitchen, where they wouldn't be disturbed, he told them about finding the diary and the last entry. "We need to watch the house and pick up Mrs. Larsen when she comes back."

"If she comes back," Browning said.

Hawke wiped a hand over his face. "There is that. From what I learned this morning, she might be at her brother's farm outside of Eagle. If you two want to sit tight here, I'll go see if he has anything to tell me about where she might be."

"You want to hand that to Herold and he can put it in an evidence bag?" Browning motioned to the book Hawke still held.

Hawke was reluctant to part with the book. It might have clues as to where the woman could have gone. But he knew it was evidence and therefore should be bagged and tagged. "Keep it at the station. I might need to read it to find out how she was mixed up with the pastor and his wife."

"We'll have it locked up at the office until we find her." Browning plucked the book from Hawke's hand and dropped it in the evidence bag Herold held out.

Before Hawke walked away, he said, "Keep looking. Mrs. Betz could have hid something in the house that Mrs. Larsen doesn't know about."

The two nodded and Hawke strode out the front door and over to his vehicle.

Chapter Twenty-seven

Driving to Eagle, Hawke wondered what Mrs. Larsen had done when she'd followed Jayne into the church. Had she gone around to the house and roused Mrs. Betz? And did the two of them conspire to kill the pastor? But how did the two get the ketamine and why did they use it on Jayne? Had they planned all along to do something to the pastor? That would be a good reason for them to have had the drug available that night.

He parked in front of a two-story farmhouse five miles outside of Eagle. The yard was well maintained and the house, though a dull gray, appeared to be kept up. The barn was a little saggy and weather-beaten.

Two border collies ran down off the porch, barking and waving their feathery tails. Hawke stepped out and let them sniff him before he walked toward the house. If the dogs were lounging on the porch, it was most likely their owner was inside.

Hawke walked up the three steps and the screen door opened. A man close to Mrs. Larsen's age with the same build and grayer hair stepped out.

"What can I do for you Trooper?"

"I'm looking for your sister. You wouldn't happen to know where she is, would you?" Hawke wasn't in the mood for pleasantries.

"I saw her a couple days ago. She comes over on Mondays and Thursdays. She cleans my house and takes care of the yard. She's done that ever since she got married." He patted the dog that walked up and leaned against his leg.

"We're trying to find her. If you hear from her, could you ask her to call me or get information about where she is and let me know?" Hawke held out a business card.

"Have you checked her house?"

"I was just there. Her car is gone and so is she." Hawke studied the man.

His brow wrinkled and he stared out at the barn. "The only other place she might be is the church, but it's burned down. There are only three places she goes. Here, home, and the church." The man shook his head. "I guess I can't help you. But if you do find her let me know. This doesn't sound like her. She's punctual and stays to her routines."

"Thank you for your time." Hawke descended the steps and studied the barn. He wondered if a Toyota Camry would fit inside.

Back in his vehicle, Hawke drove out the lane trying to decide if it was worth a try to get a look inside the barn. The man had seemed genuinely stunned that his sister wasn't at her house. She was a creature of habit. Hawke didn't think the woman would come here and implicate her brother in what she did. She seemed to care about him the way she took care of his house and yard.

He'd go to the Alder City Police Station and read the diary. Maybe that would give him a clue.

《》《》《》

Passing through Eagle, Hawke parked alongside Al's Café. His stomach had started growling when he left Paul Booth's place. He'd glanced at the clock in his vehicle. It was after two. It also wouldn't hurt to learn a little more about the brother and sister if any of the locals were having a late lunch.

He walked inside the café and was greeted by Lacie Ramsey. She and her husband, Burt, owned the café.

"Hawke, it's been a while." She placed a menu and a glass of iced tea on the counter.

He scanned the nearly empty room and walked over to the counter. He picked up the menu and the tea. "I'm going to sit over there." He pointed a corner of the menu at a table where five Eagle residents sat.

"I'll be over in a few to get your order."

"Thanks." Hawke walked over to the table and set his drink and menu down. He grabbed a chair from a table nearby and sat.

"We're not planning to rob a bank or anything," Dave Bolden said, with a laugh.

Hawke grinned, sipped his tea, and studied the menu. When he made his decision, he closed the menu and set his glass down. "I was wondering if you could tell me about Paul Booth and his sister, Suzanne."

Jess Rumple chuckled. "Well, if she hadn't married that scrooge Larsen, we would have thought they were playing house together."

Hawke studied the man in his fifties. "Why do you say that?"

"Well, she never looked at a man or even acted like she fancied one until she up and married Larsen." Jess picked up his cup of coffee.

"Did they grow up here?" Hawke asked.

Dave nodded. "Yeah, right on that farm Paul has. He got it when their parents died in a car crash. He and Suzanne were both in their twenties, I think."

The other men at the table nodded their heads.

"You say he got it. Wasn't it half to him and half to his sister?"

Dave shook his head. "She'd gone off to college and the parents left it to Paul. I guess thinking she'd get married and have a nice place of her own."

Hawke thought that sounded pretty old-fashioned but didn't voice it. "There wasn't any mention of her having a boyfriend in college?"

They all shook their heads again.

"What about any friends she might have made?"

"You'd have to ask Paul. She pretty much stayed to herself," Arlo Springer said.

"No women friends here in the county?" Hawke asked.

"Not that I can think of. She only went to church and worked the farm until she married. After that, I can't tell you what she did," Dave said.

Lacie stopped next to Hawke with her ticket book and pen poised. "I heard you were talking about Suzanne Larsen. She was in here a couple weeks ago visiting with Dr. Macklin's oldest boy. They were at the table in the corner. I didn't hear what they were talking about."

Hawke grinned. He had a pretty good idea. "I'll have a cheeseburger and fries. And thanks for the information."

"You're welcome," she grabbed his menu and headed back to the counter and window to the kitchen.

"I heard Macklin's clinic was robbed," Arlo said.

"Really? When was that?" Hawke asked, wondering if they meant the missing drug or if it was something different.

Arlo stared at him. "I heard you were the one talking to them about it. I'd think you'd know."

Hawke grinned. "I thought maybe something had happened since then." He refused to add more fodder to the gossip. Changing the subject to turkey season and the weather, his lunch arrived and he ate while one by one the others at the table left.

"Looks like you chased them off," Burt said, pulling out a chair and sitting down. He drank half the glass of iced tea he'd brought with him and smiled.

"Taking a break?" Hawke shoved his empty burger basket to the middle of the table.

"Yeah, this time of day it slows down enough I can wander out of the kitchen and relax for a bit." He nodded to the clock. "But not for long. The kids will be getting out of school pretty soon."

Hawke nodded. "How well do you know Paul

Booth and his sister, Suzanne?”

“Not well. Lacie and I moved to the county when we bought this place. We mostly just know the regulars and they weren't regulars. The sister more than Paul, but then not that often.”

Hawke left a twenty-dollar bill on the table. “Thanks for the information and the good burger.”

“Anytime.”

Hawke left the restaurant and instead of heading to Alder to read more of the diary, he headed to the Macklins to see if he could find out what Mrs. Larsen and the boy were talking about at the restaurant.

《》《》《》

Pulling up in front of the vet clinic, Hawke discovered a pickup and stock trailer alongside the building. He stepped out of his vehicle to cattle bawling. It appeared they were working on some cattle.

Following along the side of the vehicle and trailer, he found two young women hanging over a tall metal panel. They glanced his way when he hung his arms over the top of the panel next to them.

“Trooper Hawke, what are you doing here?” asked the young woman closest to him.

He studied her and smiled. “Jamie Clark, you've grown up. Are you still rodeoing?”

She grinned, showing off the gap in her smile from when a bull rammed her in the face. “I am. But I'm also starting up a small herd of cattle and the heifers needed bangs vaccinated. I don't have all the corrals and catching chute set up yet.”

“This is my partner, Sarah.”

Hawke touched his hat brim. “Pleased to meet you,

Sarah." He shifted his gaze back to Jamie. "Do you know how much longer it will take?"

"They're on the last one as far as I can tell."

And as if her words had been heard, Dr. Macklin yelled, "Jamie, get ready, they're coming your way."

"Ready!" she shouted back and the two women hopped over the panels, opening panels to make a straight shot into the trailer. Ten head of Corriente heifers came ambling down the alleyway the women had made. They calmly stepped up into the trailer and Jamie closed the door behind them.

"It was good seeing you, Trooper Hawke." She slapped the side of the trailer. Sarah must have hopped in the driver's seat because the trailer pulled forward and Jamie headed to the passenger side.

"It was good seeing you as well," he said loud enough for her to hear him.

She raised a hand in a wave and slipped into the pickup before the whole rig drove away.

Hawke followed the alleyway to the heart of the large building and found Dr. Macklin and his oldest son cleaning up.

"Trooper Hawke, what brings you back here? We haven't had any more thefts," Dr. Macklin said.

"I'm still interested in the last one. I'd like to speak with your son, if I may." Hawke's gaze didn't waver from the teenager spraying water on the cow manure in the cattle squeeze. The young man cast a quick glance at his dad but not at Hawke.

"My son? Why do you need to talk to Chad?"

Hawke said, "Chad, do you want your dad to hear this conversation?"

The young man shrugged.

"Do you think Chad took that ketamine?" Dr. Macklin turned all of his attention to his son. "Chad, did you take the ketamine that was missing?"

"No. I didn't take it." The teenager stared his father right in the eyes.

"I don't think he took it. I think he helped the person who did." Hawke added. "Am I right?"

Dr. Macklin stepped closer to his son. "Did you help someone take it? Why?"

Chad turned off the hose and stared at his dad. "There was a lady, you know, Paul Booth's sister. She was in Al's Café a couple of weeks ago. She recognized me and offered me two hundred dollars to just leave the drug cabinet unlocked on a certain day. When you acted like nothing had been taken, I figured she hadn't shown up and I'd made two hundred."

"But the other day, when Trooper Hawke came here and had me look, why didn't you say something then?" Macklin asked.

The boy shrugged. "I figured it was over and done and nothing I could do about it."

Dr. Macklin made a frustrated sound and spun away from his son.

Hawke pulled out his notebook. "I need a full account of that conversation with Paul Booth's sister."

Chapter Twenty-eight

Heading to Alder, Hawke reviewed the information he'd gleaned the last couple of days and felt good about getting closer to solving the case. If they could just find Mrs. Larsen. There was a strong possibility she had something to do with the pastor's murder since she'd stashed what she thought was a dead body in her attic.

At City Hall, he entered the building and headed down the hall to the police department.

The receptionist called after him, "Trooper Hawke, Chief Browning is at the hospital. He asked that you go there if you showed up here."

Hawke pivoted and headed back by her cubicle. "Thank you," he said and exited the building. The short drive to the hospital had his mind spinning. Had Mrs. Betz regained enough strength and stability to tell them what had happened?

Walking into the hospital, he encountered Rosa and

Jayne. "What are you two doing here?"

Jayne glanced over at Madison, the young woman who worked the intake office.

"Madison called and told me they had Mrs. Betz here," Rosa said. "I wanted to know how she came to be here but Chief Browning is making us stay out here and Madison doesn't know anything more than the EMTs brought Diane in."

Hawke ran a hand over the back of his neck. "You two should go home. I'll come tell you what we know when we discover it. But I can tell you that you are neither one a suspect at this point. We are pretty sure we know who killed the pastor." He strode on past and down the hall to the nurse's station.

Bev Archer, who usually worked nights, stood beside the nurse's station talking to Keith the daytime head nurse.

"Excuse me. Could you tell me which room I'll find Mrs. Betz?" Hawke asked. Bev jumped as the sound of his voice and Keith's gaze shot from the woman to Hawke.

"How did you know she was here?" Bev asked as Keith said, "Room nineteen."

Hawke studied the woman. Her composure which had been hard and authoritative, now appeared strung tight. "How do you know Mrs. Betz?" he asked.

"Just as the wife of Pastor Betz." She picked up a purse sitting on the counter. "I have to go."

Hawke watched her walk out of the ward. His mind buzzed trying to find a way to connect her to the crime and finding nothing that made him think she could be connected. Yet, she was very jumpy about Mrs. Betz.

"Hawke, we're in here," Herold walked down the hallway toward him.

Hawke followed the city officer into a room. Mrs. Betz lay in the bed an IV in one arm, a bandage around her head, and her other arm in a sling. One leg was also in a cast. Her eyes were open but appeared as Jayne's had when he'd found her. Only the officers sat and stood around her bed. Hawke wondered why there wasn't someone from the congregation here to keep her company.

"How's she doing?" Hawke asked a little above a whisper.

"She has a broken leg and collarbone, a gash to her head, and the doctor thinks she was drugged," Browning said.

"Ketamine?" Hawke asked.

"They don't know yet, but most of the signs seem to give him that impression. Which is the pits because she may not remember what happened to her for a few days, if ever." Browning rose from the chair where he sat. "The doctor said the older a person is the more chance they won't regain the memory of what happened to them."

Hawke realized they would have to rely on the diary and find Mrs. Larsen to ever learn the truth.

"Are we taking shifts to make sure Mrs. Larsen doesn't come in here and try to finish her off?" Hawke asked.

"That's what I was thinking." Browning motioned for them to all step out into the hall. "If we let word get out that we have Mrs. Betz and we're waiting for her to wake, Suzanne Larsen may try to get in here and silence her."

Hawke nodded in agreement. "She can't be left alone. Even if a parishioner comes to sit with her. I would trust Rosa to sit with her. She's not going to hurt the woman. That would give us some time to share thoughts and ideas without doing it in public," Hawke said.

"But could she handle herself if someone attempted to try anything?" Herold asked.

"I haven't a doubt she could handle Mrs. Larsen if the woman showed up." Hawke had a feeling Rosa didn't show up to out of the way places to help with births without some kind of protection, like pepper spray or a taser. "And she has a stake in the outcome of this investigation. She wants to be cleared of charges and have the women she's tried so hard to get justice for to feel safe."

"See if she can come sit for an hour at seven. By then you and Herold can follow any leads you've come up with and we can gather at the office with your report." Browning moved back into the room and sat in the chair beside the woman's bed.

Herold and Hawke walked down the hall to the entrance.

"Did you learn anything new?" Herold asked.

"Yes, and no. I'm no closer to finding Mrs. Larsen but she had an accomplice in getting the ketamine at the Macklin clinic. The oldest boy of the vet. She paid him to leave the drug cupboard unlocked on a specific day."

"That means the murder was premeditated," Herold said, as they walked through the doors that automatically opened in front of them and stepped out into the cool evening air.

"I'm not sure all of it was premeditated. I need to read more of her diary. I want to know what her feelings were toward Pastor Betz and his wife. And figure out if she and Mrs. Betz killed the pastor and who could have helped Mrs. Larsen put Mrs. Betz in the attic. There is no way Mrs. Larsen did it by herself." Hawke walked over to his vehicle. "I'll meet you at the office and we'll figure out what to look up from there."

Before driving to City Hall, Hawke called Rosa.

"Are you going to tell me what's going on now?" she answered her phone.

"I can't tell you more than we are looking for Mrs. Larsen. She is the one who put Mrs. Betz in the hospital and we believe the two of them killed the pastor." Hawke listened as the silence grew on the other end of the call.

"Where do you think Mrs. Larsen is?" Rosa asked, finally.

"Officer Herold and I are working on that while Chief Browning sits with Mrs. Betz. That's why I'm calling. We could use your help sitting with her while the three of us get together at seven tonight to go through what we know and how to proceed." Hawke felt his jaw clench and slowly released it. The woman had every right to refuse to help them.

"I'll be there at six-forty-five. Do you think Suzanne may show up to finish her off?" The woman said it without a hint of fear.

"She might. That's why someone needs to be with her at all times."

"Jayne and I will help spell you." Rosa's tone was

firm.

"I'd rather not have Jayne there. I don't think—"

"I'll do the thinking where Jayne is concerned and she'll be just fine. Tell Chief Browning I'll be there fifteen minutes before seven." The call ended.

Hawke knew the midwife was fierce in her loyalty toward the women she helped. But for some reason, she was even more loyal to Jayne.

On his drive back to City Hall, Hawke thought about Suzanne and her brother. Was there any other family in the area? Someone who would help her hide? He didn't think the brother would. But it wouldn't hurt to send Herold down there to check things out.

When they both parked at City Hall, Hawke stopped Herold from getting out of his vehicle. "I think it would be a good idea to take a drive down to Eagle and see if there is any activity at Paul Booth's, besides him. He didn't strike me as someone who would hide his sister from the law, but I could be off on that. She seemed to be more devoted to him than he was to her."

"Here's the key to the side door." Herold handed Hawke the key to get in a side door of the building. "When you get in, there's a key in the top left-hand drawer of Browning's desk. It opens the safe in the breakroom. That's where the diary is." Herold rolled up his window and backed out.

Hawke grasped the key in his hand and went to the side of the building. The key slid into the lock and he stepped inside in seconds. He flipped a switch inside the door and the corridor lit up. His boots thunked on the tile floor as he strode down the hall to Browning's office. Inside, he flipped on the light and opened the drawer. A key on a ring sat on top of everything else in the drawer.

In the breakroom, Hawke started a pot of coffee and then opened the three-feet-wide by five-feet-high safe in a corner of the room. There was ammunition, a couple of rifles and revolvers inside along with an evidence bag. Hawke grabbed the bag and it felt like a book. He signed the date, time, and his name to a paper attached to the bag and closed the safe.

Placing the evidence bag on the table, he poured a cup of coffee and then sat down and opened the bag. He pulled the book out and instead of hopping around, he sat back, sipping his coffee, and started reading from the beginning. There had to be a clue to either the crimes or where Mrs. Larsen might be hiding.

Chapter Twenty-nine

Hawke stood, stretched, and replenished his coffee. It was close to seven. He'd made notes the second time he read through the diary. Mrs. Larsen had written about running away with Pastor Betz and how he made her feel like a woman. Hawke had trouble swallowing his coffee when he read those entries. She also mentioned an enjoyable weekend at a quilt retreat with her niece. No name on the niece. He wondered if it was someone in Wallowa County or if a sibling had moved away and that was where Mrs. Larsen had gone to the retreat.

He walked into Browning's office and found the paper files on the case. He dug through them to find Paul Booth's phone number. While the phone rang, he checked his watch. Browning and Herold should be showing up any minute. He hoped the hour Rosa and Jayne were at the hospital nothing happened.

"Hello?" answered Booth.

"Mr. Booth, this is Trooper Hawke. Do you have a niece who lives in the county?"

"No. Suzanne never had any children."

"Do you have any other siblings?" Hawke asked, pretty sure it was a no.

"No. It was just Suzanne and I, why?"

"There's a notation in Suzanne's diary that she went to a quilting event with her niece. Do you have any idea who she could have been talking about?" Hawke hoped the brother would be as honest as he'd been so far.

"That would be Beverly. She's Suzanne's niece by marriage. Beverly's mother was Everett's sister."

"What is her last name?" Hawke asked, jotting this down in his book.

"Fowler."

The hair on Hawke's neck tingled. How much of a coincidence could it be that the pastor's last victim was a Fowler and Mrs. Larsen was related to the Fowlers, even if only by marriage?

"Thank you, Mr. Booth. You've been a huge help."

As he ended the call, footsteps echoed down the empty hall. Browning entered the room followed by Herold.

"How are things at the hospital?" Hawke asked.

"Quiet," Browning said.

"Same at the Booth Farm," Herold added.

"I just finished a call with Paul Booth. This just gets more and more interesting." Hawke told them about how Suzanne Larsen had lusted over the pastor and was related to the pastor's latest victim. "I think when she discovered the man she was coveting had raped her great-niece, she cracked and decided to do away with Pastor Betz. I'm not sure if Jayne arrived when she was killing the pastor or if her arrival hastened Mrs. Larsen to do what she'd planned. With a witness Mrs. Larsen may have improvised. We won't know until we find her. And what part Mrs. Betz may have played in the murder we'll have to wait to see until she regains consciousness."

"There's one thing that doesn't make sense," Herold said. "I don't think there is anyone in the Fowler family named Beverly."

Hawke pulled out his phone. "There is one way to find out." He scrolled through his contacts and pressed the call icon beside Darlene's name.

Several rings and she answered, "Hawke, I know you aren't home. Dani is over here helping me."

"I'm happy you are keeping her busy. I have a question for you. The other day you seemed to know a bit about the Booths. Do you happen to know anything about the Fowler family? I've learned that Beverly Fowler is Suzanne Larsen's niece. Do you know where she fits in with Tom and Cathy Fowler's family?" Hawke pulled his notebook closer and flipped the pen back and forth.

"Beverly Fowler is Tom's sister but she isn't a Fowler anymore. She's Beverly Archer. She married Wade Archer after Eloise left."

Hawke let out a curse.

"Wasn't that what you wanted to know?" Darlene asked.

"Yes, that was exactly what we needed to know.

Thank you. Tell Dani I'll be late getting home." He ended the call and held the other men's gaze. "Bev Archer is Beverly Fowler."

Browning shot to his feet. "She was coming on duty when I left the hospital."

Hawke held out a hand. "We don't know for sure she is helping Mrs. Larsen. I think we're better off giving Rosa a head's up than rushing into the hospital."

《》《》《》

Rosa sat in the chair next to Diane's hospital bed. She'd brought some crocheting and Jayne sat in a chair in the corner reading a book. They'd agreed it would be best if she sat where no one coming into the room would see her, just in case things went wrong. She had Rosa's taser and Rosa had her can of pepper spray in the pocket of her skirt. They were prepared if anyone came to do Diane harm.

The woman in the bed hadn't moved when Bev came in and checked her vitals. Rosa tried to ask questions but Bev only said, she just came on duty and didn't know anything about Mrs. Betz's injuries or how they happened.

The covers moved down by Diane's foot of her uninjured leg. Rosa stared at it as her phone jingled in her purse. She dug into the depths of her purse and pulled out the phone. It was Trooper Hawke.

"Hello," she said in a hushed voice.

"Has Bev Archer been into the room yet?" the trooper asked.

"Yes, she checked Diane's vitals. Why?" Rosa's heart started racing.

"I'm surprised you didn't think of this. She is

related to Gemma Fowler."

The connection zipped through her brain. "Oh, yes! I should have thought of that. I forgot she was a Fowler before she married." She sucked in air as she connected another dot. "And Suzanne is related to Gemma and Bev by marriage."

"I'm coming over to ask Bev some questions. Don't let her do anything other than check vitals until I get there."

The call ended. A puff of air on Rosa's cheek made her glance toward the door. It was closed but she wondered if someone had been listening to her phone call. Her gaze met Jayne's.

"Is everything okay?" Jayne asked.

Rosa nodded and glanced over at the woman in the bed. Her eyes were open but she appeared confused.

"Diane, you're in the hospital. You have a broken leg and collarbone and some gashes on your head, but you'll be fine." She leaned forward and whispered. "You're safe."

The woman only grew more confused and asked, "Where is Gordon?"

"He's—" Rosa started and realized she shouldn't tell the woman her husband was dead if she didn't remember it. "He'll be along shortly."

She caught Jayne's surprised expression and shook her head.

The door opened and Bev walked in carrying a syringe.

"What is that for?" Rosa asked, standing, barring the nurse's way to the patient.

"Pain medication. The doctor ordered it

intravenous until the patient wakes up enough to swallow pills." Bev stood right in front of Rosa, her arm raised as if she would push her aside.

"Diane is awake, so there is no need for the shot." Rosa stood her ground, hoping Jayne had the taser out and ready.

"Let me check the patient then," Bev said, moving to step around Rosa.

"Put the syringe down and then I'll let you near her," Rosa didn't take her eyes off the syringe still in the nurse's hand. The reason she became a midwife and used naturopathic remedies was her fear of needles.

The swish of the door opening caused a breeze.

"This patient will be fine while I have a word with you, Mrs. Archer," Trooper Hawke said.

Bev spun around.

Rosa sat back down in her chair. Her heart raced in her chest and she tried not to show how worried she'd been the woman would poke her with the syringe.

"Why should I go with you?" Bev asked.

"I have some questions about your niece, Gemma, and your aunt, Suzanne." Trooper Hawke motioned with his hand for her to come to him and the door.

The woman stood in one place for so long, Rosa tensed. The stillness made her wonder if Bev still planned to stick Diane with the needle.

"Mrs. Archer, I just have a few questions. If you don't come with me, I'll arrest you as an accessory to murder." Trooper Hawke's voice held empathy and truth.

Rosa was glad she'd made the decision to trust him.

Bev walked stiffly toward the door and the trooper. Rosa took that moment to glance at Jayne. She sat stiff as a rock, holding the taser in her hands.

Hawke scanned the room swiftly, noted the three women appeared unscathed, and followed Mrs. Acher down the hall to the nurse's station. There was one other nurse on duty.

"Beth, take a break," Mrs. Archer said as she dropped the syringe in the waste basket next to the desk and sunk onto the chair in front of a computer.

The younger nurse glanced from him to Mrs. Archer and back to Hawke.

"It would be a good idea if you did take a break," he said as Herold walked down the hallway.

"I have Wade in the reception area," Herold said.

Mrs. Archer's back straightened and she glared at Hawke. "Why did you bring him here?"

"In case you need some support as you talk with us. Would you like him to be brought down here?" Hawke studied the woman. He was pretty sure she didn't want her husband present.

"No." She glanced around. "I'd rather do this somewhere else. More private."

"We can take you to the police station," Hawke suggested.

Her head shook back and forth. "No. If Suzanne sees you hauling me in…"

"Then where do you suggest?" Hawke asked, crossing his arms. He'd much rather bring her to the station but if she thought Suzanne would go crazier if she saw them bring in Beverly, then he'd go wherever Mrs. Archer thought best.

"We can use the surgeon's office. It's only used when a visiting surgeon is here." Mrs. Archer stood.

"We'll have to wait for the other nurse to return. In the meantime, I'll talk to Rosa and Jayne a minute." He settled his gaze on Herold. "Keep her here until I come back."

The other man nodded.

Hawke entered Mrs. Betz's hospital room. Jayne stood, clutching her purse to her.

"Is everything settled now?" she asked.

"I'm afraid not. Officer Herold and I are taking Mrs. Archer to a room in the hospital that will be private and question her."

"You aren't taking her to jail?" Rosa asked.

"No. We have lots of unanswered questions. If she answers them and happens to be implicated in all of this, then we'll arrest her. Until we know that, we can only question her." Hawke glanced at the woman in the bed. "Has she regained consciousness?"

"Yes. For a few minutes right before Bev came in. But she's asleep again." Rosa shifted her attention from him to Mrs. Betz.

"Did she say anything?"

Rosa turned sad eyes on Hawke. "She asked for Gordon."

"If we're right about the ketamine, it could have been used on her and she may have memory lapses." Hawke didn't like that their victim and a possible suspect may not be able to remember what she'd done.

"We'll be here until someone relieves us. Suzanne is still free, correct?" Rosa asked.

"Yes. So stay on alert." Hawke left the room and

found the younger nurse back at the station.

He motioned for Herold and Mrs. Archer to start walking to the room she wanted to use.

Bev didn't move, she asked, "Could Officer Herold give my husband a message?"

Hawke nodded.

She faced Herold. "Tell him to contact Vern, our lawyer."

Herold glanced at Hawke.

"Mrs. Archer, we aren't arresting you."

"I know. But I have a feeling I'll need to talk to a lawyer after I talk with you."

Hawke nodded to Herold and waited for him to return before Mrs. Archer led them down the hall.

When Mrs. Archer and Herold turned their backs, Hawke bent, picking up the syringe in the wastebasket and using a manilla envelope sitting on the desk to drop it into. "Evidence," he said to Beth and walked down the hall after the other two.

Chapter Thirty

The surgeon's office had three chairs. Hawke had Herold take the one behind the desk while he and Mrs. Archer sat in front of the desk, their chairs facing.

"Mrs. Archer, have you been conspiring with your aunt, Suzanne Larsen to kill Pastor Betz?" Hawke started.

The woman shook her head. "No, I haven't been conspiring. But when Aunt Suzanne called me and said she needed help the night she'd killed Pastor Betz and knocked out that young woman, I didn't know that was what she wanted help with until I arrived." She glanced up from where she'd been staring at her hands as they picked at the sides of her fingernails. "I started to say we should call the police and she said, no one would believe it was an accident. And she knew what to do if I'd just help her take the young woman somewhere and leave her."

Her eyes narrowed. "I wasn't sorry for what she'd done to that bastard who professed his love of God and then used his sermons and bible teachings to sexually assault young innocent women. He deserved everything my aunt did to him." As she spoke her words came out full of anger and hate.

"Were you one of his victims?" Hawke asked gently.

She shook her head. "No. My best friend in high school was and recently my niece. I couldn't believe my brother went with Gemma's wishes to keep it quiet. He should have been storming the police station and getting up a group of men to bring that bastard in."

"Who was your best friend in high school?" Hawke asked.

"Eloise Laude. She was fun. Wade, Eloise, and I had a lot of fun together."

Hawke studied her. "You knew she was raped by Betz and you never told Wade? And then you married him?"

A wry smile twisted her lips. "I knew I would never be loved like he loved Eloise, but she had sworn me to never tell Wade what had happened. She didn't want him to know what had happened to her for fear he'd retaliate." Mrs. Archer shrugged. "Instead, I became embroiled in the whole thing." She leaned forward. "I didn't hurt anyone. I was only pulled in after the fact."

"I understand you didn't hurt anyone, but yourself. Allowing your aunt to get away with murder isn't helping her," Hawke said, noting Herold was scribbling as fast as he could in the notebook.

"Aunt Suzanne was always there for me when I needed her. I couldn't let her down. I couldn't turn her in. That predatory pastor is who made her the way she is. He promised her he'd help her have a child, but it came before she was married. She didn't want the scandal and made it go away. Then after she was married, he teased her but never made her pregnant, keeping her devoted to him." Her eyes narrowed again. "He made her a victim of his schemes. She knew he was 'helping' the younger women. She didn't realize he was actually raping them until a few years ago. Then she tried to make him stop but his poor wife hadn't been able to stop him all these years, I told Aunt Suzanne, she'd never be able to make him stop. He was a pervert that needed something cut off."

Hawke squirmed at the mention of cutting off the pastor's penis. While the man deserved it, the woman said it without remorse. In fact, she said it with conviction.

"Did she say if she'd figured out a way to get even with the pastor?" Hawke asked.

"No. Like I said, she only brought me into this the night she hit that young woman and killed pastor Betz. Then when she knocked out Mrs. Betz, she called me to help her put the woman in the attic." She held up her hands. "I swear, I knew she was still alive. But I told Suzanne Mrs. Betz was dead. I wanted her to leave and stop involving me in her actions. As soon as I was sure that Suzanne was out of town, I was going to call and report where Mrs. Betz was."

Hawke studied the woman. "I still don't understand why you didn't just call the police to begin with."

She wrung her hands and stared at him. "When I was young, I could have ended up in juvenile detention for something I'd done. Before that incident, I had been a bit of a hellraiser and brought my parents lots of grief. But when I told Aunt Suzanne what I'd done, she took the blame and told me to straighten my life out. That hers wasn't worth saving but mine was." She crossed her arms. "I owed it to her to help her out of a tough situation. She changed the course of my life and helped me get Wade when Eloise left."

"Where is your aunt?" Hawke asked.

"I honestly don't know. She said she was going to go live it up for a change." The woman frowned. "But I'm not sure how. I know that Uncle Everett left his money to Suzanne in small amounts once a month. Unless she was being very thrifty since he passed, there isn't any way she'd have enough money to live it up."

Hawke had wondered how the woman had been living since her husband died. It was apparent she'd not had a job. He stood and motioned to Herold. "Take her in and get her signature on the notes of what we just talked about." He studied the woman. "We'll have to keep you in jail until the District Attorney decides if you are an accomplice or an accessory after the fact."

The woman didn't even argue. She held out her hands. Herold drew her hands one at a time behind her back and clicked the handcuffs in place. As they walked down the hall, to the reception area, Hawke noticed Wade hovering by the entrance. He wondered how the man would cope with knowing the same person had ruined both his first love and wife's lives.

While it was a relief to know a bit about what

happened, they still didn't have the whole story. He was sure Herold would get that out of Mrs. Archer as he worked on the statement with her.

Hawke made a detour toward the room where Rosa and Jayne were keeping watch over Mrs. Betz.

《》《》《》

Rosa's head jerked up as she felt the draft of air across her face. She'd dozed off, but came awake sharply at the breeze and the sound of boots on the floor. Trooper Hawke strode into the room and stopped at the end of the bed.

"I'll take over. You two go home." The trooper didn't say anything about her having been asleep on the job.

"Did you take Bev to jail?" Rosa asked, wondering how Wade would deal with his wife being arrested.

"Herold is taking her now." Trooper Hawke sat on a stool, most likely used by a doctor.

"Did she kill Pastor Betz?" Rosa asked. "And hit Jayne?" She glanced over at the young woman sitting in the chair behind the open door.

"No, she didn't kill anyone. She's being charged as an accessory. It seems after Mrs. Larsen knocked out Jayne and killed the pastor, she called Mrs. Archer to help her with something. She didn't realize what the woman had done until she'd arrived." Trooper Hawke raised a hand to keep her from saying anything. "And she agrees she should have called the police, but she felt compelled to help her aunt."

Rosa had been sitting here thinking about how Suzanne could get Bev to help her. It had to be over the time when Bev was fourteen and she nearly killed someone while driving a car. Only Suzanne had sworn it was she who had been driving recklessly and lost her license for many years and paid a fine. Rosa had heard later that Bev had been running away from home and had stolen the vehicle to use to get away.

"And what about Diane? Who hurt her?" Rosa asked.

"Mrs. Larsen incapacitated Mrs. Betz and then called Mrs. Archer to help hide the body. Mrs. Archer did say she had planned to call the police when she realized that Mrs. Betz wasn't dead. She'd told her aunt the woman was dead to keep Mrs. Larsen from hurting Mrs. Betz more."

"And you believed her?" Rosa said and humphed.

"I didn't disbelieve her. She seemed to care that her aunt had hurt Jayne and Mrs. Betz. As for the pastor, she was very happy about what happened to him." Trooper Hawke rubbed a hand across the back of his neck. "You two go on home. I'll wait here until Chief Browning relieves me."

"With Bev out of the picture, do you really think Suzanne will come after Diane? I mean if Suzanne thinks Diane is dead and Suzanne is running, there isn't any more threat to Diane, is there?" Rosa shoved her body to the front of the chair and pushed up to stand. She'd been sitting a while and her body was ready for bed.

"I'm hoping she is long gone for Mrs. Betz's sake. But I don't want to get complacent and learn she snuck in here and did the woman more harm." Trooper Hawke stood. He waved to the door. "Go home and rest. We might need you to watch over her tomorrow."

"Just give us a call." Rosa waved her arm for Jayne to proceed out of the room.

When they were almost to the reception area, Jayne asked, "Do you think Suzanne is far away?"

Rosa had been thinking on that. "I don't know where she'd go. All she's ever known is Wallowa County. We'll go visit her brother tomorrow and see if she talked about any place special."

Chapter Thirty-one

Hawke put down the magazine the nurse, Beth, brought him and stared at the woman in the bed. She was watching him.

"Mrs. Betz, I'm Trooper Hawke. How are you feeling?"

Her eyes widened when he spoke to her. "Where's Gordon?" she asked.

"He's gone. I'm afraid he was killed and left to burn in the church." He heard her intake of breath. "Do you remember the fire at the church?"

She shook her head, before slowly stopping and staring over his shoulder. "Gordon did bad things. Worse than me. But I couldn't stop him. He'd just laugh at me and said he knew my secrets and would let everyone know if I said anything against him. After all, I was his wife and had to do as he said."

"What had you done that he could hold over you?"

Hawke asked, believing he already knew.

"I borrowed money from the charities. But I'd give it back when I won." She smiled faintly. "There was a time when I borrowed more than I returned. But lately, I've been winning. I was saving up enough to get far away from Gordon."

Things were starting to make sense. "Did you tell Suzanne Larsen about your winnings?" Hawke asked.

"After the fire, I told her I needed to go to the house and get more clothes. She caught me getting the money out of my closet. She started to accuse me of stealing from the church so I had to prove to her it was winnings." Mrs. Betz stared at the door for several minutes. "She took it, didn't she?"

"I believe so," Hawke said, wondering if the woman was telling the whole truth since just minutes before she said she didn't remember the fire and yet, she spoke of it and everything that happened later.

"I figured as much when I woke up in pain with bound hands and feet in the attic. How did you find me?"

"I got lucky. Did she give you a shot?" he asked, thinking the woman was clear of mind for having been given ketamine.

"I don't think so. But the pain made me faint as she shoved me through the hole in the ceiling." Tears came to Mrs. Betz's eyes. "I thought Suzanne was a friend. I confided in her about Gordon's indiscretions. She listened as if she cared about me and my problems. I heard what you said to Rosa. Suzanne killed Gordon, hurt that poor girl, and then she tried to kill me. What caused her to do all of that?"

"She never let on to you that she was in love with your husband?" Hawke asked.

The woman's eyes widened. "Suzanne? No, she never said a word. I never noticed her paying him any more attention than the rest of the women. Did they…" She swallowed and began again, "Did they…"

"From what Mrs. Archer said, I believe they did," Hawke said. He figured it was best to get it all out in the open now. And he had a question he needed to ask. "Mrs. Betz, the family members of the young women your husband raped were all certain you were in the room with Pastor Betz and the women. Were you?"

"Heavens no! I wouldn't have let him do what he did if I'd been in the room. No, he told the families I would be present then he'd tell me if I didn't leave them be, he'd tell the congregation I was stealing from the church."

"But you knew what he was doing to those young women," Hawke persisted.

"I had my notion, but nothing to prove it other than my husband's lack of interest in me." She twisted her head to peer out the window into the dark night. "When I couldn't produce a child, he started giving pre-marital counseling with the couples and later the husband and wife separately. When one of the husbands-to-be came to Gordon about what he had done to his fiancée, Gordon stopped doing separate counseling and began counseling the girls whose families felt they were being too wild or disobedient. And then he started giving lessons to the girls who were interested in playing the organ or being in the choir. He'd come up with reasons to be alone with them." She shuddered. "I kept wishing one of them would speak out. But they didn't. Their families either didn't believe them or didn't want to be gossiped about."

"But you could have come forward and then they would have listened," Hawke insisted.

"Yes, and Gordon would have turned them all on me saying how I stole from the charities and the poor children overseas. He could turn things around so easily and make him look like a saint and whoever he wanted to ridicule looked like they were the one in the wrong." Her eyes begged for forgiveness, as did her tone.

Hawke wasn't about to give this woman any sympathy. She had let a psychopath reign far too long in the church and this county. "You could have spoken out. Rosa would have been right beside you, as well as many of his victims. You could have done the right thing, but chose to do nothing."

He leaned back in his chair and pulled his hat down over his eyes. "Get some sleep so you can give a statement in the morning."

《》《》《》

His shoulder shook, bringing Hawke awake with a start. He shoved his hat up and peered blurrily at Browning.

"Hawke, I'm here to take over. Since you're sleeping, I take it there isn't anything to worry about?" Browning nodded toward the woman in the bed.

Scrubbing his face with his hands, Hawke willed his brain to work. "What time is it?"

"One. You said to take over from you at one." Browning held a cup of steaming coffee.

Hawke pointed at it. "Where did you get that?"

"Home. Think you can stay awake long enough to drive home?" Browning asked.

"Yeah. Did Herold fill you in on Beverly Archer?" Hawke stood and stretched. His tendons popped and his muscles moaned at having slept in the chair.

"Yeah. I know what went down." Browning sat on the chair.

"I had a chat with Mrs. Betz. She knew what her husband was doing but he was blackmailing her because she 'borrowed' money from the church to gamble. She was winning a lot lately and that's what Mrs. Larsen made off with." Hawke yawned and walked to the door. "I told her we would get her full statement in the morning."

"I'll make sure Herold is here first thing to do that. Go home."

Hawke waved a hand and meandered down the hallway to the entrance. This time of night it was locked. He had to go through the emergency area to get someone to open the door and let him out.

A young man in scrubs sat behind the emergency intake desk. He glanced up at the sound of Hawke's boots on the shiny flooring.

"Can I help you?" the young man asked.

"I just need let out of here," Hawke said, yawning.

The young man stood, walked to the door, and pushed a button on the wall. "That's all you have to do to get out of here this time of night."

"Thanks, I'll remember that, but I hope to not be in here this late again." Hawke walked to his vehicle, climbed in, and headed home. On the drive he thought about all they knew. The evidence was going to be hard to pull together to prove Mrs. Larsen, and not Mrs. Archer, killed Betz. They hadn't found any evidence so far that proved either woman did it. They would have Mrs. Archer and Mrs. Betz's statements in the morning but that was hearsay, not really evidence. They had to catch Mrs. Larsen with the evidence and get her to confess to killing the pastor. Unless he could find evidence in her house.

Chapter Thirty-two

Dani and Tuck were flying back to the lodge today. Hawke made sure he told her how sorry he was that he had been consumed by finding a killer while she was home. She just smiled, kissed him, and said, "I know you have a one-track mind when it comes to piecing together murders. I'll be back in a week and you'll be able to tell me all about it."

That was what he loved about the woman. She understood his need to discover who, what, and why one person would take another's life.

"I promise to take you out to a wonderful dinner at the Lake Lodge and we'll go for a horseback ride when you come back." He walked her out to her SUV.

"I'm going to hold you to it, because from the sounds of things, you should have this murder closed by then." Dani stepped into her vehicle and leaned out for one more kiss before she closed the door. "See you in a week."

"I'll be here." Hawke waved as she drove away. He glanced down at Dog. "Come on. Let's get the boys fed. Then I'm going back to Mrs. Larsen's and doing another search. This time, I'm going to look through all the rooms."

Hawke and Dog walked to the barn and Hawke scooped grain into three plastic troughs. At the pasture the two geldings and the mule had their heads hung over the metal gate. "I'm coming. You three are spoiled." He fed the animals and walked back into the house. Hawke opened his laptop to see if forensics had anything new for him. There was an email from Herold.

Subject line: Read this.

He opened the email. *I found this while reading through Mrs. Larsen's diary. Her husband may not have died of natural causes.*

Hawke opened the scanned document. It was a page from the woman's journal dated the year her husband died. She talked about plants she'd been growing that were poisonous and how Everett thought the Lily of the Valley was pretty. *Because Everett likes the flower so much, I made him a cup of tea for his last day on this earth and put the flower in a vase on the table. The doctor said it was his heart that failed. I could have told the doctor you needed to have a heart to have it fail, but I kept my mouth shut and pretended I was upset.*

Hawke opened the other scanned page. Here Mrs. Larsen talked about being tired of sharing the pastor with the younger women of the congregation. She confronted him and learned what he'd really thought about her. After that, she'd made the plan to get the ketamine and started writing all the different ways she could teach him a lesson.

Several of the methods made Hawke cringe and hope he caught her before she turned the tables on him.

After calling dispatch to say he was on duty, Hawke called Sheriff Lindsey to see if he could spare a deputy to be at the Larsen house while Hawke searched it thoroughly. He knew Herold was taking Mrs. Betz's statement that morning and would need to get it all typed up and in the report. Hawke would head to the State Police Office in Winslow after he did the search to write up everything they'd discovered in Mrs. Larsen's diary and whatever he came up with during the search.

Deputy Corcoran met him at the Larsen residence. "Hawke, heard this is part of the homicide connected to the church burning," Corcoran said.

"Yeah. The woman has fled the premises and I want to see if I can discover where she went." Hawke opened the front door the way he had the back, with his lock picks.

Corcoran followed him into the house and closed the door. "What are we looking for?"

"Anything that could tell us where she's gone. A photo, a word written somewhere, anything about a place." Hawke started with the small table by the door. He pulled out the drawer and dumped the contents on the tabletop. Pushing the items around with his latex-gloved hands, he didn't see anything that might give a clue as to where the woman had run.

Moving to the living room, he heard Corcoran in

the laundry room. Hawke pulled cushions off the furniture, looked under the furniture, and opened anything that could be opened. Nothing.

He walked into the dining room as Corcoran entered the kitchen.

"Nothing in the laundry room," Corcoran said, opening drawers and digging through them.

"I haven't found anything either," Hawke said, opening the drawers in a buffet. He found a map tucked in between a stack of quilted placemats. Unfolding the map, he placed it on the table. There weren't any marks on the surface. He did notice creases that didn't match the way the map folded. Following the lines, he folded the map until an area in southeast Idaho remained. It had to mean something.

Hawke pulled out his phone and called Browning.

"Hawke, what's up?" Browning's tired voice answered.

"Are you still at the hospital?" Hawke asked.

"Yeah. I'm waiting for an off-duty deputy to come relieve me. I talked the DA into paying for someone to sit with Mrs. Betz until we catch Mrs. Larsen."

"That's a good idea. How can I get someone to ask Mrs. Archer a question?" he asked.

"Herold finished his statement here about twenty minutes ago. He should be back at the office typing up his report. He could run over to the jail or you could call county and have someone ask the question."

"I'll call over there. Thanks." Hawke ended the call and dialed Sheriff Lindsey.

"Sheriff Lindsey."

"Rafe, it's Hawke. I need someone to go to the jail

and ask Mrs. Archer why Mrs. Larsen would have a map folded to the southeast Idaho area. I'd do it but I'm in the middle of searching Mrs. Larsen's house again. We have to figure out where she's gone." Hawke didn't let the desperation that swirled in his head come out in his voice. He had a feeling if they didn't catch up to the woman soon, they would never catch her. There were too many people who had their lives interrupted by this woman's actions.

"I'll go see what I can find out. You said southeast Idaho?"

"Yes."

"I'll give you a call after I talk to her."

The call ended and Hawke turned back to the buffet and finished going through the drawers. He moved to the first room off the hall. He flipped on the light. The fabric filling the shelves around the room glowed with vibrant colors. A cutting table, ironing board, and a sewing machine took up the middle of the room. Hawke groaned thinking about going through all that fabric. He started in the middle of the room with the sewing machine and cutting table. In a drawer, he found several receipts for fabric, thread, and patterns. The next drawer was as large as a file cabinet drawer. It held folders and books of patterns. He pulled out the folders and read the businesses and addresses stamped on each pattern. One read *The Quilting Retreat, Heyburn Idaho*.

Hawke strode out of the room and over to the map he'd left folded open to southeastern Idaho. He moved his finger back and forth from the southern boundary of Idaho, working his way north. There it was, Heyburn.

His phone rang as he started to Google, The Quilting Retreat.

"Hawke," he answered.

"It's Rafe. Bev said she and her aunt went to The Quilting Retreat in Heyburn, Idaho, several years ago. And her aunt had mentioned going back one day."

Hawke grinned. "Thank you. I came to the same conclusion after going through her sewing room. I'm going to call the retreat and see if she's there, and then send the local police to hold her if she is."

"Good call."

Hawke finished googling the retreat and touched the phone icon.

"The Quilting Retreat, this is Shirley," a middle-aged female voice answered.

"Hi, Shirley. I was wondering if you have a woman at the retreat by the name of Suzanne Larsen?"

"We don't but she should be arriving later today. Do you need to leave her a note?" the woman asked.

"No, we were just wondering where she'd gone. Her niece thought she might be at the retreat." Hawke said, making small talk to not have the woman tell Mrs. Larsen someone called looking for her when she arrived.

"She was here a few years ago with her niece. They were both such good seamstresses and seemed to be very close for an aunt and niece."

"Thank you." Hawke immediately called the Idaho State Police and requested they send someone to the retreat later this afternoon to apprehend a fugitive from justice on probable cause. Then Hawke went in search of Corcoran to inform him he was heading to the courthouse to write up a warrant to bring Mrs. Larsen back to Wallowa County.

Chapter Thirty-three

Not knowing when Mrs. Larsen would arrive at the retreat and be picked up by the Idaho State Police, Hawke spent the rest of that day and the next going about his usual routine. He was out patrolling the rivers checking fishing licenses and zigzagging through turkey country making sure the hunters were being ethical.

His phone buzzed. It was Rosa.

"Hawke," he answered.

"I know it's you, I called you." The woman snapped, more upset than usual.

"Why did you call?" he asked, parking on the side of the road so he didn't lose cell service.

"Jayne went home this morning and I was cleaning up the room she stayed in. There's something you need to see." The woman's voice shook as if she were scared.

"What do I need to see?" Hawke asked, wondering what could have scared the woman.

"I don't want to talk about it on the phone. When can you swing by my place?" Rosa sounded more like her bossy self.

"I'm a good hour away from Alder. If it bothers you that much, take it to the city station and I'll look at it there."

"No! I want you to come here and see. I'm not going to take this to someone who will give me the run-around." She ended the call.

Hawke stared at his phone and turned his vehicle around. Whatever she'd found that he was presuming Jayne had left behind, had the woman more upset than she'd been during the whole ordeal. The pickup fishtailed and slid on gravel as he hurried to get off the forest service roads and onto the blacktop. Whatever Rosa found must have some significance to the murder.

《》《》《》

Rosa couldn't sit still. What had Jayne been thinking? She'd tried to call the woman's cell phone several times after finding the list in the bedroom, but she was either out of service or not answering her phone.

The list sat on the coffee table. Rosa glanced at it every time she walked by. Hawke was sure that Suzanne had killed Pastor Betz and attempted to kill Diane. But then why did Jayne have this list? It didn't make sense.

She heard the crunch of tires on gravel and hurried to the front door. Trooper Hawke stepped out of his official vehicle and strode up to her door.

"What is this all about?" he asked, walking through the door she held open.

"It's on the coffee table," she said, following him into the house.

He strode to the table and glanced down at the piece of paper. He studied it for nearly a minute with the muscle in his jaw twitching before he dug into his pocket and took out his phone. He clicked two photos, pulled on a latex glove, and picked up the paper by the corner.

"Where did you find this and where did you touch it?" His gaze bore into her. It was plain he didn't like the ramifications of this any more than she did.

"It was down between the bedside table and the bed. I grabbed it by the bottom corner and glanced at it. Then I carried it out here." Rosa waved her hand. "Does this mean she did everything?"

Trooper Hawke shook his head. "I don't see how. But the crossed-out names make it look like she either killed them or set them up."

Rosa shuddered. "That's what I thought." She had a thought. "Set it back down, please. I have something she wrote. Maybe we can compare the handwriting."

The trooper studied her with a scowl on his face. "Neither of us is an expert in handwriting."

"But if we, as you say, who know nothing about handwriting can tell it isn't hers then we need to figure out who put this in that room." Rosa hurried to the kitchen where she'd recited her grocery list to Jayne who'd written it down. Back in the sitting room, she placed the list on the table alongside the paper she'd found with Pastor, wife, friend, crossed out.

It was because there were no names only the references to the people, that Rosa had feared Jayne had killed the pastor, tried to kill the wife, and framed the friend. She wouldn't have known their names if she'd made the list before coming to Wallowa County.

Trooper Hawke sat on the couch and studied the two pieces of writing. "The way she made the P and the swirl on the f. I think she did write both of these. But she could have made the list and as she met each one, crossed them off." He glanced at her.

Rosa shrugged. "True. But why isn't she answering her phone?"

"Where is she supposed to be?" Hawke asked.

"She headed home this morning. Jayne said that she'd met, if briefly, the man who'd ruined her mother's life and she felt for all the others but she needed to get back to her life and take care of her mother's legacy, the antique store."

"Exactly what time did she leave?" Trooper Hawke asked.

"It was close to nine."

"That should only have taken her four hours, five at the most if she stopped. Try calling her again." Hawke now wondered if the woman had fooled them all or if something happened on her way home. While Rosa tried to contact Jayne by her cell phone, Hawke pulled out the business card Jayne had given him and called the antique store number.

"Hello, Mom and Daughter Antiques, how may I help you?" questioned a female voice.

"Jayne?" Hawke asked.

"No. Jayne is taking care of some family business, this is Lorelei."

"Lorelei, have you seen Jayne today?" Hawke was

feeling uneasy about the woman's disappearance.

"No. She did call and said she was coming home but wouldn't be in the shop until tomorrow. Is something wrong?" Worry crept into the woman's voice.

"I don't know. She left here early this morning and should have been home by now. Did she mention making any stops?"

"No. She said we'd check out estate sales and such when she got back. I don't see her car parked in her usual spot. She lives above the shop, and I haven't heard anyone moving around up there." She sucked in a breath and said quietly, "Should I call the cops?"

"Not yet. I'll do some more digging on my end. Thank you and call this number," he recited his cell phone, "if you hear from her."

"Who are you?" the woman inquired.

"Oregon State Trooper Hawke." He ended the call and peered at Rosa's worried face. "She hasn't made it home. I've got her license plate number and car make. I'll put it out across the state and see if we can locate her car."

"What do you think happened to her?" Rosa asked.

"According to her help, she planned to be home today and start work tomorrow. That doesn't sound like someone running." He had a sinking feeling Mrs. Larsen was behind Jayne's disappearance. But how? She was in Idaho and should be apprehended by now.

"I'll let you know what I learn." Hawke strode to the door. "Keep hold of that paper so we can ask her about it." He let himself out of the house and strode to his vehicle. Once inside, he pulled out his notebook and put out an all points on Jayne's car. Then he called the contact at the Idaho State Police to see if they had apprehended Mrs. Larsen.

"This is Oregon State Police Senior Trooper Hawke. I was wondering if you had the woman, Suzanne Larsen in custody for transport back to Oregon?" he asked when his call was answered.

"We have a woman in custody who signed into The Quilting Retreat as your suspect but she doesn't fit the photo that was sent to us."

Hawke stared at Rosa's house. "Can you describe her? The woman you have in custody."

"Five-seven, short dark hair, brown eyes, slender."

That sounded like Bev Archer. He never followed up on whether or not she was held as an accessory. Had her lawyer managed to get her released? Why would she impersonate her aunt knowing what she had done? "Hold onto her. She was an accessory to the charges against Suzanne Larsen. She's been used as a decoy." Hawke ended the call and immediately called Browning and Keller to fill them in on Bev impersonating Suzanne, Jayne being missing, and Suzanne not being where they thought she was.

"We received an email from forensics today. They say the bust of the Virgin Mary was the murder weapon. They found the victim's blood in a crack. And a set of fingerprints that matched a hit and run over forty years ago."

"Suzanne Booth," Hawke said.

"Yes," Carol said.

"I've been digging into her past. Thanks. Right now, Jayne Laude is my priority with Suzanne still at large."

Best way to find out what happened to Jayne would be to follow the path she would have taken to get home.

《》《》《》

Just as Hawke entered Eagle city limits, his radio crackled. "I found a car abandoned alongside the highway three miles out of Eagle. It matches the APB."

Hawke recognized Corcoran's voice. He dialed the deputy on his cell phone.

"Hawke, are you the one who put out the APB?" Corcoran answered.

"Yeah. Where exactly is the car?"

Corcoran gave him the milepost and Hawke stepped on the accelerator as soon as he crossed the railroad tracks on the north side of Eagle. He spotted Corcoran's flashing lights within minutes of leaving the town behind.

Hawke pulled in behind the county rig and met Corcoran at the back of Jayne's car. "Did you look it over?"

"Her purse and phone are sitting on the passenger seat. Her bag is in the trunk."

When Hawke sent him a questioning look, Corcoran added, "The keys were still in the ignition."

Hawke cursed and put in a call to have someone come out and process the car. "We need to find her. She left this morning and if this is all the farther she got, whoever took her has a huge head start." He did a 360 looking all around and stopped. "We aren't that far from the Booth Farm."

Corcoran spread a map across the hood of his vehicle. "This is where we are." He moved his finger only a short distance. "That's the start of the Booth land."

"It butts up to wilderness." Hawke didn't like the idea of Mrs. Larsen taking Jayne into the wilderness and killing her. "We need to head to the Booth Farm and talk to the brother."

Hawke hurried to his vehicle and took off toward Deer Creek and the Booth Farm. They had to stop Mrs. Larsen before she took another life.

Chapter Thirty-four

Hawke and Corcoran parked in front of the Booth farmhouse. They were met on the porch by Paul Booth and one of the border collies.

"What's this about?" the man asked, crossing his arms.

"We believe your sister abducted Jayne Laude and has brought her here," Hawke said. He'd called in a search warrant while driving to the farm. He hoped someone showed up with it soon so they could search if the man standing in front of them didn't allow them to do so.

Booth laughed. "Why would my sister do that?"

"Because she killed Pastor Betz, tried to kill Mrs. Betz, and stole church money. We found Jayne Laude's abandoned car not far from here. The only person who would want to harm her is your sister."

"Do you have proof of any of this?" Booth asked.

"We do. Mrs. Betz told us how your sister hit her on the head then tied her up and shoved her in the attic of her home, to leave her to die, after stealing the church's charity collection. And we have your sister's diary telling how she planned to kill Pastor Betz, as well as her fingerprints on the murder weapon." Hawke knew they had more than enough to take Mrs. Larsen to court.

"Murder weapon? I thought the pastor died in the fire?" Booth said, wasting precious time.

"He was killed before the fire started. Are you going to let us search your farm?" Hawke was ready to bodily move the man so they could search the house.

"But why would she want to take this person, you said, Jayne?" Booth had uncrossed his arms.

"Because she was in the church the night your sister killed the pastor. Your sister gave her ketamine to make Jayne forget what she'd seen. But little by little it has been coming back to her. I think your sister wanted to tie up the one last person who could get her locked up for murder not just attempted murder." Hawke didn't like standing around talking when the woman could be getting farther away to kill Jayne.

"I haven't seen her, but Talley, my bitch border collie has been missing since noon. She sticks to Suzanne like glue when she's here." He patted the dog's head sitting on the porch next to him.

Hawke studied the male dog. "Would he find Talley if you asked?"

Booth nodded. "I guess I have no choice but to help you. If my sister has done all that you say, she is a menace to herself." He reached for the door behind him. "I'll get my hat, and we'll see if Dodge can find Talley."

Hawke retraced his steps to his vehicle and pulled out his daypack. It had a canteen, protein bars, first aid kit, climbing rope, and a crime kit. He slid his arms through the straps and buckled the straps together. By the time he walked back to Corcoran, Booth walked out of the house also wearing a day pack and carrying a shotgun.

"I'm not sure the shotgun is necessary," Corcoran said.

Booth studied him. "You two have guns, I need this in case that damn cougar I've been seeing is still around."

Hawke nodded. "We had a couple calls at the station about a cougar sighting down here."

Booth held out a blanket to Dodge. "Find Talley. Find her."

The dog sniffed the blanket, glanced at his owner, and then took off through the field.

Hawke hoped this border collie was as good as Dog when it came to following a scent.

They walked for half an hour when Dodge began running in circles in a small clearing.

"Looks like this is where Talley met up with my sister," Booth said. "See the small circles, she was happy and running around."

"Hold on to Dodge," Hawke said, scanning the ground looking for prints. He'd feel better having something they could see to follow rather than relying on the herding dog.

He found where two people entered the clearing.

By the tracks, Suzanne had been prepared to hike through the woods. There were boot tracks with an aggressive tread and shoes that only left an impression, no sole design. "They entered here." He made a perimeter sweep of the clearing and found where they moved into the trees. The dog was still excited and jumping around which made it easier to follow the tracks.

Hawke started jogging, his gaze on the ground, watching the tracks.

After another thirty minutes, the tracks ended at a creek. Hawke waded through and discovered the tracks on the opposite side. He'd feared the woman would have walked up or down the creek a distance to hide their tracks. She apparently didn't think anyone would be following them.

Then they turned west.

"I know where she's going," Booth said.

"Where?" Hawke asked, not slowing down.

"There's a kind of cave made out of boulders where we used to play as kids. Only we'd ride our horses in and pretend we were Indians."

"Is this the straightest route to get to it?" Hawke asked.

"If we went straight, we'd avoid having to scramble over a shale slide." Booth took the lead.

Hawke and Corcoran stayed right behind him. It was another hour of climbing uphill and Booth stopped.

"See those granite boulders? The opening is on the other side, the way they were hiking to it." Booth pointed to a group of boulders forty-five yards in front of them.

"You stay here," Hawke said to Booth. "Deputy Corcoran and I will see if we can get close enough to figure out what's happening inside."

"Don't hurt my sister," Booth said, his hands tightening on the shotgun.

"We will only do what needs to be done to detain her. There won't be any shooting unless she shoots first." Hawke tried to reassure the man that they weren't going in guns blazing. He wanted to make sure that if Jayne was still alive, she'd get out alive.

He motioned for Corcoran to follow and they proceeded closer to the boulders. When they were at the back, Hawke stopped to listen. He could hear a muffled voice coming through a crack between two of the boulders. He pointed for Corcoran to go around the other side and Hawke walked around the grouping of rocks to the front.

At the entrance, he spotted Corcoran. They both stayed back from the opening and listened.

"I don't understand why you are doing this," Jayne's soft voice pleaded.

"You do. You just don't want to tell me," Suzanne's voice was higher pitched. She'd come across to him as someone who was better at taking orders, but to have pulled off the murder, arson, and attempted murder, she had to have more guts than he'd given her credit for.

"Please, I don't have any idea what you're talking about," Jayne persisted.

"You woke up enough from me hitting you that I had to give you a shot. You saw me. You looked right at me. You can tell the police I killed Gordon. The bastard told me he would leave Diane and we'd go away together. He told me that for ten years. TEN LONG YEARS!" She shouted. "That night I'd been sitting in my living room holding the ketamine syringe in my hand and plotting how and when I'd kill the bastard. I'd learned from Gemma that she'd been raped by Gordon. He told me he was only making love to me. ME!" She raised her voice again and Jayne gasped. "Then you walked into that church and I knew he was going to betray me again and he was never going to go away with me. NEVER!"

"Please don't. I went there to confront him about raping my mom twenty-eight years ago."

"He wouldn't have listened. He was an addict. He was addicted to young women. He used his charm to sweet-talk their families into letting him teach them and then he used the women for his own desire. Diane confided it to me and I was nauseous. I thought Gordon used me because Diane wasn't interested in him."

A muffled screech pushed Hawke to step into the boulder formation. There wasn't a top to the area made by the boulders. The sun shone down on the two women. One, in jeans and a sweatshirt huddled on the ground, and the other looming over her in jeans, a jacket, and boots, a hunting knife in her hand.

"Suzanne, one more death on your hands is going to keep you in prison for a very long time," Hawke said to draw the woman's attention to him.

She spun around, the knife raised. "How did you find me?"

The female border collie cowered in a space between the boulders. He wasn't going to turn her anger on the innocent animal. "We found Jayne's car and tracked you."

Suzanne shook her head. "No, why would you track me."

"Because you're wanted for murder, attempted murder, and now kidnapping and attempted murder." Hawke had drawn his gun before entering. He knew Corcoran would be behind him with his weapon drawn, so Hawke holstered his.

"Suzanne, put the knife down and come out with us. Your brother is outside. He cares about you and doesn't want you to get hurt." He added, "None of us want you to get hurt."

She flashed a look over her shoulder at Jayne. "I have to stop her from talking."

When she pivoted, Hawke lunged forward, grasping the arm with the knife. He held onto the arm with both hands as the woman flailed and kicked at him. Within seconds, her free arm was held by Corcoran who clicked handcuffs on that arm. Hawke finally made her release the knife and pulled that arm behind her back. Corcoran snapped the cuff.

As soon as Corcoran had control of Suzanne, Hawke knelt in front of Jayne. She had scratches on her face and she was trembling, but he didn't think she had any major injuries.

"You're safe now." He held out a hand and she flew against him, her arms wrapping around his neck as she sobbed.

Chapter Thirty-five

Hawke and Dani parked in the street in front of Rosa's house. There were a dozen cars in and around her driveway.

"It looks like she invited the whole town," Dani said.

Hawke grinned. The women who had been victims of Pastor Betz were having a party at Rosa's while the loyal congregation had a memorial for the late pastor in the Senior Center. He and Dani had been invited by Rosa. He wondered if Jayne would be here. The last time he saw her, she'd finished giving her statement about being kidnapped by Suzanne. That was a month ago.

In that month, Bev Archer had been returned to the county and put in jail until her sentencing since she'd left the state while on bail. Suzanne Larsen was held in jail without bail awaiting her sentencing for murder, two counts of attempted murder, and one kidnapping. Because she'd confessed the trial was over quickly. And Diane Betz was doing community service for 'borrowing' from the church.

"Trooper Hawke, so good you could make it," Rosa answered the door. "And you must be the wise woman who enlightened this man to a woman's worst fear." She took Dani's hand and shook.

Dani grinned and said, "He is teachable."

The two women laughed and Hawke followed them into the house, figuring he would get more of this if he was the only male present.

To his surprise, there were several spouses of the women. They had finally told their husbands what had happened to them. It was good for their health and relationships to talk about their experience.

When everyone had a plate of food and something to drink, they sat around Rosa's backyard. Dani sat next to Hawke and Jayne sat on his right. In a low voice, Hawke asked, "That note that Rosa found after you left, why did you have it?"

Jayne's cheeks reddened. "It was the list of people Mom wanted me to talk to. Pastor Betz, his wife, and Rosa, the only person Mom called a friend because she listened and believed her. I crossed off the names after I'd talked, well, no talking happened with the pastor, but after I'd briefly seen him and he was dead, I crossed him off. Then when Rosa and I visited Mrs. Betz at Suzanne's I crossed that off. And of course, Rosa was crossed off first because I came to her first."

Hawke nodded. That made sense. And Rosa had jumped to the conclusion they were marked off because

Jayne had killed them.

Jayne put her fork and knife on her plate and twisted in her chair to look at Hawke and Dani. "What really happened that night? The one where I ended up in my car in the middle of nowhere. Did you ever find out?"

Hawke set his empty plate on Dani's and picked up his iced tea. He swallowed down the last bite of food and cleared his throat. "From what Suzanne told us after she was arrested, she was sitting in her house already in possession of the ketamine because she'd been planning to kill Betz. She saw you pull up outside the church and walk in. She thought he was meeting another young woman to assault." He took a sip of tea as Rosa wandered over.

"Pull up a chair. He's telling me what really happened that night," Jayne said to Rosa.

The older woman grabbed a stool and sat with her back to the rest of the party.

"Suzanne entered the church with the syringe. She wanted to use it on Betz so she knocked you out and he said something to her that enraged her and she swung the Virgin Mary bust at the pastor and hit him so hard it killed him. Not needing the ketamine for him and you starting to come around, she injected you," Hawke continued.

Rosa squirmed on her stool and said, "And that's when she called Bev?"

Hawke grinned and said, "Yes, that's when she called Beverly to come help her. Because of how loyal Suzanne had been to Beverly growing up, she helped her aunt. Beverly told us more details about putting the pastor in his office, locking the door, and leaving with Jayne. When they came back, Suzanne told her to go on home. That's when Suzanne set up the time-release fire. She had planned to be back home in her housecoat when the fire broke out but she waited to make sure the fire was going well and then called Mrs. Betz to say she saw her husband enter the church. She had hoped to kill Mrs. Betz in the fire, too. When she saw Mrs. Betz come out the front, she ran from where she was hiding and dropped over the body so she would have an excuse for smelling like smoke."

"Now that's devious," Dani said, with a bit of admiration in her voice.

"What were the two doing when I saw them go into Diane's house?" Rosa asked.

"Mrs. Betz was giving the money she'd stolen from the church charities to Suzanne as blackmail to not tell anyone she'd taken the money. She didn't have any idea that Suzanne had killed her husband." Hawke had stopped while writing up the report thinking how cunning Suzanne had been and what a waste she'd made of her life marrying a man who didn't love her and lusting after one who manipulated and used women.

"I felt like an idiot when I didn't recognize Suzanne. She was standing on the side of the road with the hood up on her car. I stopped to help and she pulled out that knife, shoved me in the car, and drove to where we started hiking through the trees." Jayne set her half-eaten plate to the side.

"How did she know that Jayne was heading home that day?" Dani asked.

Hawke grinned at her. "She hadn't left town. After using Bev Archer as a decoy, Suzanne had been watching Rosa's house for a chance to get to Jayne."

The young woman shuddered. "But she was on the road ahead of me. How did she manage that if she was watching me?"

"You stopped at the Rusty Nail on the way out of town. She drove on by and waited on the side of the road. She knew you were leaving because she saw you carry your bag out to your car and hug Rosa." Hawke picked up his iced tea. "Suzanne Larsen was a clever woman. It's too bad she couldn't have put that mind of hers to a better use than killing people."

Rosa picked up Jayne's plate. "You need to eat. You've become too thin since arriving here." She set the plate back in Jayne's lap.

"It's all over with. Both Suzanne and Beverly have confessed so there's no reason for a trial," Hawke said.

There was a crunch of a car pulling up to the front of the house. Rosa left to see who had come to the party late.

"Thank you for believing in me," Jayne said to Hawke. "I was a stranger, and yet, you believed I didn't kill the pastor."

"Nothing made sense," Hawke said.

"He has to have everything fit into place to make sense to him," Dani offered and smiled at Hawke.

He nodded.

Rosa walked out into the yard with Wade Archer. The man crossed the yard in long strides and stopped in front of Jayne. "I'm so sorry for everything you and your mother went through. I can guarantee that if Eloise had confided in me, we would have stopped that monster and we would have raised you as if you were our own."

Jayne shot to her feet, wrapping her arms around Wade.

Dani's hand grasped Hawke's. He glanced at her and saw tears glistening in her eyes.

As each woman made to leave, she came over to Hawke. His cheeks burned with embarrassment as each one thanked him.

"It wasn't just me, I worked with the State Police and the City Police," he'd say each time. They'd smile at him and walk away. When the last woman had left and it was just Jayne, Wade, Rosa, and Dani left, he said, "I didn't do anything special. I did my job."

Rosa shook her head. "You did more than your job, you believed in me and the women who had been violated by that man. You listened and you did something without involving all of them. While some of the men in their families are standing with the women, there are others that believe the woman must have done something to provoke the pastor to rape them. Men need to learn women's bodies are their own. Not something men own or can take without consent. You're a good man, Trooper Hawke."

When they were settled in Hawke's pickup, he turned to Dani. "At first I was skeptical that so many women wouldn't say anything about a man that they knew was hurting so many. But you and Mom made me see that the women felt as weak and vulnerable as I have on occasion when White men would gang up on me because I was Indian. There are prejudices everywhere and this was one that had to be listened to."

"Rosa was right. You are a good man, Hawke." Dani leaned over and kissed his cheek.

Hawke grinned at her and started his vehicle. "Let's go home and take the horses for a ride."

"Is that code for something?" she asked, a twinkle in her eye.

"It's code for I want to spend time with you outside." He laughed at her when her lips turned into a frown. Maybe one day he would understand women. But for now, it was fun teasing this one.

《》《》《》

Thank you for reading *Damning Firefly*. I hope you enjoyed Hawke's latest story. Please leave a review where you purchased the book. You can also leave them at Goodreads and Bookbub. Reviews are how an author's book gets seen.

If you would like to stay in contact with me or know more about my books you can go to my website: https://www.patyjager.net or get my newsletter https://bit.ly/2IhmWcm

Murder of Ravens
Book 1
Print ISBN 978-1-947983-82-3
Mouse Trail Ends
Book 2
Print ISBN 978-1-947983-96-0
Rattlesnake Brother
Book 3
Print ISBN 978-1-950387-06-9
Chattering Blue Jay
Book 4
Print ISBN 978-1-950387-64-9
Fox Goes Hunting
Book 5
Print ISBN 978-1-952447-07-5
Turkey's Fiery Demise
Book 6
Print ISBN 978-1-952447-48-8
Stolen Butterfly
Book 7
Print ISBN 978-1-952447-77-8
Churlish Badger
Book 8
Print ISBN 978-1-952447-96-9
Owl's Silent Strike
Book 9
Print ISBN 978-1-957638-19-5
Bear Stalker
Book 10
Print ISBN 978-1-957638-64-5
While you're waiting for the next Hawke book, check out my Shandra Higheagle Mystery series or my Spotted Pony Casino Mystery series.

About the Author

Paty Jager grew up in Wallowa County and has always been amazed by its beauty, history, and ruralness. After doing a ride-along with a Fish and Wildlife State Trooper in Wallowa County, she knew this was where she had to set the Gabriel Hawke series.

Paty is an award-winning author of 54 novels of murder mystery and western romance. All her work has Western or Native American elements in them along with hints of humor and engaging characters. She and her husband raise alfalfa hay in rural eastern Oregon. Riding horses and battling rattlesnakes, she not only writes the western lifestyle, she lives it.

By following me at one of these places you will always know when the next book is releasing and if I'm having any giveaways:

Website: http://www.patyjager.net
Blog: https://writingintothesunset.net/
FB Page: https://www.facebook.com/PatyJagerAuthor/
Pinterest: https://www.pinterest.com/patyjag/
Twitter: https://twitter.com/patyjag
Goodreads:
http://www.goodreads.com/author/show/1005334.Paty_Jager
Bookbub - https://www.bookbub.com/authors/paty-jager

Windtree
Press

Thank you for purchasing this Windtree Press
publication. For other books of the heart, please visit
our website at www.windtreepress.com.

For questions or more information contact us
at info@windtreepress.com.

Windtree Press
www.windtreepress.com
Hillsboro, OR